After The We

Copyright 2024 by K.D.Kinz

Original poetry by K.D.Kinz

https://www.facebook.com/kdkinz
Library of Congress: TXu 2-408-312
ISBN: 9798875578687
Cover Illustration by pro_ebookcovers© 2024
10 9 8 7 6 5 4 3 2

Acknowledgments

All my gratitude to the following alpha and beta readers…

Alpha readers:
Lois Z.
Brittany Kollmann

Beta readers:
Diane R.
Kim S.
Sue
Suzanne Noyes

Imagine coming to the realization that the person you married, the person you thought you were going to spend the rest of your life with, is neither capable nor has the desire to love you.

Imagine that person has no care or compassion for your difficulties or trials.

Imagine realizing your whole relationship was a farce.

And the only real thing they feel for you is contempt…

Maria Consiglio

After the We

K. D. KINZ

by the author of Frogs In A Pot

One

Escape

ZARAH PRESSED DOWN hard on the gas. She had to drive away from her parents' house quickly. She had told them she was contemplating filing for divorce from Joe, her husband of twenty-eight years.

They were far from supportive when hearing this news and immediately took her husband's side. There was so much wrong in their marriage. She only gave her parents a few highlights—the highlights she thought they might be able to wrap their heads around. She was so wrong.

Maybe *she* was to blame for them not believing her. She had kept the problems in her marriage a well-guarded secret over the years.

Joe's drinking was the tip of a very ugly iceberg, but it was the only circumstance she thought her parents might understand. The rest was just too unbelievable to verbalize. She warned Joe and gave him many opportunities to change. But nothing ever changed... Nothing.

Two

Twenty-eight years earlier

ZARAH'S MOTHER TOLD her, "You must move out" only days after high school graduation. "You don't need to go to college. Craig told us that he asked you to marry him. So marry him! You've got six months left to live under this roof."

Zarah's heart was not wrapped around her mother's plan for her, but she knew why her mother wanted her to leave… Zarah did not get along with her father—he had a volatile temper, and there was constant tension between them. Her twin sister, Liz, was not given the same ultimatum. Liz typically took on the role of the family peacemaker and made sure never to push his buttons under any circumstances.

Zarah had dated Craig throughout her senior year. He was someone to do things with on the weekends, and her love for him was not unlike love for a close friend. She was *not* "in love."

Some of Zarah's friends were planning to marry their high school boyfriends. It was the 70s— marrying at a young age was the rule, not the exception. And if you weren't married by age twenty-two, you were almost considered a spinster.

That summer, Zarah landed a secretarial job in an office for a company that manufactured industrial equipment. She knew nothing about gears and couplings but could type like the wind.

During her lunch hour, Zarah sat with a pencil and paper to calculate how long it would take to save from her paltry paycheck to afford an apartment. By her best calculations, it would take at least a year to save enough for the first and last month's rent, purchase some second-hand furniture, and have a modest reserve in the bank for emergencies. Even if she saved every dollar that was left after paying her mother room and board and filling her gas tank—and if nothing went wrong with her old Pontiac—she would not be ready to live on her own in the timeframe her mother had given her unless she lived from paycheck to paycheck.

Zarah met Joe on the very first day of work. He was one of thirteen men in the field crew for whom she would work. She immediately thought he was drop-dead gorgeous. He stood a couple of inches taller than she, which was nice—at five-foot-eight, it seemed that most men were shorter. He had a medium build and thick, dark hair, which he wore a little long. Zarah thought he resembled John Lennon, as he wore similar wire-framed glasses. Any time he stopped at her desk to give her an invoice, her heart would race, but in her wildest dreams, she never thought someone like Joe would be interested in someone like her.

Martha, the office gossip, informed Zarah that, as far as she knew, Joe did not have a girlfriend and lived at home with his widowed mother. She said he was a lovely young man, good at his job, and never missed a day of work. Martha was thinking of introducing Joe to her single daughter. Zarah felt a pang of jealousy upon hearing Martha's plan. If Martha's daughter and Joe started dating, her fantasy of dating him would never be.

Joe *was* seven years older than she, which felt like a giant age gap. She was intimidated. He was mature and had seen so much of the world already. He had been a soldier in the Vietnam War and had returned home only months ago. Zarah *had* noticed several fresh scars on his right arm—she hoped he didn't get them during battle.

After several months, Zarah could no longer deny that she was attracted to Joe. She even liked his name... Joseph Zoelle. He was a bit shy, making Zarah suspect he hadn't had much experience with women. Every so often, he watched her as she walked past his desk. She could not control her blushing, and she cursed her fair skin that displayed her emotions for anyone to see.

Joe began to hang out at Zarah's desk longer than necessary, and she was starting to suspect that his feelings toward her were mutual. One day, while they walked through the warehouse together, he asked her if she wanted to go out on a date. With the buzzing of the loud machinery around them, she wasn't sure if she had heard him correctly.

"What did you say?" she answered loudly.

He took a deep breath and then yelled back. "Would you like to go out with me this weekend?"

At the same time, he yelled, the loudest machine paused, and his voice was heard throughout the factory. The workers began to hoot and wolf whistle. Zarah and Joe laughed hysterically; this time, it was Joe's turn to blush.

"We will just be ourselves," he said as they returned to the office. Zarah had no idea why he said that. Of course, they would be themselves—who else would they be? She was too excited in anticipation of their impending date to read too much into the comment, and she blew it off as impending first-date jitters.

Joe drove up the driveway right on time. When Zarah answered the door, she was blown away by how handsome he looked in his brown leather jacket. She caught the faint scent of English Leather cologne through the screen door, and for a split-second, she thought she also detected the smell of cigarettes. But that couldn't be... Joe was not a smoker—he must have stood near someone smoking.

"Come in, Joe," she said calmly as she let him in. His wide eyes scanned her up and down.

"Wow, you look nice, Zarah."

He had been very reserved around the office... He was not as shy as she once thought.

"Thank you, Joe. You look nice, too. I love your leather jacket."

Zarah's family slowly strolled into the living room to check out Zarah's date. Even the elderly family dog waddled up to sniff the new visitor.

"Joe, this is my mother Rita, my father Charlie, and my sister Liz. That cute little fur ball is Tillie. Everyone, this is Joe."

Joe exchanged uncomfortable small talk with Zarah's parents. At the same time, Tillie provided much-needed comic relief after determining that Joe was okay and sat down on his feet, hoping he'd pet her.

"Awww, Tillie!" Zarah laughed. "You're going to get Joe all full of dog hair, you silly girl!" She bent down to kiss her dog on the head.

"Are you ready to go? I made reservations." Joe said nervously. He sensed tension in the room and wasn't aware that Zarah's family was none too happy with her for breaking up with Craig to date this strange new man.

Zarah suspected the car had just been washed as they walked toward his brand-new blue Buick. He opened the passenger door, and Zarah felt like a princess as she stepped into the sparkling-clean car.

"I'm sorry, Joe. My family is upset with me. I broke up with my high school boyfriend last week. They all thought I was going to marry him, and they're *not* happy that I'm going on a date with someone else. Don't take it personally."

"It did feel like I was under a microscope in there."

"My twin sister Liz liked you!" she added cheerfully.

"She's your twin? There's no resemblance."

"We're fraternal twins. I got the blonde hair and height; she got the brown curls and girly figure."

"Well... I like *your* curves," he said as he raised his eyebrows. Zarah felt her face flush.

"I've been told I'm built like a boy," she laughed. "When I was a kid, my nickname was 'Stick.'"

"You don't look like a stick to me," Joe said overtly flirtatiously.

"Well, thank you! I've always hated that nickname!"

"Your name is unusual... I've never met a Zarah before," he added.

"Elizabeth and Zarah are biblical names," she answered flatly.

"Is your mother a religious zealot?" he asked jokingly.

"Hardly!" She stopped herself from saying more. She didn't want to explain their family dynamics on their first date—she didn't want to scare him away.

That evening, Joe took Zarah to dinner at an Italian restaurant and then to see the blockbuster movie *The Exorcist*. She was reluctant to see the film, and by the time it ended, she wished she had never laid eyes on it.

After the movie ended, Joe drove Zarah home, followed by a quick kiss on the cheek. He asked if she wanted to go out with him again. She replied with a definitive "Yes."

Zarah exited the car and began walking toward the front door, only to realize she had forgotten her house key in the excitement of getting ready for her date. She turned back to flag Joe, but he had already left and was driving quickly up the road.

"Why didn't he wait for me to get into the house?" Zarah said into the darkness. Nobody had thought to leave the front porch light on. She rang the front doorbell several times until it dawned on her that her parents had gone out for the evening. She heard Tillie whimpering on the other side of the door.

Finally, she went to her sister's bedroom window and pounded hard. Still half-asleep, Liz slid the bedroom window open.

"Why are you standing outside in the dark?" she asked.

"Joe just dropped me off. We saw *The Exorcist,* and I'm scared shitless out here. I imagine that the devil is hiding behind every bush. Let me in!"

"Why didn't he walk you to the door? That was rude!"

"Elizabeth, I don't know! Please... Stop asking stupid questions and let me in!" Zarah only called Liz by her given name when she was irritated with her.

Every time Joe picked Zarah up for another date, his eyes lit up when he saw her as if he had never seen a prettier girl in all his life. He freely complimented her on the outfits she chose to wear and how she styled her hair. Zarah had never considered herself beautiful, but with Joe's generous praise, she began to feel beautiful—if only in his eyes.

Her nineteenth birthday was approaching, and she was keenly aware that the days of living under her parents' roof were numbered. What were the chances that the love of her life would arrive when she needed him? Neither of them had mentioned anything long-term, but Zarah felt their relationship was heading in that direction.

Joe and Zarah still lived at home, so they found a secluded parking spot every chance they got and made out in his car. Joe's kiss was *different*. He gently circled Zarah's mouth with his lips, but his lips never made complete contact. Zarah didn't have much experience in this area but realized this was not typical. She had always dreamed of a passionate kiss… A kiss that would leave her breathless. That kiss never happened with her high school boyfriend— Craig's kiss did nothing for her. But she admired many things about Joe—she would overlook this shortcoming. She was sure that, in time, he would learn to kiss with more passion.

Joe had never mentioned any former girlfriends or relationships, and Zarah thought that, at his age, he should have had at least one or two serious relationships in his past. One evening, as they walked hand-in-hand through a local park, she thought it was the perfect time to bring up the subject…

"Have you had any girlfriends, Joe?"

"While I was in Nam, my fiancé Jean married my best friend, Mike," he said with a serious demeanor.

"Oh my God, Joe! That must have been terrible for you. While you were away serving your country, they fell in love?" Zarah was horrified at the thought.

"Yes."

"Have you had any other relationship since then?"

"I think that once, when I was stationed in Hawaii, I had sex with a woman…" His voice trailed off as if he was sorry he had mentioned it.

"Joe," Zarah chastised. "How can you *not* know that you had sex?"

"Well, I was pretty drunk."

"This isn't any of my business, and don't answer if you don't want to, but did you consummate your relationship with Jean before you left for the war?"

"We were saving sex for marriage."

"So… What you're telling me is… You may or may not be a virgin?" Zarah half-laughed.

She regretted asking the question the moment it left her lips. He could turn the tables and ask her the same thing. She *had* slept with her high school boyfriend but was not ready to admit it this early in their relationship.

"I don't know, Zarah. Can we please change the subject?" He was irritated with her line of questioning, and the conversation abruptly ended.

Zarah could not stop thinking about Joe when she wasn't with him. Going to work was not an effort but a thrill because he would be there. She no longer felt shy around Joe and sometimes flirtatiously walked past his desk to get his attention before bending over to do some filing.

On a Saturday evening, Joe and Zarah were at a local pub and were sharing stories about the past week. It had been an incredibly hectic week, and they were glad it was behind them.

Up to that point, they had kept their relationship a secret from everyone in the office, but their fondness for each other was becoming more challenging to conceal.

"I don't care if people know we're dating, Joe. We always talk to each other, and I believe it's becoming obvious to our co-workers."

"One of us will have to quit then. It's against company policy for employees to date," he explained.

Zarah knew it would be *her* who would have to quit. She barely earned over minimum wage, whereas Joe made a decent living.

"Let's keep it quiet for now. At least until I find another job."

Zarah cringed at the thought of circling jobs in the "want ads" of the local newspaper, but at the same time, she was thankful that she had had the foresight to take secretarial classes in high school. She was qualified for almost any secretarial position and now had some experience to add to a resume.

In the dim light of the pub, she focused on the scars on Joe's forearm as he reached the bar for his beer mug. She gently placed her hand on his arm and ran her hand down over the scars.

"Joe, what happened to your arm?" she said softly.

Joe's facial expression went blank. He pushed his beer to the far side of the bar and, without one word of explanation, walked out of the pub, leaving Zarah alone.

Zarah felt like a stupid child. Did she upset him? She wasn't sure. She asked herself if she had said something wrong. Since they began dating, Joe never once brought up the subject of the war. It was as if he was never there. Should she have known that he didn't want to discuss it?

Zarah sat by herself for what seemed like forever. Every so often, the bartender glanced in her direction and asked her if she was okay. She just smiled and said, "Everything is fine." But everything was *not* fine, and her mind was racing in different directions.

She had two options… Call a taxi or sit patiently and wait. But wait for what? For all she knew, Joe went home. After an hour passed, she put on her jacket and took her purse from the back of the barstool. She caught the bartender's attention.

"Do you have a phone I could use? And a phone book? I need to call a taxi."

At that moment, the door opened, and Joe walked back into the bar.

His hands shook as he pulled bills from his wallet and tossed the money on the bar to pay for their drinks.

"It's time to go," he said coldly.

The ride home was disturbingly silent as neither of them spoke. Zarah knew she would never bring up the subject of the war again. Something terrible had happened to him, but she was sure that, in good time, he would trust her enough to tell her.

"Good night, Joe," she said when he shifted his car into park in her driveway.

"Good night," he said while staring straight ahead.

"Joe…"

"I'll be busy with my mother tomorrow, so I'll see you Monday."

He was still angry with her. She exited the car and watched as he drove up the road. She formulated a plan… *Monday, I'll talk to him at work. I'll apologize and promise I'll never bring up the subject of the war again.*

As she was getting dressed for work, Zarah overheard her parents in the kitchen discussing taking Tillie to the vet later that day to have her put down. Tillie was curled up in her bed on the kitchen floor. She was shaking, and her breathing was irregular and labored.

"Don't touch her!" Her father, Charlie, commanded from his seat at the breakfast table when Zarah entered the room.

Zarah was *not* going to have it. She had to leave the house in no less than five minutes to make it to work on time, and she knew this would be the last time she'd ever see her beloved Tillie again.

Zarah had always considered Tillie to be *her* dog…

The narrow room at the Humane Society was stacked with cages on both sides, and dogs barked at her and Liz as they timidly walked through the room in search of the dog they would take home that day. Liz stopped at a cage and instantly fell in love with an incessantly barking black lab.

"No, Liz! I get to pick out the dog. It's my communion money, not yours! You already spent your money on stupid stuff. That dog is too loud!"

Zarah fell in love with Tillie when she saw her shaking and cowering in the far corner of a cage. It felt like an eternity as six-year-old Zarah waited for an employee to take Tillie out of her steel prison cell. Zarah clutched her new puppy, and she paid the cashier seven dollars.

Zarah ignored her father's warning, sat on the floor, and covered the dog with a blanket. As she bent over to kiss her dog goodbye for the last time, she felt the hard slap of her father's hand across the side of her head. Her neck instantly burned from the jolt, and it took a moment for her to regain composure.

"I told you not to touch her!" Charlie screamed as if to justify why he *had* to hit her.

She stood up, pushed the hair out of her face, then walked out of the house. She did not say a word, and she did not let him see her tears. She lived every day in fear of his temper and couldn't wait to afford to move out and start a life of her own.

They had been dating only four months when Joe proposed marriage. Without hesitation, Zarah threw her arms around his neck.

"Yes! Of course, I will marry you! I would marry you for your last name alone!" she teased. Her name would become Mrs. Zarah Zoelle, and she liked the sound of it.

"Craig is coming to the reception today…" Rita bluntly announced to Zarah only twenty minutes before they were due to leave for the church. Liz concentrated on removing

Zarah's wedding dress from its zipper bag. The two girls had spent the morning fixing each other's hair and putting on makeup.

"You invited Craig to my wedding reception? Without asking me? Mother, I don't want him there! His attendance at my wedding reception is inappropriate!"

"You broke his heart, Zarah! He refuses to attend the wedding but *is* coming to the reception!"

Zarah could not imagine a guest at her wedding reception she wanted less. She was not heartless—she felt terrible about how their relationship had ended. The break-up had not been graceful. Once Zarah had stopped dating him to date Joe, her parents often invited Craig over and lavished him with praise and affection. They told Craig that their daughter was a foolish girl and he was a far better man than Joe.

"He's coming as **my** guest," Rita said with finality, then turned and left the room. She may have just as well used a gavel to end the conversation.

"Don't let her ruin your big day!" Liz whispered to her sister.

On that day, one month after her nineteenth birthday, Joe and Zarah were married before one hundred friends and relatives in the Catholic church Zarah had grown up in.

After the priest announced them, "Husband and wife," Joe leaned over and quickly kissed her. The photographer somehow managed to capture the split-second kiss on film.

Joe's brother Henry was the best man, and one of his duties was to drive the newlyweds from the church to the reception hall—a twenty-minute ride away.

Zarah's wedding dress was bulky, and she required assistance from her new husband to tuck her into the car's back seat. The photographer snapped pictures of the laughing couple as they struggled to get control of her fluffy white dress. Someone had painted "Just Married!" on the car's rear window and tied tin cans to the bumper. Zarah strongly suspected that her sister had been the mastermind behind the cheesy decorations.

As they rode in the backseat to the reception, Zarah gazed up at Joe—he was so handsome in his black tuxedo. He looked briefly her way but was distracted by what was straight ahead through the windshield.

She wished he'd look at her again. He had yet to tell her she was beautiful in her wedding dress. She expected him to compliment her after they stepped up to the altar hand-in-hand. She expected him to look at her and whisper, "You look beautiful, Zarah." Instead, he briefly smiled and nodded his head.

"Joe," Zarah said impatiently.

"What?" He snapped.

He maintained his focus as if something exciting was happening on the road ahead. Zarah peered out the front windshield—there was nothing extraordinary to see.

She took a deep breath and decided to ask him the obvious… "Joe, how do I look in my wedding dress?!" Where was the praise he had generously lavished upon her over the past ten months?

Zarah was humiliated. This should not have been something a bride needed to ask her new husband. She did not want compliments, but she knew a groom *should* compliment his bride on their wedding day. He should have also been holding her hand in the back seat as they rode to their wedding reception, and he should have been gazing and smiling at her like she was staring and smiling at him. What had happened? Why was he treating her this way?

"Joe!" she half cried this time.

"What, Zarah?!" he answered sharply as if he was answering a naughty child.

She was not going to get an answer. She turned her face to the window—away from him. It was the first time he had spoken to her in that tone. She began to cry softly and couldn't stop the tears from running down her face. She would have to duck into the restroom to fix her makeup before the reception.

What has changed? Why is he acting like this?

Henry overheard Zarah crying. "Is everything okay back there?" he asked concernedly.

"She's fine," Joe answered firmly. Henry knew from his brother's tone not to push for further explanation.

This was the last thing she expected on what should have been the happiest day of her life. As if a switch had been flipped, the compliments Joe had so freely given her had abruptly stopped. She felt that, for some reason, he was angry with her—at the very least, he was annoyed with her. What did she do wrong? Should she tell Henry to stop the car and let her out? That would be ridiculous... A crying bride all alone on the side of the road. What would their guests think when told the bride was not coming to her wedding reception?

Two weeks into their marriage, Zarah sat at the kitchen table in their apartment with a pen in hand. It was a Saturday, and Joe had gone to work. She began to write feverishly—her frustration flew from the pen's tip onto the paper. She wrote down everything that crossed her mind and had no idea when she would stop. Finally exhausted of her anger, she set down the pen...

Joe,

Something happened on our wedding day. You changed after we said our vows. Before we were married, you were loving toward me, and you showered me with loving words. After the ceremony, you could barely look at me. You didn't even dance with me at our wedding reception! The photographer had to find you and pose us together as if we were dancing, but you turned and left the second he took the picture.

You drank so much at the reception. I was surprised you didn't pass out! I would have liked one glass of wine, but a bride should not have to go to the bar and order herself a drink! Where were you? You should have been at my side! We barely spoke two words to each other the entire evening!

Are you angry with me? You're a different person now. Why did you marry me? I'm so confused and don't think I can live like this!

The letter went on for several more pages. Zarah knew that the marriage should be ended, and she stated so clearly toward the end of the letter. She knew that he had used her... for some reason... But why? He now acted as if he were far superior to her as if she meant nothing to him.

Zarah's mother had always taught her not to make waves, to sweep everything under the rug, and move on as if the bad things had never happened. She was raised to believe that speaking up for yourself was not ladylike and was considered bad behavior...

Zarah's father, Charlie, was volatile when he was stone sober and worse when he was drunk. Her mother, Rita, walked on eggshells to not anger him. He would fly into a rage over minor infractions... Something as insignificant as the neighbor's dog in his yard, the paperboy forgetting to deliver the newspaper, or a meal not prepared the way he wanted would release his fury.

Every week, his temper flared when he accused Rita of having an affair, which was merely a figment of his suspicious imagination. It was he who cheated on his wife and not the other way around.

His anger was always right below the surface. If he was drinking, Zarah and Liz knew to stay far away from him and not return home until he was passed out on the couch.

Rita learned that it helped to keep silent when Charlie escalated. As soon as he raised his voice, she became mute. She rarely talked back or gave him additional fuel for the fire. But her plan wasn't foolproof. On occasion, she received bruises or a black eye, which she learned to conceal with makeup artfully.

Zarah and Liz ran like the wind when they sensed their father's rage escalating. Occasionally, he took off after them, removed his leather belt, and beat them with it.

Zarah always prayed she would hear her mother cry, "Charlie, stop!" But she never did. Rita was never anywhere to be found—she was locked in the bathroom… taking a valium.

Sometimes, Charlie felt remorseful after hitting his daughters, and he would come home after working all day in the factory with a bouquet tucked under his arm to present to whoever had been the unfortunate recipient of his violence.

"Awww, isn't that sweet, Zarah. Your father bought flowers for you!" Rita said to her in a sing-song tone of voice.

Zarah stared blankly at her mother. Didn't she have a clue that this wasn't right? Didn't she see that he abused them? Didn't she understand that her husband was unstable? Was her mother willing to tolerate anything to keep the family together?

"Zarah, you're being impolite! Thank your father for the flowers!" Rita said sweetly, but Zarah knew it was an order, not a suggestion.

Rita appeared satisfied when Zarah accepted the bouquet and mumbled "thank you" under her breath. Accepting the gift was the path of least resistance. If she did not, she would get lectured by her mother that the bible states we must learn to forgive and forget. As a young teen, she had heard that lecture way too many times and could *regurgitate it verbatim. Simply telling her father that she did* **not** *want his fucking bouquet was not an option.*

When Charlie left the room, Zarah shoved the flowers in a vase and never looked at them again. If she did, she was afraid they would burn her eyes.

His rage would surface again—it was not if, it was when.

Rita spent her days sitting at the kitchen table smoking Pall Malls, drinking coffee and talking on the phone. Zarah overheard her mother's conversations with her grandmother, but she never heard her complain about Charlie to her—not once. Brownish-gold streaks of nicotine ran down the kitchen walls. Rita did little to no housework and spent her days smoking one cigarette after another.

After writing the letter to Joe for over an hour, Zarah ripped it into shreds, went outside, and threw the pieces into the garbage dumpster outside their apartment building. Her mother would never let her return home, but she could *not* move back in with her parents anyway. She had found a better-paying secretarial position one month before they married, but her income would never support an independent life. She couldn't ask Liz to share an apartment with her either—Liz was dating Cameron, and it sounded serious. She was trapped. She had no other choice than to make her marriage work.

Zarah could not explain it, but she still loved Joe despite his indifference toward her. She loved the Joe she fell in love with—the Joe who existed on some level and would eventually return. Maybe the wedding and setting up the apartment had been stressful for him. She would give him time to get over it all. She would wait.

Zarah let her family believe that Joe was the perfect husband, and she consciously decided to keep her problems with Joe to herself. She did not want to disappoint her sister, who thought Joe walked on water.

Her mother had always said, "You made your bed. Now you lie in it." Zarah figured this was one of those times she'd have to do just that. Besides, she didn't want to admit to her mother that her choice of a husband had been flawed… Like hers was. She would **not** give her mother that satisfaction. Zarah wanted to prove that she was more intelligent than her mother had been. After all, Joe wasn't violent like her father. He *was* dark and distant, but he didn't seem to have a violent bone in his body.

Zarah told herself that she loved a mysterious man—his darkness was seductive. Maybe he *was* superior to her. He had secrets, but she convinced herself he would confide in her… someday… when he was good and ready.

Zarah kept their apartment clean, did their laundry and cooked their meals. After washing the dinner dishes in the evening, she'd collapse onto the couch with a magazine or a book while Joe sat in his recliner with a can of beer in one hand and the TV remote in the other.

When they had sex, Joe did not open his eyes, and he occasionally said crass things that shocked her. Sex with Joe was not intimate; it was primal, and sometimes, the things he wanted to do in bed made Zarah feel dirty. She told herself, *This is what married people do. They experiment, and they push sexual boundaries to new limits. I have to step up to the plate and go with it.*

To outsiders, they looked like a happy, young couple. But Zarah lived each day wondering… Where was the man who adored everything about her?

Three

Babies

FOUR YEARS INTO their marriage, Zarah became pregnant with their first child. The couple bought an unpretentious home in the suburbs with a modest downpayment and moved out of their tiny apartment. Zarah quit her secretarial job four days before the baby was due to be born.

Zarah did not have one maternal instinct in her body. She felt nothing but unrelenting nausea and an uncomfortable weight gain. Other pregnant women would put their hands on their bellies and speak lovingly about their unborn child. But Zarah could only fake those emotions, and that scared the hell out of her.

After twenty-three hours of labor, Zarah's son was born. The nurse bathed, wrapped the baby in a blanket, and presented him to Zarah. He struggled to lift his head, then locked his eyes on hers for a few seconds before dropping the weight of his heavy little head back down onto her chest.

How did he know to lift his head and search for her eyes? That magical moment in time would change Zarah forever. She had no idea that love at that intensity even existed. Her fear of not being a good mother vanished as if it had never, for one moment, been a concern. She would devote herself to the baby. She would be the kind of mother that she would have wanted if she had been given the choice.

Her second son was born two years later, and Zarah was enraptured in motherhood. She felt blessed that she didn't have to work during this critical time in her sons' lives so that she could focus on raising Damon and Drew... her two precious boys.

Zarah was good at making money stretch and always bragged that she could "make a dollar squeal," but not much money was left after the bills were paid. She sewed or bought the boys' clothing at rummage sales, and most of their furnishings were second-hand. She saved enough money every summer to take the family to a cabin in upper Michigan. Lavish vacations were out of the question.

Joe made an adequate living, but over the years, Zarah became painfully aware that he showed *no* incentive to move up the corporate ladder. His lack of ambition disappointed Zarah. She knew that if the family were to thrive financially, it would be up to her to make that happen.

She enrolled in evening courses toward a degree in nursing. When Joe came home from work, she would quickly tell him what she prepared for their dinner, get into her car and head straight for the college campus.

She cleaned and cooked during the day while the boys played, and she studied her nursing books when they took their afternoon nap. She loved her life as a student, but it was exhausting.

Zarah had no idea how her decision to become a nurse would affect her future. She thought only about how nice it would be when they had a second income and she could contribute more to the family than just cooking and cleaning. She had grown accustomed to Joe's indifference toward her, and motherhood and nursing books were enough to fill her days.

Four years later, Zarah graduated with a degree in nursing and shortly after was hired for a part-time, third-shift position in the neurosurgical ICU at Lansing General Hospital. Being hired directly into an ICU fresh out of nursing school was rare. Still, despite raising two children while simultaneously attending classes, she graduated near the top of her class, which looked impressive on her resume.

Four

The club

ZARAH HAD DREADED the arrival of this day... Her fortieth birthday. Even the number sounded dowdy. After crawling out of bed and walking toward the bathroom, something felt different. Something she did not recognize yesterday... the last day she was thirty-nine.

Joe had become progressively more distant over the years. They lived parallel lives under the same roof, and they may as well have lived on different planets. Zarah focused on raising her boys and on her career. Her mother had taught her not to rock the boat. She must have been a mindful student, for that was precisely how she had lived the last twenty-one years.

Her husband's quirks crept into their marriage occasionally. Zarah had become an expert at stuffing all his oddities into a tidy mental box and placing it high on a tidy mental shelf. In all the years they had been married, she never considered that someday she would have to deal with everything she thought she had so cleverly tucked away.

That day, her fortieth birthday, was different from every day before. It was as if someone knocked on her front door and told her she was now a member of an exclusive club. She was persistently aware of the oddness that was her husband's personality, but for the first time in their marriage, felt as if she'd had enough, and for some reason —on her fortieth birthday—she was no longer afraid to tell him so. That morning, she could tell her husband to "go to hell" without batting an eye. Maybe forty sounded dowdy, but she thought the wisdom she had gained (since the innocence of her twenties and thirties) might be worth the trade-off.

Joe lost his edge… if he ever had one. In recent years, he floundered at work and couldn't hold down a job for more than a year. Zarah had high hopes that, after she began working, her income would launch the family into a better financial position. It did for a few years, but now Zarah's paycheck supported the family.

She critically studied herself in the mirror. She had let herself go. She had put on a few pounds, looked soft, and her once blonde hair had grown a mousy brown. She didn't want to look her age, but she felt every one of her forty years.

In the past, Zarah had remained faithful to Joe. The thought of an affair never crossed her mind. She did not believe she was attractive anymore, and she wasn't aware of another man ever giving her the time of day—it was almost as if she had become invisible.

Zarah worked with brilliant doctors; some were attractive men, but their relationships remained strictly professional. She had a crush on one of the surgeons, Dr. Bluett, affectionately dubbed Dr. "Blue Eyes" by the nursing staff. She gave him no hint of her feelings, but anytime she had to discuss a patient with him, her heart raced, and her palms got sweaty.

What would her life have been like had she married a man like Dr. Bluett? He was brilliant and respected by everyone who knew him. She enjoyed watching him walk through the ICU with a string of residents following behind like ducklings. They clung to his every word. To them, he was God.

She laughed at the fleeting thought of trying to balance an affair on top of all that was going on. Her boys and her career were all she needed to fill her days. She wasn't the type of person who could be unfaithful, and a relationship with Dr. Bluett was merely a fantasy. She was stuck in her marriage to Joe; besides that, the doctor had recently married.

After showering, she picked out her scrubs for the day. Her birthday was no excuse to miss a day of work. She hated spending so much time away from her two teenage sons, but she did love her job. Her co-workers were like an extended family, and she loved the fast pace of the ICU and the challenge of keeping a patient alive from minute to minute. She was a kind nurse but could be firm when needed. Her co-workers loved her as much as she loved them, and over time, she preferred to go to work over spending an evening at home alone with her husband.

On her evening break, Zarah would typically call Joe to ask how everything was going. The boys were involved in many activities, but she, of course, could not be there to enjoy their activities while working, so she relied on Joe to tell her what was happening in her absence.

Sometimes, Joe's voice was slurred when he answered the phone. Over time, she figured it out... He was drinking. He had always loved his beer, but when she was at work, he had the freedom to drink whatever and however much he wanted. She eventually stopped calling him on her break. Hearing his slurred speech twisted her stomach and made it hard for her to concentrate on her job. If she ignored the situation, it wasn't happening, and she would not have to deal with any of it.

During family dinners, Damon and Drew mostly conversed with each other and with Zarah—rarely did they include their father in any conversation. She didn't think the boys meant to exclude him—they just unconsciously didn't include him. When he was sober, he didn't have much to say, and when he was under the influence, the opinions he interjected were contrary and bordered on rude. As a rule, the two boys chatted away during dinner, almost like they had a language all their own. They were always excited about their rock band and the new music the band was learning. Damon had become incredible on the keyboard, and Drew mastered the guitar. Zarah enthusiastically threw her two cents into their conversation when she could get a word in, but Joe quietly ate his dinner as if his mind was in a different place.

As they sat around the dinner table, their three-year-old Jack Russel terrier Rosie danced around on her hind legs, begging for handouts. She would jump high enough to see the food on the table if dancing didn't get their attention. Her silly head would appear for a split second when she was air-bound. The little dog did anything to get their attention, and her antics elicited laughter at nearly every family meal.

Five

Nothing funny

OVER THE YEARS, Zarah and Joe had remained close friends with Jean and Mike. Jean... The woman who betrayed Joe while he was away fighting a war—the woman who had married his best friend. And Mike... Joe's best friend—the man who fell in love with and married his fiancé Jean.

Zarah had always been curious... What circumstances led Jean and Mike to fall in love with each other? Did they harbor guilt for what they did to Joe? Did Jean have any feelings left for Joe? Zarah had always thought it was big of Joe to have forgiven them. He had kept them in his life and remained friends after their ultimate betrayal. Jean and Mike's son Christopher was getting married, and Zarah looked forward to the event.

Jean and Mike were as close as family, maybe more so. There were bowling leagues, camping trips, and Lions and Tigers games to attend. The four were as involved in each other's lives as two couples could be, and the story of their betrayal faded away over the years as if it had never happened.

A handful of times, Zarah asked Joe a follow-up question about the time he was betrayed. Joe's answers were consistent…"Leave it alone, Zarah," "I don't want to talk about it," or "It was so long ago… I don't remember anymore." His evasiveness left her as bewildered as she was before she asked.

Zarah chose a long floral dress to wear to the wedding and spent time fixing her hair and putting on makeup. She had been lifting light weights for the past few years and maintained her blonde highlights. As usual, she hoped her husband would give her a scrap of a compliment that evening. But of course, she knew that would not happen, and she quickly shook off the notion.

After the ceremony, Zarah sat next to Jean as they watched Jean's son and his new bride dance to the song, *You Look Wonderful Tonight.* Ironically, the song made Zarah feel sad whenever she heard it. It had been many years since anyone told her she looked wonderful, and she wondered what it would be like to be the woman for whom Eric Clapton wrote the song. She had learned that anticipating a compliment from Joe was equally painful as the disappointment of not getting one.

"Your little boy is all grown up, Jean," Zarah told her friend.

Jean reached over and squeezed Zarah's hand, and together, they watched the newlyweds dance. They had their entire future ahead of them. Zarah said a silent prayer that their lives would be filled with joy.

In the twenty-five years she had been friends with Jean, Zarah had never mentioned the subject of "the betrayal." She knew Jean as well as she knew anyone—Jean was more like a sister than a friend. Zarah knew that she probably should leave well enough alone, but if there was even a shred of guilt left in Jean's heart, she wanted to ease her mind and free her from it. She wanted Jean to know that there were no hard feelings and that she had forgiven her and Mike long ago.

The band went on a break, and except for voices and laughter, the reception room was relatively quiet.

"Jean," Zarah said softly to her friend. "I've always known that you were engaged to marry Joe before he left for Nam. He told me what happened... You fell in love with Mike when he was away fighting the war. I want you to know that I'm okay with all of that, and I believe that Joe is okay with it, too. It was a lifetime ago."

Jean looked puzzled. "Zarah... What are you talking about? I never even *dated* Joe."

"He told me that... You were his fiancé... You and he had plans to get married when he returned from the war. That, when he was gone, you fell in love with Mike... And you married Mike instead." Zarah stumbled over her words.

"I don't know what to say, Zarah... That is not true."

Many years ago, Joe had lied and kept up the ruse. But for what reason? What would a lie like that prove? That he had had a girlfriend in his past? Did he think she'd never find out the truth?

"I need another glass of wine," Zarah said emphatically. She was a light drinker, and she knew that another glass of wine could make the room spin—but at that point, all she wanted to do was to shut up the little voice that was screaming inside her head.

After the reception, Zarah and Joe walked up to their hotel room. In the elevator, the strong scent of alcohol emanated from him. He leaned over and whispered in her ear...

"How about a little hotel sex?"

"I don't think so, Joe. You're inebriated."

"I was just having fun, Zarah! Everyone else was drinking! It was a goddamn wedding. Aren't I allowed to have fun? It was an open bar! And I saw you drinking, too… But that's different because you are 'The Perfect Zarah!'" he said sarcastically as he made air quotes.

"I'm far from perfect, Joe, but I can stop after one or two drinks!" She would say nothing more—she'd never win this argument.

After they climbed into bed, he pulled her close and began to run his hands up and down her back. Even though he had taken a shower and brushed his teeth, the scent of alcohol still exuded from every pore.

Zarah laughed.

"What's so funny?" Joe asked.

"Nothing… I'm sorry, I was thinking of something that happened tonight," Zarah lied. She had no idea what made her laugh. Jean's words, "That is not true," resonated in her mind.

He continued to run his hands over her body, and he kissed her in his odd sort of way. She felt her entire body starting to shake as she attempted to suppress the laughter that was rising to the surface.

She had no idea what was happening to her. There was nothing funny about the situation. It was a laughter from deep inside that she could not explain. It felt as if someone or something else had taken control of her body.

"Sit on top of me," he ordered in a slurred voice.

She did as requested. She was now holding back with every ounce of her strength. He grabbed her hips, closed his eyes and began to moan. She could no longer hold back, and she burst into full-blown laughter.

"What the fuck?!" Joe yelled as he pushed her off and tossed her to the side of the bed. He was disappointed. He would not have "hotel sex" tonight. He turned over and was snoring within minutes.

"You won't remember this in the morning, dear husband," Zarah whispered sarcastically as she got out of bed.

She slipped her dress back on and exited the hotel room into the dark summer night. She released the gales of laughter she had held back when she stepped outside the building. Nobody was around, and she was grateful—if anyone heard her, they would think she was absolutely nuts. She belly laughed as if she had just heard the funniest joke of her life. But nothing was funny. Nothing was humorous. Everything was weird, strange, surreal.

All composure was lost. Maybe she was losing her mind. She sat down on a bench and held her cheeks as they ached from all the laughing.

Reality finally came crashing down... She had caught her husband in a twenty-five-year-old lie.

***

"Have a seat, Joe," Zarah pointed toward a white wrought iron chair on the back patio of their home, then sat down directly across from him.

Several months had passed since the wedding of Jean and Mike's son. Zarah had never confronted Joe with the lie she discovered that night, and she was unsure why.

Over the years, Zarah would occasionally push Joe for answers. Why did he change so abruptly right after they were married? Why did they stop having any meaningful conversations? Why did he drink to excess? He consistently stood his ground and gave her no insight as to why he was the way he was. Sometimes, she would almost scream in despair, but he responded with barely a word.

"I have something to say, Joe. We've been married for twenty-five years. The boys are on their own, and I don't believe they know about the problems in our marriage. Maybe they have figured some things out, but I have kept my anger toward you a secret. They are incredible kids, and I never wanted our problems to affect them."

Joe sat quietly—his facial expression remained blank. He had grown accustomed to their marriage. He knew Zarah would occasionally push him for answers, but he could live with that.

"Recently, before I take my shower in the morning, I check the levels of alcohol in the bottles in the liquor cabinet. After my shower, I recheck the levels. In the fifteen minutes I am in the shower, the levels in one or more of the bottles drop by an inch or more. That is some f'ing serious drinking, Joe. You are sneaky when I'm not around. I hate that I have become suspicious, and I feel the need to spy on my husband. I'm not your wife. I'm your mother. And I believe that my suspicions have been correct... You are a full-blown alcoholic."

Joe continued to stare straight ahead with his arms folded across his chest.

"Why are you drinking so much, Joe? Why?! And I know you smoke—I can smell it on you. Don't you care about your health?!" She had raised her voice and was aware that the neighbors might overhear. She took a deep breath and composed herself.

She had tried everything to get him to stop drinking, and despite being a healthcare provider, her husband was the one person she felt incapable of helping. If she could only amputate the "addiction" part of his brain... and the part that kept secrets.

"I dumped whatever alcohol was left in the cabinet, Joe. There wasn't much left. It's all gone now."

He remained stubbornly mute. She almost wanted to slap him to elicit a response. But she had to hand it to him... His commitment to keeping his secrets was impressive.

"Joe, what I am getting at is… My feelings for you have changed. I have loved you—more than I should have—despite never feeling loved by you."

He said nothing. Not a muscle twitched as he stared straight ahead.

"Joe! Do you understand what I said?! I said that my feelings for you have changed. I don't think I love you anymore!"

"I heard you," he finally replied.

"Do you have anything to say about this situation?" she asked.

"You don't love me. There's nothing more to say."

"You've put me through hell with your drinking! Have you ever noticed that I don't call you from work anymore? That's because I can't stand to listen to your slurred speech!"

He began to push up from the chair to leave.

"Wait!" Zarah took a deep breath. "There is a point to this conversation that I am getting to…"

He sat back down.

"I am giving you a chance to change. You can fight for this marriage or not. It's up to you. You can stop drinking. You can confide in me all your deep, dark secrets, or it's over…. Our marriage will be over."

"I'll change." His voice was barely perceptible. Zarah questioned if she had heard him speak or if his answer was her wishful imagination.

"I can help you," Zarah offered in a kind voice.

"I'll do it myself." They sat for a while in silence. The only sounds were the birds singing in the trees surrounding their home.

"Are you through?" he asked.

"Yes."

He stood up from the table and walked back into the house. Zarah felt a twinge of hope. Accepting her offer of help would have bolstered her confidence. Reaching for the bottle was his only coping mechanism.

She had called him out. She had clearly stated her exasperation. She had no idea how much time she would give him to make the changes in himself necessary to save their marriage. She would have to see a whole new Joe, or she would have to see the Joe she only caught glimpses of many years ago.

Six

Not my son

JOE'S NEW JOB in sales required him to travel. He would leave on Monday and not return home until Friday. Zarah felt a little guilty that, when he left, she felt nothing but relief. The house was empty with both boys away at college, and she was thankful she had precious little Rosie to keep her company. The moment he returned home on Friday evening, her heart sank. She could barely force a smile or say, "Welcome home."

Zarah was all too aware that the time Joe spent away from home meant he was doing whatever he wanted. That would not have been a problem if she had trusted him. But he had not stopped drinking after she had given him the ultimatum over three years ago. Zarah did not keep up her end of her bargain either. She once again donned her rose-tinted glasses and stayed in the marriage. She wasn't aware of many couples that divorced at this stage of life, and the thought of divorcing her husband was still something she thought she could never do.

Zarah immersed herself in her career, and on the days that Joe was working from home, she could hardly wait to leave the house for the hospital.

At Zarah's request, Joe began to sleep in Damon's old bedroom and moved his toiletries into the boys' former bathroom. It was as if Zarah had drawn a chalk line down the middle of the house. Living separate lives inside the same home was a solution that seemed to work.

Drew was coming home from his sophomore year at Michigan State on spring break. Zarah was scheduled to work that day, so it was up to Joe to pick his son up at the bus stop.

Right before she was about to leave for work, Zarah walked into Joe's home office to remind him that he had to go in thirty minutes to make it to the bus stop in time to pick up Drew. Joe appeared to be deep into his paperwork, and he did not acknowledge Zarah when she spoke. She watched him reach for his coffee cup and slowly lowered it to the floor.

Zarah instantly knew what was happening.

"What's in that cup?" she firmly asked.

"Coffee."

"Let me see it!"

"It's fucking coffee, Zarah. Please leave me alone. I'm busy here."

"Why would you find it necessary to hide your cup from me if it's only coffee, Joe? Let me see that cup!" she demanded. He ignored her and continued reading the papers in front of him.

Zarah's mind began to calculate... *If he is to leave in thirty minutes to pick up Drew, he will be adequately drunk after drinking a mug full of alcohol.*

She had ignored his drinking, even after threatening him that the marriage would be over if he didn't stop.

How many times has he driven drunk, and I've ignored it? But now, because it involves my son, I'm angry. She was ashamed of herself when she finally admitted that ignoring Joe's drunk driving was putting other people at risk.

"You will *not* pick up Drew today, and you will *never* pick him up again!"

Zarah called Liz, told her that Joe couldn't pick up Drew because of a work emergency, and asked if she could pick Drew up at the bus stop. Liz gladly agreed to help out. When Zarah hung up the phone, she wished to tell her sister about her miserable life with Joe, but too much time had passed. Why upset her when Joe might eventually straighten himself out?

In hindsight, when would the right time have been to tell Liz? Zarah was, by nature, a happy person. Raising her boys gave her great joy—that part of her life was never a lie. Zarah had her own life to distract her from her husband's issues. She lived for her sons and career and ignored the elephant in the room, her husband, in all his oddness.

In his typical slurred speech the following day, Joe said he had to "go to the post office." Zarah watched him through a crack in the blinds as he drove away from the house. The post office would have been a right turn at the end of their street... Joe turned left.

Zarah did not believe anything he told her anymore, and she found herself suspicious of nearly every word he spoke. Last week, he went to the post office and did not return home for two hours. The post office was two blocks from their home, and the trip should have taken him fifteen minutes. Zarah didn't bother asking him where he had been —she didn't need to listen to another of his fabrications.

She picked up her phone and dialed the local police department.

"My husband just left the house—he is driving drunk."

"Your husband or your ex-husband?" The dispatcher asked.

"We live in the same house, but we are separated."

"Legally separated?" the dispatcher inquired. Zarah could not determine why that mattered and detected sarcasm in the dispatcher's voice.

"I am not trying to get him in trouble. I'm trying to stop him from killing himself or someone else."

Zarah thought that she heard the dispatcher snicker.

"We cannot stop every ex-husband that an angry ex-wife reports."

Zarah gave the dispatcher Joe's name and license plate number, but she had no confidence anyone would intervene. The dispatcher did not believe her and thought she was out for revenge. Joe had become an adept drunk driver, and there would probably be no overt reason for the police to pull him over... And they certainly would not pull him over simply because "an angry wife" had reported him.

Seven

The contract

THE VERY LIFESTYLE Joe led *had* to be damaging his health. Zarah approached her husband one evening as he relaxed in his recliner with a beer.

"Joe, can I take your blood pressure?"

"Stop it, Zarah. I'm fine." He didn't try to hide his annoyance.

"If you are fine, you have nothing to worry about."

Zarah placed her stethoscope into her ears, wrapped the cuff around his arm, and inflated the cuff. As she watched the needle pulsate downward, she consciously kept her jaw from dropping open.

"218 over 116!" she announced. "Joe, you need to see a doctor! You have severe hypertension!" Her husband was a ticking time bomb.

"I'm fine," he sounded bored and continued watching television.

"Hypertension is a *silent* killer, Joe. You *have* to see a doctor. You have no choice!"

"I said, I'm fine!" He spoke with force. Only an act of God would get him into a doctor's office.

The stench of cigarette smoke on her husband was the rule and not the exception. Zarah had never seen him in the actual act of smoking, nor did she ever see a pack of cigarettes on him. At one point, she conceded and told him to smoke on the back porch. That Joe found it necessary to do everything secretively was in itself more disgusting to Zarah than the actual act of smoking itself.

As a last-ditch effort to save their marriage, Zarah proposed a contract. If Joe agreed to it and worked toward its terms, their marriage would stand a fighting chance. If Joe sufficiently progressed, she might regain something that no longer existed in their marriage on any level... respect. At that point, there was none left.

If Joe had failed to agree to the contract, she would have had to consider other options, but she had no idea what her next move would be. All she knew was that she would have to do something.

It read:

• Stop drinking. If necessary, consider enrolling in a treatment program.
• Attend AA meetings.
• Join a smoking cessation program.
• Establish yourself with a medical doctor. Schedule yearly exams.
• Talk to a professional about the time you served in the war.
• Go to marriage counseling *together.*

It was a tall order, but she didn't care. His habits turned her off, and without some changes, his habits were going to kill him.

That evening, she presented the contract to him, and for the first time in their marriage, she evoked a response, but it was far from the reaction she had anticipated...

"I'm going to be homeless!" he cried out after reading the contract.

"Joe, what are you talking about?! Why are you going to be homeless?" His reaction made no sense whatsoever.

"I've always known that I would end up homeless!" he cried again.

He began to pace back and forth in the living room—not unlike an animal trapped in a cage.

"I don't understand your line of thinking... I want you to be healthy and our marriage to survive! We live separate lives, Joe. We don't talk, and I have *no* idea what's happening in your head!"

Joe continued to pace. Exasperated, Zarah grabbed his arm and stopped him in his tracks.

"Joe, could you please look at me?"

He made eye contact but was uncomfortable—it was an effort.

"*Why* must you drink all day? What is it that you're trying so hard to numb? What is so horrible?! You don't talk to me, so I can't help you. It's only a matter of time before you get into a drunk driving accident! That is the direction you are headed! You are killing yourself, and you could kill someone else! You need professional help, Joe."

"I don't *want* to live," he said just above a whisper as he pulled free from her grip.

"You'd sooner die than stop drinking?! You have a lot to live for, Joe. After everything that's happened... I am still here! God help me, but I am still here! And you have your sons! We could have grandchildren someday. Does alcohol mean more to you than your family?!"

Sadly, Zarah knew the answer to her question. If she were a gambling woman, she would never bet on Joe getting sober. He was hardcore, and he knew of no other way to be.

He paced for several more minutes, stopped and took a deep breath.

"Okay, give me the goddamn thing. I'll sign it."

Zarah was amazed—she finally elicited a reaction, even though his response was pitiful. His irrational fear that he would become homeless (if he did not comply with the terms of the contract) could work in her favor.

"I don't expect this will be easy, Joe, but we'll do it together. And we'll find a good marriage counselor."

Zarah put her hand on his shoulder. She hated to see him reduced to this. But maybe this was his rock bottom, and she could help him crawl out of his pit.

That evening, she quietly went into the bottom drawer of Joe's nightstand to retrieve their only gun, then hid it in the trunk of her car. In the morning, she would take it to the local police station and tell them to dispose of it. When they ask her why, she'll tell them that she suspects her husband may be suicidal. She won't mention that she had pushed him to his limits and wasn't sure what he might do.

Eight

Through the window

ZARAH LAUGHED WHEN she realized it had been exactly one year since Joe agreed to "the contract."

He had displayed a feeble attempt to fulfill the terms for several weeks. He went to a doctor and was prescribed medication for his hypertension. But last week, Zarah counted… Only three pills were missing from the original bottle, and he never had the prescription refilled. During the past year, he told Zarah he was taking the medication every morning. He said that he occasionally went to the doctor's office to monitor his blood pressure and told Zarah what his blood pressure reading had been that day. She believed him.

He had never stopped drinking and instead began using mouthwash to mask his breath. Zarah had no clue where he was hiding the booze. She kept no alcohol in the house, yet he was in a perpetual state of some level of drunkenness, and he consistently smelled like a dirty ashtray.

There was no more denying… Her marriage had been a sham filled with threats and broken promises. She could no longer count all the chances she'd given him. Why had she re-drawn her line in the sand so many times? Only four years ago, she sat in the backyard with him and told him that her feelings had changed—she was no longer in love with him. He had no change after that, and she continued with the status quo.

At nineteen years old, she did not possess the maturity to recognize the quirks in Joe's personality as warning signs. She saw him only as a handsome man who loved her. And truth be told, he was her subconscious ticket to move out of her parents' home.

Damon and Drew were busy with their own lives. Zarah and Joe rattled around in the quiet, empty house. There was no longer music blasting up through the floorboards as it once did when the boys' band practiced, and the piano in the living room sat silent. Joe and Zarah spoke to each other only when necessary, accentuating how eerily quiet the house had become.

Zarah was convinced that her little Rosie felt sympathy for her, and maybe the dog understood the gravity of the situation better than any other soul on earth. Zarah was Rosie's alpha, and Rosie was Zarah's shadow. They were physically separated only when Zarah had to work.

In the past few months, Rosie had become bloated and sick. Zarah found herself cleaning up after her multiple times a day, and she knew that the day was coming when she would have to say goodbye. Rosie did not seem to be in pain, but recently, she had begun to grunt whenever Zarah reached down to pick her up as if bracing herself for certain discomfort.

With her children grown and gone, Zarah's career became her main focus. She was still attractive—maybe more so now than in her early forties. People often guessed her to be much younger than her actual age. She worked out regularly, and she took long daily walks. She usually brushed her hair into a ponytail and wore little make-up, but she never left the house without putting on hoop earrings of some design.

Through a friend, Zarah found a marriage counselor. Joe refused to go with her, so she went to the appointments alone. The counselor, Dr. Foxen, was a former Catholic priest who left the church because he had fallen in love and gotten married. Zarah didn't know if his history would work for or against her, but he had come highly recommended.

Although she was raised Catholic, Zarah no longer practiced the faith. She didn't like that men in pointy hats wrote the church rules. She had read the bible from cover to cover, and nowhere did she find anything that stated you should confess your sins to a priest, not eat meat on Friday, or that, for a fee, you could be granted an annulment after a long term marriage ended—even after children were born into the union. How could men make those decisions? Who gave bishops and cardinals God-like authority to make those calls?

Zarah felt closest to God when she walked in nature. Talking to Him directly felt far more natural than sitting in a confessional booth and telling your sins to a man behind a screen. She had raised her boys in the Catholic church and saw that they received all their sacraments, but from that point on, she left them to make their own decisions. They were good people, and she felt confident they were on the right path.

On her first appointment with Dr. Foxen, Zarah curled up in a big chair across from him. She spoke rapidly as she explained the state of her marriage. An hour was insufficient to tell him everything that had led her to this point. Her final sentence spoke volumes to the counselor...

"I don't want to break up the family." She stared down at her folded hands.

"Zarah... *nobody* should be this unhappy. Nobody," Dr. Foxen spoke with concern.

Zarah expected he would give her advice on how to *save* the marriage. He was, after all, an ex-priest. She was surprised that his advice was to the contrary.

"Zarah, you've been through a lot. Before we meet next week, I want you to do something... I want you to take a week off of trying to 'fix' your husband. As long as he doesn't harm you in any way, observe his behavior. Don't obsess about watching him; only observe him... As if you're watching from a distance. Your husband is *not* your responsibility."

"But he is! If he gets behind the wheel and has an accident when he's drunk, that will reflect on me... and on our children! He could kill someone, then we'd have to live with that!"

"Have you tried calling the police when he leaves the house?"

"Yes... They blew me off."

As she walked back to her car, she felt something foreign... She had never told anyone about Joe before today—not even Liz. For a moment, she thought she had done something wrong—her mother would have *never* approved of her discussion with the counselor. She had kept everything locked inside, and for the first time in her life, she had confided in someone. The emotion she was feeling was peculiar. The words... "Your husband is not your responsibility," resounded in her head—that thought had *never* occurred to her before. She finally recognized the emotion she felt... It was relief.

"Why did I do that?!" she whispered as she approached her car, "Why did I cover for him all those years?" She shook her head in disgust. She knew why she did it... She did it to protect him. But maybe it was more than that. Maybe she concealed their problems for selfish reasons so their marriage would appear normal, even perfect, to the outside world. She would have to think about that.

She turned her face up to the clear blue sky and felt the sun's healing warmth on her skin. In her mind's eye, she saw herself clawing out of a deep, dark hole, struggling to the surface and breathing as if she had just run a marathon.

A huge chapter of her life was behind her, and another chapter was about to begin. She wished she had a crystal ball. In the past hour, she had told Dr. Foxen everything, and she would bet good money that the doctor's ears were still burning.

Joe's cousin Emma called, and Zarah answered. Emma asked if she and Joe were going to their nephew Jason's wedding in Dayton in two weeks and would it be okay if she hitched a ride with them? The invitation to the wedding hung under a magnet on the refrigerator—it mocked Zarah every day as she did her best to ignore it.

"We are not going, Emma." Zarah definitively said. It tugged at her heartstrings to miss Jason's wedding—she had watched him grow up. But she could not imagine spending a weekend in a hotel room with Joe.

"Why not!?" Emma was confused. In the past, Zarah and Joe went to all the family functions. Zarah also loved planning family gatherings, often for no particular reason.

"Emma, I hope you are sitting down. I have to explain something to you… Joe and I live separate lives. We live in the house together, but I no longer consider us married."

"What?! That is ridiculous!" Emma yelled into the phone. "You've been married for a long time! You two need to figure this out!"

Zarah maintained her composure. Emma was in her seventies and grew up at a different time… a time when getting a divorce was something to be ashamed of.

"I don't expect you to understand, Emma, but we have serious problems. And I *have* been trying to 'figure it out' for years!"

"Zarah, I am begging you… come to Jason's wedding! You can't do this to the family! Are you thinking of divorcing Joe?"

"Emma, I'm sorry. I can't…"

"Just come!" Emma interrupted. "We'll have fun! I'll stick with you the entire time. Tell Joe that he has to sleep on the floor."

"I'm not sure, Emma…" Zarah felt herself giving in.

"Zarah, you can't split your family up! What are you thinking?!"

"Okay, okay. I'll talk to Joe," Zarah conceded.

"I'll find other travel arrangements for myself so you two can be alone."

During the drive to Dayton, Zarah and Joe spoke to each other only when necessary, and not knowing when he last drank, Zarah did the driving.

"I'm going out for coffee," Joe stated not five minutes after they checked into their hotel room.

Zarah doubted that it was coffee he needed, but she would be glad to have some space. She had had enough of him in the silent four-hour car ride. The hotel room was cramped, and they were not due to meet his family for several hours. She brought along a novel. Reading for pleasure was a luxury she rarely allowed herself, and she relished the thought of laying on the bed and losing herself in someone else's drama for a change.

He returned two hours later. She didn't bother to ask him what had taken so long.

The twenty or so family members who arrived from out of state agreed to meet in the hotel lobby at four o'clock. That would give them an hour to visit each other before driving to the restaurant where the rehearsal dinner would be held.

"I have to leave for a few minutes," Joe stated for a second time since arriving at the hotel. He had showered, put on a sports coat and tie, and was ready for the evening.

There was an apparent nervousness in his voice, and she suspected that he must be highly addicted. Being away from home and his hidden supply of alcohol was rocking his world.

"Why do you have to leave *again,* Joe?! We will go downstairs to the lobby to meet your family in ten minutes! Where do you have to go that is so important?"

"I need to get another cup of coffee." His excuse was weak, even for Joe.

"There is free coffee in the lobby!" Zarah informed him.

"That coffee is terrible."

"How do you know that? You haven't tried it!" Zarah was well aware that she was wasting her breath.

"I want a *good* cup of coffee," he argued.

"Another one… in three hours. You can't live without another 'good' cup of coffee. Since when have you become a coffee connoisseur?"

He blankly stared at her.

"Go," she flatly answered.

The door closed quickly behind him—he wasted no time leaving. She was exasperated. She would go down to the lobby and greet his family by herself. As far as she was concerned, he could show up whenever he wanted to.

Minutes later, Zarah was ready for the evening. She had bought a floral sundress for the occasion. She locked the door behind her and walked toward the elevator. She could hardly wait to see Joe's relatives—many of whom she had not seen in years.

Joe's family had become *her* family. She had grown close to them, and it sometimes scared her that if she divorced Joe, she would lose them—they would no longer be a part of her life. It hardly seemed fair. Only one of her in-laws was aware of their marital problems... Emma. But Emma would not betray her confidence. Emma just hoped the whole mess would go away.

She waited for the elevator—it was taking forever. Directly to the left of the elevator was a porthole window... She stepped forward and looked through it. It looked down on the lobby one floor below, and she saw her in-laws gathering. They were hugging and laughing—they were not known to be a quiet group. They'd be happy when they saw her, and she anticipated receiving a hug from each and every one of them.

Zarah suddenly saw Joe enter the lobby from the main lobby doors. He walked toward his relatives, conversed with them for a minute, then left the group and walked directly up to the reception desk. He said something to an employee; then the employee handed a small object to him from under the counter. Zarah could not make out what it was.

He then quickly turned and walked back out the lobby doors. Some of his relatives looked at each other and shrugged their shoulders—they didn't understand why he had so abruptly left.

Zarah quickly walked over to a large window that overlooked the hotel grounds in the same direction her husband was heading. She immediately spotted Joe and watched as he approached a man standing beside a large ashtray and lighting a cigarette. They spoke briefly; then, the stranger handed Joe a cigarette. Joe reached into his pocket and pulled out a matchbook (the matchbook he had asked the hotel clerk for).

"Guess it wasn't caffeine you needed, husband. You needed a nicotine fix," Zarah whispered sarcastically into the window.

Zarah stood as if frozen. She had never seen him smoke before—he looked like someone else, not her husband. He was relaxed talking to the stranger, and they seemed to have a lot to say to each other—certainly more than he had spoken to her on their four-hour drive to Dayton. The stranger snuffed out his cigarette and exchanged additional words with Joe. They laughed as if they were old friends.

As if mesmerized, Zarah couldn't break her stare through the window—she was peering into his private world. He was alone. She watched him pull his phone out of his pocket and intently studied the screen.

He took one long, last drag and snuffed out his cigarette. Nervously, he put his phone back into his pocket, then turned and began to walk quickly *away* from the hotel.

"Where the hell are you going, Joe?" Zarah whispered into the window.

He walked faster and faster until he reached the end of the driveway, then crossed to the far side of the street. She stood at absolute attention, trying not to blink, to absorb every detail of that moment.

A car drove up alongside Joe, slowed down, and came to a stop. Zarah squinted, but she could not see the driver's face. When Joe approached the car, several trucks drove by, obscuring her view. Seconds later, when the trucks cleared, the vehicle was gone... and so was Joe.

"What the hell!" she said to herself. "Did he just get into that car?!"

Her heart was racing. She took several deep breaths and tried to compose herself. She walked back to the elevator and pressed the down button. She would step off the elevator in a few moments and enter into the gathering. She knew that they would immediately ask her where Joe went. She would say, "He's become a coffee enthusiast, and he went to find a cup of coffee." They'd all laugh and point out that there is a coffee pot with free coffee only steps away from them. She would then tell them, "He wants a *good* cup of coffee." Nobody would doubt her. Lying for Joe had become second nature; she was very good at it.

She would not confront her husband that weekend with what she saw out the window. She'd talk to Dr. Foxen next week. Better yet, she'd insist that Joe accompany her to the next therapy session. After all, Dr. Foxen was a marriage counselor, and she should not be attending marriage counseling sessions by herself. She would confront Joe about what she saw when they were both in Dr. Foxen's office and Dr. Foxen, in all his wisdom, would help guide them through this inexplicable situation.

Dr. Foxen was surprised to see Joe enter the room with Zarah for her standing Wednesday morning session. Zarah had given Joe no choice this time. It was either, "Come to the next marriage counseling session with Dr. Foxen, or I *am* filing for divorce."

Joe seated himself on the far end of the couch. He wore a jacket even though it was nearly eighty degrees that day. He crossed his arms across his chest and could have only appeared more defensive if he was donning a suit of armor.

"It's nice to meet you, Joe." Dr. Foxen reached out to shake Joe's hand. "You can remove your jacket if you'd like."

"I'm good," Joe replied.

"It's warm in here, Joe. Why don't you hang your jacket on the hook by the door?"

Zarah immediately scolded herself for making the suggestion. Even to her ears, she sounded more like a mother than a wife.

"I said I'm good," Joe replied curtly.

"Well, I have to say that it's very positive that you are *both* here today," Dr. Foxen said enthusiastically. "What has been going on with you two in the past week since we last spoke, Zarah?"

Zarah was curled up in her favorite chair—the chair that always seemed to hug her. But today was different—she could not find a comfortable position.

"We went to a wedding in Dayton," Zarah stated in a monotone.

"And how did that go?" the doctor asked.

"We set boundaries before we left. We got a room with two beds and agreed not to discuss our problems with the family. It would have ruined the entire weekend for everyone and not been fair to the bride and groom." She took a deep breath and continued...

"We were in our hotel room for five minutes when Joe told me he had to leave to get a cup of coffee; then he returned two hours later. After he showered and dressed for the rehearsal dinner, he told me he had to leave... *again...* to get another cup of coffee. Apparently, he has become a coffee enthusiast," she said sarcastically.

She redirected her tone and adjusted her posture to face her husband.

"What you aren't aware of, Joe, is that I saw you through a window. I saw you bum a cigarette off a total stranger."

Joe didn't flinch. He remained in the exact position he originally sat down in. She thought he *must* be sweating profusely inside his jacket. He sat mum for minutes as the counselor, and Zarah waited for him to respond.

"Joe," Dr. Foxen broke the silence. "Do you have anything you want to say to your wife?"

"I'm stupid," he finally answered.

Dr. Foxen and Zarah quickly exchanged glances. They waited for Joe to give further explanation, but those two words were all he had to say.

"May I go on? There is more, *much* more."

"Of course, Zarah. Continue."

"I then watched you, Joe, after you extinguished your cigarette. I watched as you walked *away* from the hotel. You nearly broke into a run. When you reached the end of the driveway and crossed the road, you disappeared. Did you get into the car that stopped next to you? Where did you go, Joe?! You didn't return for over an hour!"

She could not look in the direction of her husband any longer and stared into her lap at a tissue she held tightly. She thought she would cry when she explained what she saw—but her eyes were dry.

Dr. Foxen was speechless. Zarah wished he would say something, anything, to break the silence. Something wise. Something that would explain away what she saw the day her husband vanished before her eyes.

"Joe," Dr. Foxen finally spoke up. "Can you explain this to your wife? Where did you go? Don't you think Zarah deserves an explanation?"

Again, Zarah and the doctor waited for Joe to answer.

"I'm stupid."

"Oh my God! Are you a fucking broken record?!" Zarah nearly screamed. "Don't you have anything else to say?! Where did you go, Joe!"

She wanted to jump off her chair and pound him with her fists. Maybe then he would talk and reveal his secrets, and she would get some answers. She took a few deep breaths and did her best to regain some composure.

She felt as if she was watching a movie—a bad one. One she would turn off if given the choice. How did she allow herself to be fooled for so many years? What did she love about this man for so long? A man who never loved her back and was indifferent toward her throughout their entire marriage.

On some level, Zarah had always been aware that Joe had a darkness about him. In her naïveté, she convinced herself he was mysterious. She thought that, eventually, she would help him find peace and happiness. She would help him discover a revelation about himself. For so long, she had believed she would succeed at bringing her husband out of the shadows. Now she understood... She had been fooling herself to avoid the inevitable.

What had happened in her life to make her this complaisant? Why did she give this marriage so much of her energy? Her husband was sick—sicker than she ever imagined. He would need years of therapy, and she knew she would have to hold him at gunpoint to get him to go.

For the rest of the session, Zarah felt sorry for Dr. Foxen. He tried his hardest to be helpful, but he struggled, and nothing he said from that point forward was useful, and he knew it. His job was to save marriages, but he knew that this one should be ended. The remainder of the session was one of the most uncomfortable hours of Zarah's life.

Joe sat in the same position for the entire hour with his arms folded across his chest. Beads of sweat freely rolled down his forehead, and he never spoke another word.

After they left Dr. Foxen's office, Joe stuffed his hands in his pockets and walked straight toward his car. She was glad they drove separately. She watched as he walked up the street. She thought she should care more, but she could not have cared less. Would she even cry if he fell off the face of the earth? At that point, she doubted it.

She pulled her cell phone out of her pocket and dialed. Liz answered.

"Liz, can I stay with you for a while?"

"What's wrong?!" Liz's sibling intuition shifted into high gear.

"I'll explain when I get there. You might want to have a glass of wine ready... One for each of us."

As she packed her bag to leave, she felt her heart breaking... Not because she was leaving Joe but because she was leaving Rosie behind. She couldn't take the sick dog into her sister's home—she needed to be cleaned up after multiple times a day. Joe would take care of her. He was home all day and loved the dog as much as she did.

Rosie whimpered at Zarah's feet as she packed her suitcase. The dog was intelligent—something was different this time. Zarah wasn't simply getting dressed for work. The suitcase meant that Zarah was going away. The dog tipped her head from one side to the other as she tried to make sense of the situation.

Zarah knelt beside her precious companion, took her in her arms, and buried her face in her fur. She had no idea how much the dog could understand—maybe she knew more than Zarah gave her credit for.

She walked down the stairs with her suitcase, placed it by the door, and then walked directly to her husband's office.

"I'm leaving," she flatly stated.

"Where are you going?" Joe looked horrified. He spoke in a tone that used to tug at her heart but no longer influenced her one way or the other.

"I'm going to stay with Liz for a while. Please, take care of Rosie," Zarah choked out.

"Zarah! You don't have to do this!" he pleaded.

"I *do* have to do this. I need time… away from you. Our marriage has been a living hell. You haven't kept one promise you've made, and I don't know who you are anymore. And truth be told, I don't think I've *ever* known who you are."

"Please, Zarah, don't leave me!"

"Give me one good reason I should stay!" She put her hands on her hips.

"You're my wife! We are married!"

"Joe, If you'll admit to me where you went that day at the hotel… If you tell me whose car you got into, who you met, and for what reason... If you explain why you are always disappearing... Then I'll consider staying."

"Zarah..." He said nothing more. Whatever it was he was hiding would remain locked in him forever.

She felt nothing but the need for distance when she turned her back and walked out of his office. How do you love someone who lives a double life? A secret life? It is so secret that a wife is not allowed knowledge of it.

Rosie whimpered as Zarah walked toward her suitcase. Zarah had never spent more than a few days away from her beloved dog, and they had never parted like this before. Zarah dropped to her knees.

"Rosie... Mommy has to go away for a little while. I can't take you with me." She gently took Rosie into her arms. Rosie didn't move a muscle and stared at the door as if she was telling Zarah, "Take me with you."

The grief of leaving Rosie behind was almost enough to make her stay, but the need to escape from Joe was far greater. She had to go quickly, or her tears would rise to the surface—she had to maintain control of the situation.

Rosie was becoming more bloated by the day, and her grunting sounds were now heard when she walked across a room. Zarah couldn't do it... She couldn't leave her.

For the past twelve years, Rosie had been her shadow. She had been at the door waiting for her every time she returned home from work at midnight. Rosie insisted on sitting on Zarah's lap whenever they went for a ride in the car. She slept next to her. It was almost as if the dog was connected to her by an invisible string. When Zarah was troubled, the dog sensed it. Rosie was her guardian angel in a dog's body.

It felt impossible to leave. The dog needed Zarah more now than ever. Zarah should be at Rosie's side to help her through her final days. Rosie should die in her arms, and Zarah's face should be the last Rosie sees before taking her final breath.

Zarah held her dog as tightly as she could without causing her discomfort. She could no longer hold back her tears—she had never felt this conflicted in all her life. Rosie was so much more than a dog.

Joe walked into the kitchen.

"Zarah, you've got to stop this nonsense."

"It's not nonsense," she said as firmly as she could manage.

She had tried everything to save their marriage. She had redrawn her line in the sand more times than she wanted to admit to. She had ridden the rollercoaster with Joe for far too long. The memory of him walking away from the hotel gave her all the strength she needed to make her next move. She set her precious Rosie down.

"How long will you be gone?"

"I can't answer that." She wasn't being evasive; she had no clue. She picked up her suitcase, turned the doorknob and walked out.

After backing down the driveway, she stopped and looked back at the house. Rosie was watching her through the front window. She locked eyes with her dog.

"Oh, my little Rosie... I'm sorry, I'm so sorry," she cried into the windshield. The timing could not be worse. Rosie's face in the window may be the last time she would ever see her, and the sadness of leaving the dog behind would haunt her for the rest of her life.

She broke eye contact with Rosie, put the car in drive... and drove away.

Nine

Time away

ZARAH MELTED INTO her sister's welcoming arms. Liz took the suitcase from her hand and led her to the kitchen table. For the past few years, Liz had suspicions that everything was not as perfect as her sister had let on.

"It seems silly to have a glass of wine this early in the day," Zarah said.

"Well… It's five o'clock somewhere," Liz attempted to lighten the mood. "I'm going to make you something to eat."

"I'm not hungry," Zarah answered.

It was apparent to Liz that her sister had recently lost weight along with her appetite. Liz began to make a sandwich for her anyway.

"Zarah, you can stay with me for as long as you'd like… But what about Rosie? You love that dog as much as you love your kids!"

"Rosie is sick. She's incontinent. I couldn't do that to your beautiful home. Joe will take care of her. He may not love me, but he loves the dog."

"Don't say that, Zarah. Joe loves you! But who will care for her when he leaves on a business trip?"

"That's not a problem. He's working strictly from home these days."

"So, Zarah… What's going on? In case you forgot, I'm your twin! We have 'woo-woo' intuition with each other, and I've sensed for quite some time that you're not happy."

"I don't know where to begin…. It's mostly his drinking —it's gotten progressively worse over the past few years. He can't hold down a job for long because every company he works for eventually figures out that he is drinking on the job. You've always thought that Joe walks on water, so I've kept things to myself… to spare you the disappointment. I didn't want to tell you about all the crazy that has been insidiously creeping into our marriage."

"But you've always been so crazy in love with Joe, Zarah!"

"I *was* madly in love with him… For a long time. I wore my rose-colored glasses for the first twenty years of our marriage. But something happened about the time I turned forty. I began to see him in a different light. The boys were getting older, and I had a career. Without even realizing it, I created a life for myself that was independent of him. Somewhere along the way, I fell out of love."

"You should have told me, Zarah…" Liz's voice trailed off, and Zarah knew she had let her sister down.

"I used to wonder if it was all in my head—if I was making too much of things. Or that maybe I had an overactive imagination. If I didn't admit what was happening, then it wasn't happening. I wasn't only hiding things from you, Liz. I was hiding things from myself."

"You've always seemed so happy…"

"I *am* a happy person. I have my sons and my career, which was enough to make me feel like I had won the lottery. I pretended that Joe's indifference toward me didn't matter. He could be as standoffish as he wanted, and I looked through it. I never *had* his love, so I never knew what was missing."

"I love Joe, but *you* are my sister, and I love you more. He has hurt you, so he will also have to contend with me now."

"Liz, just treat him the way you always have."

"Why, Zarah? Why are you protecting him?"

"Because old habits die hard. What is the definition of inertia? Nothing changes because that's the way it's always been. Look up inertia in the dictionary—you'll see my picture right next to the definition."

"Zarah, I won't let you beat yourself up."

"We appeared to be living the American Dream to the outside world. I should have had a white picket fence around my house!" Zarah laughed, but she wanted to cry.

"Zarah… You've always seemed to 'have it all.'"

"I've never 'had it all,' Liz. Joe does not walk on water. And my marriage is an f'ing mess…." Zarah's voice trailed off.

"Here, take a sip," Liz slid Zarah's glass of wine closer to her. Zarah did as told, then began to tell Liz the events that had changed their marriage. The floodgates had opened—Zarah could not stop talking. Liz listened intently to every ugly detail.

"Liz, it was a huge mistake keeping all of this to myself. If I could go back in time, I would have told you. But for my life, I cannot imagine when the time would have been right to have confided in you. I could have used your support over the years."

"What about the boys? Are they aware of what's going on?" Liz asked.

"I'm sure they're aware their father drinks too much—that I could *not* conceal hard as I tried. I never came right out and said, 'Your dad has alcoholism,' but they heard his slurred speech and smelled the vodka on him as well as I did. I called them both last night to tell them I will stay with you for a while."

"How did they react?" Liz wanted details. She never had children, and she loved Zarah's sons as if they were her own.

"They seemed to understand. Drew suspected something was going on for a long time. He said he once saw me putting a lock on the liquor cabinet. When he asked me why I was doing it, I told him, 'The lock isn't for you.' Damn, that was so many years ago, Drew was probably only thirteen at the time."

At that moment, Cameron walked into the kitchen. He bent down and hugged Zarah.

"Zarah, I wasn't eavesdropping, but I overheard your conversation from the other room."

Cameron, a self-proclaimed recovering alcoholic, had not touched a drop of alcohol in over twenty years. Liz and Zarah sometimes asked themselves if he indeed had alcoholism or if he was helping people to overcome their addictions.

"My life is exactly like the frog in a pot metaphor… The water temperature kept heating up, and I never knew when to jump out. I stayed until the pot was boiling. Now I suspect he's involved in a risky lifestyle, so I have no choice anymore."

"Well, you don't know that for sure," Liz reassured her.

"Then what the hell is he up to? He's not only under the influence 24/7, but he disappears! For hours at a time! And if I ask him where he was, he gives me a weak explanation. I don't believe a word he says anymore. I've moved my boundaries more times than I care to admit. There's nothing more I can do to help him. Everything has been tried… numerous times, and I'm afraid he's beyond saving."

"Do you think he'd ever do anything to hurt you?" Cameron said wide-eyed.

"Not intentionally. I installed a deadbolt on my bedroom door. He sleeps in Damon's old bedroom. We both live in our half of the house. He's never physically hurt me, but sometimes I'm afraid he's thinking of harming himself."

"Then you *are* afraid of him, Zarah," Cameron surmised.

"Let's just say I sleep better with the door locked."

"Is he home now?" Cameron asked.

"I have no clue. 'The police' have moved out, so he's free to come and go as he pleases without explaining himself to anyone." Zarah half-laughed.

"I'm going over to your house," Cameron said as he grabbed his car keys. "I need to talk with my dear brother-in-law. Don't tip him off that I'm on my way. I'd like to surprise him."

Cameron waited at the front door for Joe to answer. He saw Joe's car through the garage window and knew he was home. He suspected Joe was ignoring the doorbell and wanted Cameron to give up and go away. He pounded harder and yelled, "Joe! Open up! It's me, Cam!"

The front door finally opened, and a smiling Joe welcomed Cameron into the house.

"How are you, Cam?" Joe said as he patted his brother-in-law on the back.

"I'm good. Joe… What is going on with you? You must be aware that your wife is at my house, and she's pretty upset."

"We are going through a rough patch," Joe said, trying to make light of the situation.

Cameron smelled alcohol as Joe spoke, but then, he had smelled alcohol on Joe's breath for years.

"A 'rough patch' Joe? This sounds a little more serious than a rough patch."

As if the wind had been knocked from his sails, Joe flopped down on the couch and covered his face with his hands. He did not want to discuss this with Cameron… or anyone.

Cameron thought his brother-in-law appeared much older than his years. His face was red and tensed, and his eyes were bloodshot. He looked as if he was experiencing excruciating physical pain.

"Joe! Talk to me! What the hell is going on?!" Cameron demanded. Joe dropped his hands and stared at the floor.

"She thinks I drink too much," he said flatly.

"And what do you think, Joe?"

Cameron was good at this. Joe was not the first person he would counsel about his addictions, and he would not be the last.

Cameron began to tell Joe what his own life was like when he was actively drinking. How, as a younger man, he attempted to drink his problems away. When he felt stressed, he drank. When his boss was on his ass, he drank. If a girlfriend broke up with him, he drank himself into a three-day bender. Drinking, he explained, was the coping mechanism he used to numb anything negative that he was feeling. But after a while, everything that happened, ever so slight, felt like a personal attack, and he no longer needed a reason to drink. His very breath was negative because he had grown to hate his life. It was a vicious cycle that he thought was impossible to break.

Cameron went on to explain how AA works and how to follow the twelve-step program to achieve sobriety. He gave Joe a copy of The Serenity Prayer, and he offered to be Joe's sponsor.

"It's a life-long commitment, Joe. Sobriety doesn't happen overnight."

Joe accepted Cameron's kind offer of help and promised to meet him at the next AA meeting.

"You may have convinced yourself that drinking is the only way to cope with life, but once you step away from alcohol, you'll eventually see it for what it truly is... It's the devil, Joe—a devil you buy in a bottle. It's a slow path to your demise. It's much easier to numb yourself than it is to feel. But it's okay to feel, Joe. It may be the hardest thing you'll ever have to do, but working through emotional pain *is* the only real coping mechanism. Alcohol puts your problems 'on hold.' You can drink a case of vodka; when the case is empty, the problems will still be there... only worse. Drinking not only hurts you, but it hurts everyone who loves you. It's an endless spiral to nowhere, and not everyone will travel down that dark path with you."

"Zarah wants out of this marriage, that's for sure," Joe replied.

"Joe... Put yourself in her shoes. If she were the alcoholic, and she refused any help you offered, how long would you stay by her side?"

"Forever. We took vows."

"You did, but those vows have been broken—possibly beyond repair. You are sick, but Zarah is sick, too."

"Why is Zarah sick? She looks fine to me! She has a fancy career and all her fancy friends from work. She has a life, and her life does *not* include me."

"Zarah is sick because she's co-dependent on you. Drinking has excluded Zarah from a normal life with you. Creating a life independent from you was her survival mechanism. Would you prefer she drank her life away right alongside you?"

"No, of course not. That's ridiculous," Joe replied.

"Then you have to understand why she's done what she's done."

As Cameron drove away from Joe's house, he was confident he had made his point to his brother-in-law. Joe sincerely listened to every word he had said and, with a warm handshake, accepted his offer to be his sponsor.

Weeks later, Cameron glanced toward the meeting room doorway in the hope of seeing Joe walk in. Joe never attended even one of the AA meetings, as he had promised.

When Zarah wasn't working and Liz was gone for the day, Zarah cleaned and organized every cabinet and closet in Liz's house. Keeping her hands occupied soothed her mind. After several weeks, there was no cabinet or closet that she had not transformed—Liz's clothes were organized by color, and her spice rack was in alphabetical order.

Zarah continued to see Dr. Foxen every week and relished the hour when she was free to say anything on her mind. Her sister always took her side, but Dr. Foxen was impartial, and he spoke his mind when he felt that Zarah needed to see a situation from a different perspective.

After living with Liz and Cameron for five weeks, Zarah's phone rang. It was Joe. She had not heard a word from him since she'd left, and she was surprised that, upon finally hearing his voice, she felt absolutely nothing.

"Come home, Zarah. Rosie misses you."

"The dog misses me? What about you? Has anything changed? Or will I walk back into the same shit storm that I walked out of five weeks ago?"

"I have changed, Zarah. I promise you. Since you left, I've been working on myself. You've given me a lot to think about."

"You didn't meet Cam at the AA meetings..." she flatly stated.

"I don't need that. I did it myself," he reassured her.

Thirty minutes later, Joe was driving up Liz's driveway. Zarah watched through the blinds as he gingerly lifted Rosie out of the car. The dog instinctively knew that Zarah was in the house and waddled to the front door as fast as possible. Her tail wagged so fast that it blurred. Zarah opened the door and took her precious Rosie into her arms. Joe misinterpreted Zarah's tears of joy as if they were meant for him.

"My little Rosie, I will *never* leave you again," she whispered to her dog.

Zarah would always appreciate the haven that Liz and Cam provided. Living there had been the right move. The time away from Joe and the weekly counseling sessions with Dr. Foxen had helped. She knew she had some big decisions ahead of her. After all, who leaves a marriage after twenty-eight years? Did the time she spent away change Joe in a meaningful way? He sounded sincere this time. Had he felt the sting of facing his demons without her?

Ten

Fresh start

DURING THE TIME she stayed with her sister, Zarah had an idea. Now that she was back home for a few weeks, it seemed the perfect time to present the idea to her husband…

"This house is far too big for the two of us. Let's move to a suburb near the city. I'd be closer to work, and you could set up another home office for yourself."

Their home *was* too big for them and far too quiet since both boys had moved out. It was filled with memories—both good and bad. It was the home that Damon and Drew grew up in, and it was the home where Zarah and Joe had grown further and further apart.

The only thing that Joe and Zarah seemed to do well in recent years was work on home projects together, and to Zarah, those were the times when they were the happiest in each other's company.

"We should find a fixer-upper!" she said, hoping he'd agree.

Zarah thought a move like this would end in one of two ways… She hoped that Joe would become so involved with home renovations that he would pull himself together and forget about drinking. However, the most likely scenario was that nothing would change. The outcome she *never* considered was… Everything would change.

"Has Joe stopped drinking since you returned home from your sister's house? Is he still disappearing for hours at a time?" Dr. Foxen inquired. He didn't say it, but he didn't have to. The doctor would have bet his bottom dollar that Joe hadn't changed at all, and he thought Zarah was giving her husband far, far too many chances.

Zarah wanted to prove to Dr. Foxen that leaving her husband for five weeks had changed him. Instead, all she heard when she spoke was her voice smoothing things over and making excuses.

"He's been much nicer to me since I've returned home. I don't smell booze or cigarettes on him, and I haven't noted any slurring in his speech. So maybe I did scare him straight by leaving."

"What about when you're working, Zarah? What does Joe do in your absence?"

"I… I don't know," she stammered.

"How is a new house going to save your marriage?"

"Working on home improvement projects is the only time we seem to like being together. If this plan doesn't work, then…" She had no idea how to finish the sentence.

"Then…" Dr. Foxen interjected, "Will you re-write your line in the sand? Again?"

Zarah asked Joe to come with her to look at several potential new homes, but he had to stay home and work. Zarah and a realtor spent several days touring homes in the suburbs of Lansing. On the third day of searching, they walked into a circa 1950 Lannon stone ranch in a nicely maintained older neighborhood.

The house needed a lot of work. Zarah was pleasantly surprised that the kitchen had been recently renovated and had newly installed cabinets. She opened one of the cabinet doors and saw that sawdust from the installation remained.

"Wow, the owners didn't even have the gumption to clean out these cabinets," Zarah whispered to the realtor.

Zarah noted that every other room needed significant attention as they walked through the house. The basement had an outdated recreation room and a small second bathroom.

The house had a stale odor, and everything installed in the 1950s (including pine paneling, green broadloom carpeting, and scalloped ceiling light fixtures) was still present. It could take months or years to bring the house up to a modern standard... Which fit nicely into her plan.

"The house *has* good bones, but it's a hot mess," the realtor admitted to Zarah.

"This could work..." Zarah replied cautiously as she made a mental list of everything that would need to be done to make it habitable.

Zarah instinctively knew this *was* the house she and Joe would renovate. The house that might bring him out of the dark place in which he lived. He needed a project, a purpose. She would keep him so busy that he wouldn't have time to take a drink, smoke a cigarette, or go wherever it was he disappeared to. As a bonus, she would be only ten minutes from work—a nice break from the grueling fifty-minute commute she had driven to Lansing General for many years.

Later that same day, Joe and Zarah met the realtor at the house. Joe agreed... It had good bones, but it needed a ton of work. He reluctantly consented to make an offer on the house. If the offer were accepted, they would move from a spacious, modern home to a small, run-down fixer-upper.

Their offer was accepted the following morning.

The arduous task of paring down their belongings and furniture began. Half of everything they owned would have to be sold or donated because their new (old) house was half the size of their current home.

Rosie didn't understand what was happening. Strange people were coming into her home and taking away pieces of furniture. Moving boxes were stacked against the walls. Zarah knew all the commotion was confusing to her sick and elderly dog. Zarah always kept Rosie close to her and gave her lots of love and attention.

One month later, after closing on the Lansing house, Zarah and Joe put the key in the lock, opened the door, and stepped inside. Their jaws dropped open... The former owners had left nearly everything behind. The house had a musty odor and was filled with shabby (cat hair-covered) furniture, old rugs, unused cleaning supplies, multiple cans of paint, and car products. They had even left their personal files and photo albums; the bathroom drawers were filled with toiletries.

"It didn't look this bad during the showing!" Zarah exclaimed.

Zarah eventually found out from the neighbors that the previous owners were in financial trouble, and they fled the state to escape the collection agencies. Joe and Zarah were on their own for the cleanup process. They had bought the house "as is" but never expected "as is" to mean they'd bought a house filled with garbage.

Zarah set Rosie on the front passenger seat every time she drove a carload of boxes to their new (old) home. When they arrived, Zarah lifted Rosie from the SUV and gently set her down on the driveway. Rosie cautiously entered the house—the scent of the prior owner's cat was in the air, and the "hunt" to find it began. The dog sniffed every room with her tail down between her legs. Zarah had to laugh. Of course, there was no cat, but even if there were, Rosie would freak out if she found one. Zarah was becoming hopeful that Rosie was beginning to like the new house—she had never known any other home than the one she lived in since she was a puppy.

Sadly, Zarah soon realized Rosie would not make the final move to Lansing. She could barely get out of her bed and had stopped eating and drinking. The grunting noise was now audible with her every breath.

The veterinarian was kind as he gave Rosie the two injections that would end her life. The first injection sedated her, and the second stopped her heart from beating. Zarah held Rosie in her arms through the procedure, and Joe sat at the back of the room.

"Rosie!" Zarah heard Joe cry out as Rosie took her final breath. Joe had loved the dog, too. She had given them twelve years of love and laughter, and often, Rosie's antics were the only thing that made them laugh.

While growing up, Damon and Drew had taught their dog many silly tricks. Rosie was quickly trainable, more than willing to perform her tricks for the family, and thrived on their undivided attention. Rosie's ultimate joy was going for a "ride in the car" unless the car was pointed toward the veterinarian's office.

Zarah called her sons that evening to give them the sad news. They had lost one of the best friends they ever had. Joe and Zarah didn't have the dog in common anymore, and Zarah hoped that planning the renovations for their Lansing home would give them something to talk about that would fill the enormous void Rosie's death left behind.

Zarah ordered a dumpster to be delivered, and emptying the house began. Not one thing the prior owners left behind was worth keeping. Liz and Cameron arrived and pitched in. Joe seemed engaged in the project, and neither Zarah nor Cameron could tell if he was drinking.

It took Zarah and Liz two days to thoroughly clean the kitchen while the men carried out all the former owner's furniture and tossed it into the dumpster. While they worked, they left the windows open to let the fresh air in and musty air out.

"This kitchen is now sterile!" Zarah was elated. "I can cook in here!"

"What about the bedroom?" Liz whispered.

"What about the bedroom?"

"You and Joe have slept in separate bedrooms for a long time. Are you going to set up separate bedrooms here, too?"

"This move represents a fresh start—we will sleep in the same bed." Zarah was trying to remain positive.

They still had room left in the dumpster, so they pulled up the old carpeting and were pleasantly surprised to find hardwood floors hidden underneath. The wood floors were rough, but Zarah thought they could be sanded and refinished. Next, they removed all the outdated light fixtures and filled the dumpster.

After several days, the transformation was incredible. Even though the house was screaming for renovations, it was clean. The house felt like a fresh canvas where she and Joe would create something new and beautiful... A project that could save their marriage.

Eleven

Nobody's there

FOUR WEEKS PASSED quickly as Joe and Zarah packed multiple carloads of their belongings and drove back and forth to their new (old) Lansing home. The movers arrived early and loaded their furniture into a moving van. Zarah stood in the driveway and watched as they pulled away with the truckload of their worldly possessions. Joe followed the moving van in his car. He would unlock the Lansing house to let them in when they arrived at their destination.

Zarah walked back into the empty house for the last time—the silence was deafening.

It was the home that her boys had grown up in. She could still hear the echo of their voices and the sound of their feet as they flew up the stairway for the first time and enthusiastically claimed which bedroom they wanted as their own. Rosie was a puppy then, hot on their heels and as excited as her human brothers.

Damon, by nature, was laid-back and took life in stride. In contrast, Drew was intense and competitive. They were two years apart but were the best of friends. They rarely fought, and even in a quarrel, Zarah always answered...

"You both have good brains. Figure it out yourselves."

Zarah swore, the day Drew was born, that she would not get involved when the boys fought—unless she saw blood. Her plan worked well; they never brought their problems to her as they grew up.

Her greatest joy came from watching her sons develop as musicians, and for many years, the music of her gifted sons filled the house with joy.

Zarah could still recall the floors vibrating under her feet from the music of their rock band, and she smiled at the memory of watching her dishes vibrate across the countertops as the music blasted up through the floors.

Over the years, she had carried many trays of food down the stairs to feed her hungry boys and their bandmates, and she had driven her van packed with their musical equipment and four excited boys to all of their "gigs."

Raising the boys in the Springfield house had been the greatest joy of Zarah's life—she thanked God for every minute of the experience. She was honored to be their mother and was proud that they were now on their own and making their way in the world.

But blended with the beautiful memories were how she struggled to keep all the balls in the air.

As she gazed out on the back patio for the last time, she remembered how she had told Joe several years ago that she didn't think she loved him anymore. She had been right—her feelings for him had died a slow and agonizing death.

She loved her sons, her dog, and her career, which had been enough to fill her days in the beautiful home she was about to leave for the last time. She paused, then turned around. She scanned the kitchen where she had made thousands of meals... The dining room where she had served Joe and the boys their dinner... The memory of little Rosie dancing around the dinner table begging for a handout and the hysterical laughter that followed. She scanned the living room where she and the boys had set up the Christmas tree many times and the ghostly space the piano had once occupied. She would have given anything at that moment to hear Damon play just one more song.

She would soon close the door on a beautiful life with a terrible underlying existence. Her failing marriage did not take the joy of raising her sons from her. She would always have that joy in her heart—it was hers.

She closed the door and swallowed hard... *This must be the definition of bittersweet.*

That night, in their new house, Joe and Zarah slept in the same bed for the first time in years. During the night, her foot accidentally touched his—she recoiled and moved closer to her side of the bed. It had been long since she felt anything remotely physical toward him, and she concluded... That part of her was dead.

She would continue on full steam with the renovation project and hope her feelings toward her husband would change. At that point, she had to admit that even if Joe would stop drinking, there might be too much water under the bridge for her to want to make their marriage work. If he miraculously "fixed" himself, she'd have to "fix" herself into someone who wanted him. Could she possibly be that naive again?

Joe set up his office in the basement rec room. His current job required part-time hours, but the home renovation "to-do" list was lengthy and should fill his days.

Zarah thought that this time, she was right, and the move was what they needed to create new memories and leave the ugly ones behind. If her marriage somehow succeeded, it would only be because they recreated themselves and found a way to fall in love—maybe for the first time.

One of the things Zarah loved about the new house was that it had a large, covered patio out the back door that had ample room for their patio furniture. To Zarah, sitting outside and watching the birds felt like heaven. One of the first things she did when they moved in was to hang bird feeders within eyeshot of the patio. She also hung hummingbird feeders and a grape jelly feeder for the orioles. She made a mental note to plant a native flower garden the following spring, then added the project to the "to-do" list on the refrigerator.

They lived in their Lansing home for several weeks when a summer storm rolled in. Joe was sitting outside underneath the covered patio.

From the kitchen where she was preparing dinner, Zarah heard Joe yelling. She could not make out what he was saying. She opened the door to see what was going on. The rain was falling hard on the fiberglass roof. Joe was alone, and Zarah had to speak loudly to be heard over the sound of the pounding rain.

"Joe, what's going on? I heard you yelling."

"I'm not yelling," he flatly stated as he stared at the rain falling off the side of the roof.

She closed the door and left him alone while preparing their dinner. Several minutes later, she heard him yelling again. He sounded terrified. What was happening?! She dashed to the back door and opened it again.

"Joe! Who are you talking to?!" She was frightened. Was someone in the backyard? Was someone hurting him? But there was no one around—he was alone.

He turned his head, locked his eyes on hers, and answered coldly…

"Who are YOU talking to?"

She quickly closed the door. Was he hallucinating? Was he drunk? Was he out of his mind? Did the pounding rain on the fiberglass roof sound like gunfire? Was he having flashbacks from the war? Or had he pickled his brain from many years of marinating it in alcohol and could no longer differentiate reality from fantasy?

Her heart was pounding. How would she let him back in the house? She had to think fast. They had been sleeping in the same bed since moving into the Lansing house. He was not in his right mind, and she did *not* want to sleep with one eye open.

She grabbed her car keys and got into her car. As she backed down the driveway, she made a mental list. First, she would buy a deadbolt. Then she would install it on the bedroom door tomorrow—when he told her he was "going to the post office," as he did every afternoon. She would have to work fast, but she knew what she was doing—she had done it once before. She would also buy a can of pepper spray and always keep it in her bra.

Later that evening, she would ask Joe to set up a cot for himself in his basement office, and then she would slide her dresser tight against the bedroom door before going to sleep that night.

Twelve

The first secret

SIX WEEKS OF living in their down-sized house had brought about many changes to the house, but no changes toward improving their marriage.

The hardwood floors had been refinished, and the windows and light fixtures were replaced. There was still a long list of projects ahead of them, but the house was clean and livable.

Even though Zarah had downsized their belongings, she intentionally retained some things that her sons would recognize from their childhood and used them throughout the house. As a result, Damon and Drew seemed to love the new house their parents had moved into, mainly when Zarah served them dinner on familiar dishes and when they saw family photographs displayed on the walls.

Joe could fix things if he put his mind to it, but Zarah was also a handywoman in her own right. She knew how to wield a hammer and use many tools—skills typically associated with men.

While Zarah was growing up, her father, Charlie, had a workshop in the garage, and Zarah took an interest in many of his tools. When she was eleven, she asked her father for instructions to use his wood-turning lathe. After he instructed her, she spent hours on the loud machine turning chunks of wood into candle sticks, then painted her creations in various colors to match the bedspread in her room.

Her father was a different person inside the workshop— he was patient and calm. Zarah enjoyed their time together in the workshop, especially when he explained the steps of building something as simple as a birdhouse. But she always knew that the father-daughter connection she felt toward him was limited to their time within the confines of the workshop. Once they stepped out, Charlie became Charlie again.

As their "to-do" list shortened, Joe withdrew into himself and once again became increasingly indifferent toward Zarah. The move was her last ditch effort, and keeping Joe engrossed in renovation projects was doing little to help him overcome his demons.

Early one morning, Zarah overheard a phone conversation between Joe and his most recent employer. From what she could surmise, Joe wasn't bringing in enough business and was being released from his third job in three years. Zarah did not blame Joe's boss for firing him. His mind never seemed to be on his work, and he never did anything more than he was required to do.

She often encouraged Joe to show initiative and take classes toward a degree to make his resume more competitive in the job market. But the answer he gave her was always the same… "Learn to be happy with what you've got, Zarah." What Zarah "got" was an apathetic husband, and after a while, she stopped encouraging him.

Zarah prepared herself for what she knew was coming. Whenever Joe was between jobs, his drinking would be at its worst. That day, he did not mention the phone conversation with his boss to her, and for the next week, he went about every morning as if he had a full day of work ahead of him.

Joe had always maintained a separate checking account and charge card to keep his work expenses separate from his family's. Zarah never thought much of it. They had many problems, but money never seemed to be one of them. Thanks to her steady income, they had saved slowly and steadily over the years, and their bank account was sufficient to help pay the boys' college tuition and provide Joe and Zarah with a decent retirement.

It was a scorching summer day, and Zarah was grateful that the home's ancient AC unit was still working. She returned to the kitchen and put the handful of mail she retrieved down on the counter. She ripped open the Master Card statement and expected to see a high balance because of the many charges they had recently made toward the home renovations.

Puzzled, she scanned the bill—she didn't recognize *any* of the charges. She then realized... She had mistakenly opened Joe's charge card bill instead of her own.

At that moment, Joe walked through the kitchen.

"Joe, I'm sorry I accidentally opened *your* Master Card bill. What is this charge for friendfinder.com?" Zarah asked curiously as she pointed to the line on the statement.

Joe quickly snatched the bill from her hand.

"I don't know."

"You don't know what the charge is? Look, it's right there..." She pointed at the bill.

"I said, I don't know," he said with determination as he turned and walked away.

Zarah stood as if frozen. She heard his office door close tightly behind him.

Three days later, Joe informed Zarah...

"I figured out what that charge for Friendfinder on my Master Card was for... I was searching for someone that I served with in Nam."

In all the years they had been married, Joe had barely spoken the word "Nam," much less mentioned any friendships he had during the war. He never maintained communication with anyone he served with.

"Okay," Zarah answered with feigned agreement.

She felt an intense suspicion rise. She only held the bill for seconds before he took it from her. What else was on the statement? She did not have enough time to study it. What else was he charging?

Whenever Joe was between jobs, Zarah paid his business charge card bill with money from their joint checking account. He still had not admitted to her that he had lost his most recent job.

Joe had come in from his morning "run." He went out for a run every morning. He didn't resemble a runner—he didn't have the sleek physique you would expect from someone who ran every day.

"I'm going to take a shower."

"Okay," Zarah answered flatly.

When she heard him turn on the shower, Zarah made a beeline to his top bedroom drawer, where he kept his wallet. She felt like a crazy woman. She felt foolish that she had trusted him to have a separate checking account and charge card for many years. And why did it take her so long to figure out he was up to no good?

She found his wallet, then fumbled as she pulled out his Master Card and jotted down the number. She ran to her computer. Joe took fast showers—she had only minutes to look up his statement.

She entered his charge number into the Master Card website. Damn. She would need his password to go any further.

After Joe got dressed, he told her that he was going to the post office.

Zarah watched through the front window as he drove down the street. When he approached the end of their road, he turned left—the post office was to the right.

She felt an adrenaline rush as she once again ran to her computer. Her fingers flew on the keyboard as she entered "friendfinder.com" into the search bar. She navigated to the information page but quickly discovered she would not get any information unless she joined the site. She found a phone number to call with questions and jotted it down.

She stood by the front window to watch for her husband's return. She didn't want him to catch her while she made the call. She dialed, and a man answered...

"Good morning, friendfinder. How may I help you?"

"Hi, good morning. I have a question... Would Friendfinder be a good website for me to search for a friend? I'm trying to find an old friend I served with in Vietnam..." she lied.

"Ma'am... this is a dating website. It can't look people up by their names. Everyone who joins remains anonymous."

She thanked him and hung up the phone. Her hands were shaking, and she felt the blood drain from her face.

"A dating website?! While I was trying every single thing I could think of to fix this damn marriage, he's been on a f'ing dating website?!" she said to herself.

The last time Joe had "left for the post office," he was gone for three hours. She had time, and she knew what her next move had to be. She logged back onto her computer and joined friendfinder.com.

It was almost too easy. There were only four men registered in their zip code. She began to read each profile.

The caption on the third profile caused her heart to skip a beat...

"Cold and Lonely Man in Lansing"

She scanned the profile...

"Your place or mine. Looking for friendship or more! New to Lansing. Would love to see the city with you."

"Oh my God... this has to be him," Zarah whispered. She recognized the sentence structure. The commas were placed incorrectly, and the spelling was at a fifth-grade level. She had seen these exact grammatical errors in his writing before. It was almost as if he had lost the ability to construct an intelligent sentence in the past several years. There was no doubt in her mind... "Cold and Lonely Man in Lansing" was her husband.

Nervously, she continued to scan the page, and the following sentence she read almost brought her to her knees...

"Interested in men *and* women."

Zarah never had a panic attack, but she thought she might be on the precipice of one.

"Men AND women?!" She yelled into the computer screen.

"Men!? He's fucking gay?!"

She had to leave for work in minutes. She had to pull herself together. How would she get through this day? She had a ten-hour shift ahead of her, and today was the first day of five. How would she get through the next fifty hours of work? She *had* to stay focused on her work—there was no room for error. Her mind *could not* be on her problems.

She heard the garage door open. Joe was home. She closed her computer and went to the kitchen to pack a lunch. Joe walked in.

"I'm leaving for work in a few minutes," she told her husband.

"Okay," he answered curtly. As he walked past her, she caught the all-too-familiar whiff of alcohol and cigarettes.

She wavered on confronting him with her discovery, but what would that accomplish? Was she surprised? Did she, on some level, suspect something like this all along? Was she exhausted? Or maybe she just no longer gave a shit.

She got into her SUV and began to drive toward the hospital. She was thankful for the short commute she now enjoyed.

"He's gay," she stated matter-of-factly to herself. "Or is he bi?"

There were things in the past that made her suspect that her husband's sexuality was in question. She thought back to an incident that happened many years ago...

Zarah had a pleasant conversation with a young, overtly gay man. She found him delightful and more than knowledgeable about what paint color was the most popular, and he went well with the carpet sample she held in her hand. Joe was not with her at that time. He was somewhere in the back of the hardware store with the boys. When she met up with Joe, she told him about her conversation in a hushed voice.

"I just had a conversation about paint colors with the nicest young gay man. He helped me choose these beautiful color swatches." She fanned the swatches out to show her husband. "And the funny part is, he isn't even an employee. He was looking at paint swatches for his own project and then helped me with my choices. He was so helpful!"

"Where is he now?" Joe asked. His inquiry took Zarah aback. Why did that matter?

"Well... he was up front, in the paint department. I have no idea where he is now."

She bent over to explain some of the tools to her young boys, who were asking questions, but she purposefully kept one eye on her husband. He made a beeline toward the front of the store. Minutes later, he was nowhere to be found. She began to walk around the entire store, dragging the boys by their hands, and couldn't find Joe anywhere. As she stood in the checkout lane with a can of paint in her hand and her boys at her side, her husband approached from the direction of the far right side of the store.

"Where were you?" Zarah asked firmly. There was no reason for him to have disappeared for thirty minutes—no reason that made any sense to Zarah.

"I was looking around," Joe answered curtly.

A red flag went up in Zarah's mind, but just as quickly, she suppressed it. She had two young sons to raise. If she had rose-tinted glasses in her purse, she would have taken them out and put them on. She put the idea out of her head that her husband might like men. It was ridiculous. They were married, and they had a family. It couldn't be. She laughed at herself for entertaining the thought and told herself to stop being paranoid.

Thirteen

The gift

THREE DAYS AFTER discovering that Joe was on a dating website, Zarah had yet to tell him what she had found. Part of her felt sorry for him. He had been suppressing his true self and not living an authentic life. He was born into an era where being gay was something to keep hidden and be ashamed of.

But another part of her felt severe anger. Yes, he was not living an authentic life, but at the same time, he was using her to appear "normal." For their entire marriage, Zarah had been Joe's beard.

Zarah did not care if a person was gay or straight or if they were white, black, or any shade in between. She had worked with people of every race and every conceivable lifestyle. Over the years, she had worked with the best and worst people, eventually concluding that people ran the gamut. They fell somewhere on a scale of "wonderful to horrible," and in Zarah's estimation, race, lifestyle, and even socioeconomic status didn't play much of a factor where people landed on the scale.

Zarah worked with many openly gay people, and they were well-represented in her circle of friends. The difference was that her gay friends were honest about who they were—they were living authentic lives, and Zarah fully supported them.

Zarah knew that Joe would conceal his true self from her until his dying days. On the other hand, she suspected that if he *is* active on the dating website he subscribed to, he must not be afraid to tell his "dates" who he is... and what he wants.

It was midnight as she got into her car after her ten-hour shift ended. She had finished her fourth day of a five-day work rotation. She was already mentally exhausted. How would she gather the strength to work one more day? As she exited the parking structure, she drove into a heavy rain.

In the past, she put everything up on her imaginary shelf and went on with her life. This time, her coping method wasn't working. Over the past few days, she focused on her work, but the moment she punched out for the day, her troubles came crashing down off the imaginary shelf.

"It's all been a lie!" she cried into the windshield. "What else is he up to?! What's going on in his secret world?!" She wiped her eyes with her sleeve and drove to the sound of the beating windshield wipers.

"Please... dear God," she whispered. "Help me."

What did she want more than anything? If she was going to pray and ask the "All-Knowing" for help, she needed to verbalize precisely what she was begging for. *Please help me* sounded childish. She was a grown woman. She needed to ask precisely what she wanted. Maybe her indecisiveness over the years confused the All-

Knowing. She had no clear goals. Perhaps she *had* been divinely helped over the years. She had managed to get an education, find an incredible career, and raise two awesome sons. The hand of God had guided her through the turbulent years, but now she wanted something specific. She wanted to tap into a strength she had never experienced.

"I've made a terrible discovery about Joe." She spoke quietly again into the windshield—as if sitting in a coffee shop with a friend. "I'm ready... To learn *everything*. If there is anything more to discover about my husband... Please... I want You to show me **the truth**," she said more firmly. "Don't think I can't take it! I can! I'm not afraid! Please... show me **the truth**!"

Was she losing her mind? Scolding God as if this was somehow *His* fault. *She* had made all her own decisions. Nobody had held a gun to her head to marry Joe, and nobody forced her to stay in the marriage. This was *her* fault—this was all on her.

No other cars were on the road, and it felt like her SUV was floating across a calm sea. It was both eerie and mesmerizing, and she had to shake herself to keep in reality.

Then she heard it... It wasn't a sound... It wasn't a voice. What she heard did not enter through her ears. It was a straightforward word placed gently into her mind as softly as a feather landing...

"Hoorah"

Hoorah, the word soldiers cried out when they were going into battle. The word she had heard Joe say hundreds of times when he wrestled with the boys when they were little. She hadn't heard the word in over twenty years.

When Zarah got home, she tiptoed into the house and went straight for her laptop. She went into her bedroom and locked the door. She again logged into the Master Card website with her husband's charge card number. She then entered the password: *hoorah*. This time, the screen did not read "incorrect password," it paused for a few seconds as it logged into Joe's charge card account, and she began to read…

Fourteen

More secrets

NOTHING WAS MORE hygge than the chair in Dr. Foxen's office—it seemed to hug her when she sat down into it. She had a lot to tell him.

"He's gay," she stated.

Dr. Foxen locked his eyes on hers.

"He's gay? Tell me what happened. How did you find this out?"

"Something surreal happened. The password to his credit card account just fell into my head… like a gift."

"And?" The doctor wanted details.

"And… I logged into the credit card website and successfully opened his charge card statement using the correct password."

"Who gave you the password?" he asked curiously. Zarah pointed to the ceiling.

Dr. Foxen leaned forward in his chair. "What did you find, Zarah?"

"It makes me sick to tell you what he's been charging."

"Take a breath, Zarah," he suggested.

"He has been buying vodka... *a lot* of vodka. He has a subscription to a porn website. He also has a subscription to a dating website, and..." Zarah stopped.

"Take your time, Zarah." He slid a box of tissues closer to Zarah, but she didn't need them. Her eyes were dry. She took a deep breath.

"I found his profile on the dating website he subscribes to. Dr. Foxen... he is searching for men *and* women."

"He's bisexual." The doctor stated the obvious. "How long has he been active on the dating website?"

"I went back eighteen months in his statements—as far back as the credit card website allowed. He's been making these charges for at least that long, so I don't know exactly how long he's been living a double life. And here is the funny part... when he's in between jobs, I pay his charge card bill with the money I've earned from our joint checkbook—no questions asked! I've been supporting his covert lifestyle! When I presented him with the stupid 'contract' last year, he was already deep diving into his secret world!"

"Zarah, I have to ask you something difficult... have you had sex with Joe during this time?"

"It's been a while, but yes, I have..."

"Zarah, you're a nurse, so you know what I am going to suggest..." Dr. Foxen said in his kindest voice.

"I know, doctor. I know."

"I also want you to consider talking to your sons about alcoholism. There is a possibility that they have inherited the tendency to become alcoholics."

Zarah shuttered at the thought that her two precious sons could end up with the same fate as their father. They were still in college, and she knew they "partied" a lot. She hoped they had developed better-coping skills besides numbing themselves and would have the sense to recognize if or when they began to resemble the example their father had set for them.

Fifteen

Past humiliation

ZARAH HAD ALWAYS thought that laying spread eagle on the gynecologist's exam table, with her feet up in the stirrups for a yearly gynecological exam, had to be about the most humiliating position a woman could be in. She was wrong. The *most* humiliating experience is laying on the exam table, spread eagle, feet in the stirrups, while waiting to be tested for every conceivable sexually transmitted disease known to humankind.

"Am I the first middle-aged woman to request this type of testing?" Zarah choked out.

"No, of course not," the doctor answered kindly.

She pulled herself together as she drove home. She would never sleep with Joe again. His lifestyle put her life at risk. There would be no more attempts to save her marriage. She did not have one more trick to "fix" someone who could not be fixed. Even if she did, she wouldn't use it.

She was done. She had asked for the truth, and she got it. By learning the truth, she acquired the strength and courage she needed to forge on in the days ahead.

Over the years, she and Joe had been fiscally responsible, and they managed to save a fair amount of money. In a divorce, they would equally divide their assets. At one point in time, that thought bothered Zarah—she had worked hard to build their savings over the years. But now she could not care less. Giving Joe fifty percent was a small price to pay for her sanity.

After two weeks of unemployment, Joe had finally admitted to Zarah that he had lost his job. Would a judge order Zarah to pay Joe maintenance? It angered her that, because of the choices *he* had made, because of the alcohol *he* had pickled his brain with, she may now have to live on a tight budget for the rest of her life to support him.

Her first instinct was to go home, walk into the house, and tell him that she had just been tested for sexually transmitted diseases... That she had discovered *all* his secrets... And that she had all the proof she needed to divorce him *on her terms*.

She would use her head and approach this rationally. She clicked on her left turn signal in an about-face and drove toward the courthouse.

The woman across the counter asked her if she had a lawyer. Zarah said she did not. The woman handed her a thick packet of papers to fill out and told her to return the papers to her when completed, along with a check for $175.00. If she had any questions, there was someone who would help her. It was as simple as that.

Sixteen

This isn't happening

SHE HAD THE documents in her hand and knew exactly how she would present them to her husband. Joe's car was in the garage, and he was probably at his desk half-heartedly searching for a job. Zarah was afraid that his reputation preceded him, and every company in his industry was aware that he was an out-of-control alcoholic with little to no ambition.

They had managed to live together in the house for two months. Zarah laughed to herself at her "plan" to keep Joe so invested in the renovation projects that he would forget all about his vodka. Her plan hadn't succeeded for more than a handful of days.

Zarah entered his office and slammed the papers down directly before him.

"What is this?" Joe asked.

"I went to the courthouse. We will be legally separated as soon as you sign this."

"What the hell, Zarah! I'm not signing this!" Joe emphatically stated.

"If you don't sign, I will have you served," Zarah said in a definitive tone. "Please... sign them. Spare me the trouble and expense of having you served."

Joe never thought Zarah would become strong enough to stand up to him. He felt he could skate through their marriage for the rest of his life. He thought she had adjusted to their unconventional lifestyle; she would remain in the dark, and he could do anything he wanted behind her back. He had no idea that she was now aware of his clandestine existence.

Zarah stood with her hands on her hips, facing him. There was a change in her demeanor that he did not recognize. He never liked that she was happy in her career or had developed strong relationships with her co-workers. He did not enjoy watching her grow as a person. He wanted her to stay the meek housewife who wanted nothing more than to care for his home and children. Over the years, he witnessed Zarah becoming more independent, and her career seemed to mean more to her than their marriage.

"Zarah... I am financially nothing without you!"

"That's all you have to say?!" She held back a laugh. She had a long list of his indiscretions that she could have effortlessly listed at that moment... But she did not. Telling him what she knew at that point would serve no purpose. It would kill him. He could go off the deep end. She'd keep the reasons for the divorce focused solely on his drinking.

"Joe, I have filed for legal separation so you can remain on my health insurance. You need help. You need to see a doctor for a physical exam. My insurance plan also covers psychiatric help."

"I'll stop drinking," Joe said barely above a whisper, hoping she would believe him this time.

"Sign the papers, Joe."

She had happy memories of their early days together but had to stand firm and not let those memories weaken her. She had once loved him… desperately… ridiculously.

Joe handed the papers back to Zarah. "I'm not signing this."

Two days later, the doorbell rang at eight o'clock in the morning—the sheriff had arrived.

"Mrs. Zoelle? I'm here to serve your husband for legal separation."

"Oh my God… He is still sleeping. Can you come back later?"

"If I leave now, I won't be able to return for days."

"Come in." Zarah reluctantly opened the door. The sheriff sensed her sadness—he hated this part of his job.

"Follow me," Zarah instructed.

He followed her down the stairs to the basement, where Joe had set up a cot in his office. He usually slept till late morning.

He was fast asleep, and Zarah felt like the cruelest person who had ever walked the face of the earth. She would have to wake him. He would be shocked at Zarah standing over him with a strange man in uniform at her side.

As she approached her sleeping husband, her heart raced. She had never seen him asleep on the cot before. That sight was pitiful. She reached down and shook his shoulder.

"Joe, wake up."

Joe sat up abruptly—his face still puffy from sleep. Being banished to sleep in the basement office had been degrading, and it always took a few extra swigs of vodka to fall asleep. He was most likely still under the influence.

She had been given the gift of his password and discovered his secret life. She would be eternally grateful for that knowledge. It gave her the strength she needed at that moment—she had no choice.

"Joe, the sheriff is here to serve you," she said in her most assertive voice.

"Are you Joseph Zoelle?" the sheriff asked.

"Yes." Joe's voice was weak.

"Mr. Zoelle, you are served," the sheriff said as he handed Joe the court-ordered documents for legal separation.

Zarah left the house immediately after the sheriff. The memory of startling Joe awake would haunt her forever. She could not face him that morning when he walked up the stairs to the kitchen. She did not want to hear him beg her to stop the proceedings. She did not want to hear one more promise he would never keep.

Her shift wasn't due to begin for two hours, so she drove to the mall to pass the time. The smell that floated from the food court made her sick to her stomach. She hadn't eaten much in weeks. Would her appetite ever return? Her friends had been telling her that she was losing too much weight. She stood on the scale just yesterday and was stunned. *I'm going to die. I'm going to wither away and die.*

Seventeen

Two weeks later

JOE HAD FOUND an apartment, and he seemed almost giddy as he packed up his rental truck that morning. Zarah did not expect that attitude from him.

"Zarah... Do you mind if I take this set of dishes?"

"Take whatever you want," she answered. "I don't care."

She didn't care if he took every single item in the house. As far as she was concerned, the end of their marriage was only minutes away, and if she were left with one plate, one fork, and one cup, she would survive.

Last night, she had a dream... Her house was on fire. She tossed everything of value out the bedroom window and into the mud. Then she climbed out the window to escape the smoke and landed on top of all her things. She struggled to pick them up, one by one. She could not run from the fire with the weight of the possessions in her arms. Finally, she dropped everything, realizing the things she once held dear were only obstacles. She then ran as fast as she could away from the flames, and as she ran, she looked up and saw a million stars.

Joe's truck was loaded, and he returned to the house to say goodbye to his wife of twenty-eight years…

"I'm leaving now. I'll unload the stuff into my apartment, then return for a second load… and that should do it."

He didn't seem to be sad—he seemed relieved. He would no longer have Zarah to contend with. He would no longer have to see the disappointment in her eyes. He was free to do whatever he wanted… with whomever he wanted.

"We have an appointment with Byron Town tomorrow evening," she reminded him. Byron was their financial advisor. They planned to go through their investments with Byron's assistance and divide everything in half. They both agreed that there would be no need for a lawyer. Neither one of them wanted more than their fair share.

"Joe, please take advantage of my health insurance. Otherwise, there's no reason to keep this a legal separation."

Joe said nothing as he stared at the floor before Zarah's feet.

"I have to leave in a few minutes for work, so I'll see you tomorrow evening at Byron's office." She had nothing more profound to say. Everything had been said.

"I have furniture being delivered tomorrow afternoon, but that shouldn't take too long," Joe explained. "I should make it to the meeting on time."

They stood in silence for what seemed like forever while Joe contemplated hugging Zarah goodbye.

Zarah could not imagine how he was going to survive on his own. She had made all his meals, kept his house clean, and made his life appear normal to the outside world. Who would do that for him now? She was glad that she had done the laundry the day before—at least the clothing he packed was clean.

Zarah broke the silence…

"Well, goodbye." She did not attempt to walk toward him, so Joe knew a hug goodbye was out of the question.

Joe searched for the final words he would say to his wife on what was possibly the most profound day of his life…

"Zarah… It's me. I know it's me. I did this to us."

His words hung in the air. The saddest words Zarah had ever heard. She did not reply.

Joe turned and walked out. She heard him crank the radio to a rock station before shifting the truck into reverse.

She went to the front window and watched him drive down the street and out of the neighborhood.

"Will he finally be his authentic self? Or will he continue to live behind the facade of a straight man? Maybe he'll drink himself to death," she whispered into the blinds. If he "comes out of the closet," she would be astonished. He was used to living behind a lie and didn't know of any other way to be.

Zarah navigated the parking structure. She didn't find a spot to park until she reached the top level. She walked mechanically to the stairwell, headed up to the fifth floor, and then walked briskly for five minutes until she reached the time clock outside the ICU. She had repeated this routine thousands of times before.

She punched the button on the wall that opened the big swinging doors. Her co-workers were already gathered at the assignment board and were waiting for her arrival so they could complete the patient assignments.

As she walked toward her co-workers, the room began to spin, and her knees became useless.

"ZZ!" she heard her co-workers call to her as if they were far away. She felt someone grab her by the arms.

Until now, she had not told anyone at work what was happening in her personal life except for one person, Jack, a fellow nurse and a close friend, and Jack would certainly maintain her confidence.

They had all observed Zarah's weight loss, and they surmised her blood sugar had dropped due to not eating. One of the nurses ran to get orange juice and crackers.

"ZZ... Are you okay?" she heard Jack as if he was miles away. She opened her eyes and saw her co-workers standing in a circle, looking down at her.

"Did I pass out?"

Jack helped her to her feet and led her to a chair.

"Drink some juice, ZZ," Jack said kindly. "And don't stand up until you've finished eating those crackers."

Zarah fought back tears with every cracker she bit into and every sip of juice she took. It was time to tell the rest of her co-workers what was going on...

"Joe moved out today."

Eighteen

Think I'm just happy

FOR THE FIRST time in her life, Zarah was alone. What would she do now to reinvent herself when all she had ever known was Joe? Joe, Joe, Joe. Her entire adult life had been focused on Joe.

She slept in that morning—she didn't fall asleep after yesterday's shift until nearly two a.m. She poured herself a cup of coffee, then turned around and leaned against the countertop. She let her eyes glide across the kitchen… soon to be *her* kitchen, after she buys the house from Joe. She had to admit, it was beautiful. The custom-built cabinets were a work of art, and the built-in china cabinet, with her grandmother's set of china, arranged strategically inside, sparkled with the morning sun.

If Rosie were still alive, they'd sit on the couch together while she drank her morning coffee. She'd be kissing Rosie's furry little head and telling her what a good dog she was, and she'd get many dog kisses in return. Her heart still ached at the memory. She wondered about getting another dog, but with the long hours she worked, a dog would be left alone all day, and then she would return home exhausted with no energy left to take a dog for a walk. She expected to be picking up more shifts—she wanted to continue with the house renovations, and that would take a good chunk of money. Getting another dog at this point was out of the question.

When she opened the cabinet to get her coffee cup that morning, there were bare spots on the shelves where Joe had removed things from the previous day. She spent that morning rearranging the cabinets so she wouldn't be constantly reminded of the day he moved out whenever she opened a cabinet door.

She continued combing through every drawer and closet in the house and packed things that Joe had overlooked. Her hands could not move fast enough as she searched every nook and cranny in the house. She found his military duffle bag under the basement stairway. She wanted nothing left in the house that reminded her of him. She put everything in her car and would give the boxes to him later that day when they met at Byron's office.

She dusted, polished the mirrors, vacuumed the carpets, and washed the floors. She finally stood back and scrutinized... She was satisfied—any evidence that Joe had lived there was gone. It was as if he had never lived in the house at all.

This was what it felt like to be calm. She wasn't responsible for Joe any longer... Should she get down on her knees and apologize to God for dumping Joe back on His lap?

She pushed the power button on her stereo, and the music instantly filled the room...

🎵 *I'm not like you, but I can pretend*

The sun is down, and I have a light
The day is done, and I'm having fun
I think I'm dumb… or maybe I'm happy

The music reverberated off the walls of the nearly empty room. She outstretched her arms and turned her face to the ceiling. She felt as if energy was entering her very core, and her heart was surrounded by pure love.

♪♪ *My heart has broke, but I have some glue*
Help me to breathe and mend it with you
We'll float around, we'll hang out on clouds
Then we'll come down… and soothe a hangover

She didn't want the music to end. She closed her eyes and began slowly twirling around in her stocking feet on the shiny hardwood floor, then started dancing as if no one was watching.

She was alone. It was blissful. It was heaven. She had become a warrior of sorts… She was a kind warrior but would not hesitate to keep people at arm's length if they were not worthy of her love. Never again would she let darkness back in.

♪♪ *I think I'm just happy*
I think I'm just happy
I think I'm just happy

Joe was no longer her problem *or* her responsibility. Where was life about to take her? Divine intervention had helped her out of the mess that was her marriage, and divine intervention would not abandon her now.

She felt no hatred toward Joe. She wished him well and prayed he'd overcome his demons. Knowing the truth about him was all the closure she needed. She could move forward. She would not waste one more second on the "what ifs."

She walked into Byron's office. Joe was already seated with him at the table. She trusted that Byron would be fair when splitting their assets.

"I have some boxes in my car for you, Joe," Zarah explained when Byron momentarily left the room.

"Thanks, I didn't realize I missed anything. I hope the boxes will fit into my car."

She could smell the alcohol on his breath when he spoke, and the slurring of his speech was even more pronounced. *He must be enjoying his newfound freedom.*

Was alcoholism an illness or a choice? She had vacillated on that question during their entire marriage. Every time he bent his elbow to take a drink, he made a choice. On the other hand, the alcohol permeated every cell in his body—it was the first thing he thought of when he woke up, and it was the last thing he thought of before he closed his eyes to sleep. Maybe it wasn't an illness *or* a choice; maybe alcohol was the devil he couldn't refuse.

Two hours later, Joe and Zarah walked out of Byron's office, financially independent of each other. Zarah bought the house from Joe, which left Joe with most of the money and investments. There were still title changes to be made on the house and cars, but everything had been split fifty-fifty. It was the most uncomplicated, most amicable divorce Zarah had ever known.

Nineteen

A cup of coffee

ON A CRISP autumn day, Zarah was pushing her lawnmower and doing her best to mulch the leaves that had fallen from the trees. Out of the corner of her eye, she saw a young man waving from the end of her driveway. She turned off the mower—she couldn't imagine what he wanted. He explained that he lived a few doors down. He was trying to save money for college, and would she want to hire him to mow her lawn?

A week later, there was a knock at Zarah's front door. A man she had never met before introduced himself as Gary. Gary lived with his wife just up the street. He said he had recently retired and was starting a handyman business. He said he was a "jack-of-all-trades" and charged a reasonable hourly rate. Zarah took him on a tour of the house to show him all the projects she had on her mind. There were a lot, but Gary didn't flinch.

Days later, another knock on Zarah's front door brought her the pleasure of meeting Mr. Marvin. Mr. Marvin told Zarah that he heard she was a nurse and thought she might need his snowplowing services. Winter was fast approaching, and he wanted to organize his client list. He told her that because she was a nurse, he would plow her driveway first thing in the morning and again in the evening for no additional charge. He wanted her to "be ready to leave for the hospital at any given moment." It was apparent to Zarah that, for some reason, Mr. Marvin loved nurses.

Zarah could not believe her luck. She told her co-workers that she now had "all her guys." She had Lawn Boy, Gary the Handyman, and Mr. Plow aligned and ready to work. She could afford to pay the three men who had miraculously entered her life by taking several extra shifts every month. It was almost as if someone was watching out for her.

Zarah had much to accomplish outside before the weather turned frigid. She hired a tree service to trim up the jungle of overgrown trees. She tore off the old shutters that had faded over the years. Then she bought a power washer and blew off fifty-plus years of thick, black mold that concealed the true beauty of the Lannon stone house.

The prior owners had kept all their old windows, screen doors, and miscellaneous pieces of lumber stored high up on the rafters in her garage. The rafters were bending under the weight of all the junk. Zarah got up on a ladder and dragged every single item down. Sometimes, she found her only option was to let the old windows crash to the concrete garage floor—their weight was more than she could handle.

Next, she pulled fifty-year-old shelving off the garage walls and took a carload of dried-up paint, auto supplies, and miscellaneous products (that the prior owners had left behind) to a recycling center. She bought several heavy-duty shelving units and neatly organized her gardening tools and other outdoor supplies. The shelves had casters, and she could easily slide them out to sweep behind them whenever needed.

She power-washed the garage floor, painted the garage walls, and then, a few days later, rolled a coat of dark gray epoxy paint onto the floor.

During the winter months, Zarah turned her attention to the inside of the house. She spent weeks scraping old paint off the moldings. She lost count of how many paint colors were slopped on the woodwork. Her efforts paid off—the once-neglected woodwork looked almost brand new.

She was ready to repaint the interior of the house. She chose white ceilings, light gray walls for the living room, and a medium shade of gray for the kitchen, bathroom, and bedrooms. Liz came over after work every day to help out. The sisters talked all the while they painted. It was then Zarah realized she no longer needed Dr. Foxen. She had "graduated" from him. Talking to her sister and several trusted friends gave her all the support she needed.

One month after Joe moved out, he called Zarah and asked if she would like to meet him for coffee. She agreed… She felt she owed him that much, and what could it hurt?

Zarah walked into the coffee shop and immediately spotted Joe as he waved to her from his table. As she approached, he stood from his chair and gave her a polite hug. She held her breath as he did—she did not want to inhale.

"Please sit, Zarah," Joe said as he pulled out a chair.

"Well, this isn't uncomfortable at all," Zarah said jokingly to quell any tension. "How are you, Joe?"

"I'm good. May I get you a cup of coffee?" he asked.

"Yes, I could use the caffeine. I've got a lot to do today." Zarah didn't mention what she had to do, but continuing with the painting project was foremost on her mind.

Joe returned within minutes and set a cup of coffee before her.

"Thank you," Zarah politely smiled. "So, Joe, I assume you are all settled in your apartment?"

"Yes! It's very nice. My new living room furniture looks great, and the apartment's location is perfect. There are parks and restaurants within walking distance. Thanks, by the way, for the things you packed for me that I missed on moving day."

"You're welcome."

"I don't have any photographs," he added. "I left all the photo albums with you."

"Well, next time I see you, I will loan one of the books to you. We can share them. Someday, I will scan them and give you a full set."

"That would be great," he smiled.

She couldn't figure it out... Was he happy or sad? When he spoke about his apartment, his face lit up. But when he mentioned the family photos, his face went pale.

"So, tell me about your family!" Zarah said lightly. She missed Joe's extended family. She missed his mother, his siblings, their spouses, and all the nieces and nephews she had watched grow up. They had all been a part of her life since she was nineteen. That they were Joe's blood relatives and not hers made no difference.

"There isn't much to tell," Joe answered. "Not much is going on."

Zarah was the person in their marriage who kept in contact with Joe's family. She called his mother weekly. Had he talked to any of his relatives since he moved out? Had he told his mother they were separated? She highly doubted it.

"How is *your* family?" Joe inquired.

"Well, Liz is good. She comes over nearly every day after work to help me on one project or another. I don't know what I would do without her." Zarah stopped going further—she didn't want to discuss the house with Joe. She felt that anything she would say could be misconstrued as bragging. Besides, the house was hers now—it was her private domain.

"How are your parents?" Joe asked.

Zarah laughed to herself. She strongly suspected that Joe already knew how her parents were—despite everything, her parents were Joe's number one fans...

The day before Zarah filed for legal separation, she drove to her parent's house to inform them of her plans. When Zarah began to explain Joe's alcohol addiction to them, they began to scold her. They denied that he had alcoholism. They accused her of overreacting. After all, they had "never smelled booze" on Joe, and "What is wrong with having an occasional beer? Lots of men like their beer!"

Zarah did not explain anything more condemning to them. She didn't tell them that she discovered he preferred men. She didn't tell them that she had to be tested for sexually transmitted diseases. She didn't tell them that she had been paying for his vodka, gay porn and dating website for longer than she cared to admit. She didn't tell them that he had grown increasingly aloof as the years rolled by or had never once complimented her meaningfully.

Zarah sat on her parents' sofa, staring at her folded hands on her lap. She felt small, insignificant, and not unlike a naughty little girl. She was not surprised at their reactions and laughed to herself that she expected any moral support from them. Believing that they would be understanding, that they would have hugged her and told her everything would be okay, and hoping they would have given her a soft place to land and a safe place to talk were only wishful thoughts.

No matter what her father did in his younger years, her mother ignored it. His philandering, his drinking, and the violence he inflicted upon them were all forgotten the following day and never spoken of again. The "bouquet of flowers" was all it took for her mother to sweep everything under the rug, rewrite their history, and move on as if nothing had happened.

"Nobody breaks up a marriage of twenty-eight years, Zarah!" Her mother scolded. "You are going to embarrass us if you go through with this! What will we tell people?! We love Joe! He is so good to us!"

"Mom, he is NOT good to ME!" Zarah cried out in defense, but if her mother heard her plea, it made no difference in her mindset.

"Do you have a boyfriend, Zarah?! Are you having an affair? Is that what this is about?!" her father yelled at the top of his voice. Zarah felt as if a fire had been lit inside her. She was not like him! She had never cheated on Joe the way he had cheated on her mother! She wanted to hold up a mirror in front of his goddamn face.

"No!" Zarah's heart was pounding rapidly, and her palms were sweating.

"You need to see a psychiatrist!" Charlie screeched.

"I have a counselor! He is wonderful! Joe went with me only one time... Look, I'm a grown woman, and you are both speaking to me as if I'm a child! I don't know what I was thinking coming here... I thought you should know my plans before I file with the courts tomorrow."

Her parents continued to scold her—each one talking over the other. She was not about to decipher their verbiage. It was overwhelming. She got up from the couch and walked out without saying another word.

She drove away from their house as quickly as she could. Her tires kicked up gravel as she pulled out of their *driveway. She knew they would immediately call Joe and tell him how much they loved him. He would eat it up and play the part of the sorrowful victim—the soon-to-be ex-husband—for all it was worth. He would bask in the glow of their unconditional love. They would reassure him that he would always be a part of their family.*

"My parents are fine. I thought that maybe they would have contacted you by now…" Zarah said with a feigned lilt in her voice. She hoped that Joe would admit they had contacted him and confirm her suspicions.

"Yes, your mother has called me several times. And actually, I was at their house for dinner last Saturday," Joe said calmly. "It was so good to see them."

"How nice!" Zarah was incensed, but her voice and facial expression did not give her away. She continued…

"We were together for a long time. My family became your family, and your family became mine. Can we promise to inform each other if anyone gets sick or dies?"

"I have no problem with that," he answered.

Losing Joe's extended family was something that Zarah had thought of as their marriage crumbled, but she couldn't fathom how hard it was going to be to lose them until it became a reality. The absence of Joe's family in her daily life felt like the death of someone she had deeply loved, and the magnitude of the void was far greater than she had ever anticipated.

"How's Ruth?" Zarah inquired. Joe's mother, Ruth, had been living in a nursing home for the past year. Zarah used to visit her every week, but since their legal separation, she stopped going.

"She's good. Her hearing is worsening, but she is about the same otherwise."

"Does she know about us, Joe?"

"What about us?"

"That we are separated? Did you explain that to her?"

"No, I did not."

"Oh my goodness... Well, I'll visit her next week. She must be wondering what happened to me." Zarah felt terrible. "Did she ask you where I've been?"

"I told her you were working."

"Joe, you should have told her we are separated! She's *your* mother. I should not have to be the one to break this news to her."

An awkward silence followed as they both searched for something else to say.

"Have you had any luck finding a job?" Job hunting was a sore spot for Joe, and Zarah regretted asking the question the moment it left her lips.

"No, I've had no luck finding a job," he answered with finality. He leaned back in his chair and crossed his arms over his chest. Only ten minutes into their conversation, his defenses were up. He scanned the restaurant as if something or someone else was far more interesting than having this conversation with Zarah.

"Well, I'm sure you'll find something soon," she added reassuringly. She did not want this to end badly.

"I'll find a job, Zarah, Jesus Christ! Should I get a job in a grocery store as a stock-boy? Or maybe get a job at a gas station... Would that make you happy?"

"Joe, I didn't mean to upset you. I was only making conversation. You have plenty of money and probably never have to work another day if you don't want to." She had done the math... Wisely spent, his share of the money could pay his rent and expenses until he would become eligible to collect Social Security.

She'd have to change the subject and the mood quickly. But finding a "safe" subject to talk about was proving difficult.

"Well, I suppose you've heard that our son Damon has a serious girlfriend!"

"Yeah, I heard." Joe uncrossed his arms and leaned forward.

"I think that this girl might be 'the one!'" Zarah said enthusiastically.

"'The One,' huh. I thought I had found 'The One,' too," Joe said sarcastically.

"He is our son, Joe. Can't we be happy for him together?" Zarah was becoming exhausted from trying to make a semi-pleasant conversation. There was one more thing on her mind, and she knew that what she was about to ask might set him off—but everything seemed to set him off.

"I need to ask you something, Joe, and please don't get angry with me… Have you taken advantage of my health insurance? Have you made any doctor appointments? I'm concerned about your blood pressure." She lied. She was more concerned about his alcoholism.

"No, I have not," Joe said with finality. He leaned back in his chair and crossed his arms again. Were all men this defensive, or was it only him?

"Then why did I file for legal separation? If you don't use the insurance soon, I will convert the separation to divorce. Joe… please… make a stupid appointment with a doctor. Be honest about your drinking when you go and…"

"Quit telling me what to do, Zarah!"

Zarah saw something disturbing in his eyes. It was the same expression on his face that she saw the day he was hallucinating on the back porch and asked her, "Who are *you* talking to?"

She picked up her coffee cup, took a few sips, and tried to gather her thoughts. She was making no headway with this conversation—meeting with him had been a bad idea. She needed to end the conversation as quickly as possible, but first, she needed to de-escalate the situation. Both of them had been speaking a little too loudly, and several patrons in the coffee shop had focused their attention in their direction.

"I'm not sure why you asked me to meet you here today, Joe," Zarah asked calmly.

"Can't I have a cup of coffee with my wife!" He again spoke far too loudly.

"Joe… *please…* lower your voice," she whispered.

"I thought that, by agreeing to meet me, you were willing to work on our marriage!" he yelled.

Nearly everyone in the coffee shop was looking in their direction.

"Joe, I have to go." Zarah quickly grabbed her purse off the back of her chair and walked briskly toward the exit. Joe was hot on her heels. She walked straight toward her car with Joe close behind.

"Zarah! How do you expect me to live without you!"

"Go home, Joe!" Zarah fumbled with her purse to find her keys.

"For God's sake, Zarah… we've been together since we were kids! You can't do this to me!"

"You don't need me. Go home!" Zarah pleaded.

She glanced at the window of the coffee shop. They were putting on quite a show as all heads were turned and intently watching them through the windows.

"They're all watching us," Zarah said in a more controlled tone.

"I don't give a fuck. Let them look!" Joe screamed as he slammed the hood of her car with his open hand, startling Zarah and causing her to jump away from him, but she refused to show fear of any kind.

"You don't want to play this game with me!" Zarah said confidently to his face.

"Zarah, stop all this nonsense, and let me come home! Things will be different this time! You've made your point! You've proven you can go to the courthouse and fill out divorce papers. You've shown me how dramatically you can slam them down on my desk in front of my face! You've even proven your capability of letting a sheriff enter our house to wake me from a sound sleep… To serve me divorce papers! Do you have any idea how horrible that was, Zarah?! That's what nightmares are made of! That was rock bottom for me!"

The veins in his forehead protruded, and she thought his blood pressure must be through the roof.

"No, that wasn't your rock bottom, Joe. I can still smell the alcohol on you! Why must you live in a constant state of numbness?! We could have had it all, but you broke us, Joe! You did this to us. It was ALL YOU!"

Zarah had so much more ammunition she could have used—she could have told him everything she had discovered about him. But she didn't. She didn't want to scream out ugly things that could never be taken back. Or was she still protecting him—if only from himself?

She got into her car and hit the lock button. With shaking hands, she managed to get the key into the ignition. As she drove away, she glanced into her rearview mirror… Joe was standing motionless in the parking lot, watching her drive away.

Twenty

A confident man

AS SHE STOOD with her fellow nurses in front of the assignment board, she caught a glimpse of Dr. Blue Eyes walking out of a patient room. She felt her silly schoolgirl heart begin to race. Her hero worship for the man was still there, and her emotions were beyond her control whenever he was in her sight. He unexpectedly looked up from the chart in his hand, caught Zarah's stare, and met her stare. Instead of averting her eyes, as she had done many times before, she held eye contact... for several seconds longer than she should have.

He is married. This is ridiculous.

The hospital gossip was that Dr. Bluett and his wife were separated—again—but Zarah knew better than to rely on hospital gossip.

"Earth to ZZ!" she heard the shift coordinator loudly say. Zarah had *not* been paying attention and hadn't listened to a word the shift coordinator had said. The stare from Dr. Bluett had caused a high-pitched ringing in her ears. She immediately focused on the assignment board and shook herself out of the hypnotic trance.

Zarah sat down to get report on seventeen-year-old Andy from Jack, his first shift nurse. She loved sharing a patient with Jack. Not only was he one of her best friends, but he was an incredible nurse. He was gifted with an almost electric personality that exuded positivity to his patients and their families, which helped create a healing atmosphere.

They spent nearly an hour reviewing Andy's case—no detail could be glossed over. Andy had six separate IV pumps infusing, he was intubated, he had an intracranial pressure monitor inserted into his brain, he had a feeding tube, and he was on a cooling mattress to keep his body temperature artificially low. Everything being done focused on keeping Andy's brain from swelling further.

Two weeks ago, Andy had fallen from the second story of his home as he attempted to sneak out of the house in the middle of the night to attend a party. The following morning, his father found him lying unresponsive in a pool of blood on the concrete patio.

Through the sliding glass doors of Andy's hospital room, Zarah could see that Andy's family had already gathered around his bedside. Last evening, Zarah had called Andy's father with encouraging news... Andy had opened his eyes "on command" several times. The family was eagerly anticipating another sign of consciousness. Zarah knew that probably would not happen today. His intracranial pressure trended up during the night, and the third shift nurse found it necessary to give him medications that would keep the pressure on his brain within safe limits.

"I don't understand, Zarah..." Andy's father, Matt, asked. "The doctors have told me that Andy's brain scan has improved... why isn't he waking up?"

"The brain is very complex. Sometimes, a patient with a terrible brain scan is alert and behaves normally. Other times, a brain scan looks pristine, and the patient remains in a coma." At that time, Zarah did not mention what else she knew… Sometimes, the patient is never the same as they were before the accident—and sometimes, the patient never regains consciousness. She knew that brain injuries ran the gamut, and no two patients with similar injuries ever had the same prognosis.

"When will you take him off this cooling mattress? He's going to freeze to death." Matt was beginning to lose composure.

"He is sedated, Matt. He can't perceive the cold. His intracranial pressure is perfect now, and we want to keep it that way. The brain lives inside a 'closed box' that is your skull. If the brain swells, there is nowhere for the swelling to go. Everything we are doing is important for Andy's brain to heal. I assure you, he is not experiencing any discomfort."

Matt left his eldest son's bedside only to go home to shower and sleep. He was back every morning, bright and early, right after he got his other four children off to school.

Zarah made small talk while she cared for Andy to ease some of Matt's anxiety. She knew that sometimes you care for the family and the patient. Matt began to share bits and pieces of his personal life, too. He talked about the challenges of raising his five kids on his own since his wife passed away three years ago. Zarah talked about gardening and her home renovations.

Matt was a nice-looking man—he had a cowboy-like roughness about him that was attractive. She never mentioned the subject of a husband or her marital status, and Matt never asked. She still wore a simple silver wedding band—she was still technically married.

Zarah pushed the curtain aside, then slid open the door to exit Andy's room. She closed the door behind her and saw Dr. Nathanial Bluett walking toward her. She assumed he wanted to talk to her about Andy, their in-common patient.

"Hi, Dr. Bluett. I'm sure you heard that Andy followed a few simple commands for me yesterday evening."

"That's encouraging!" he exclaimed in his sexy English accent.

Dr. Bluett was the surgeon on call the morning Andy arrived via helicopter, and he performed the eight-hour emergency craniotomy on Andy in the hope of saving his life.

"ZZ," he added. "Tell me if I'm wrong... Were you checking me out the other day?" He asked quietly so that no other staff would hear. His eyes studied Zarah's face for her reaction. She opened her mouth but managed only a stutter...

"I... umm..."

"It sure felt as if you were looking at me." He smiled as if he had won a lottery. "Am I wrong?"

"No, I mean yes. Yes, you're mistaken. I wasn't checking you out!" She felt her face flush.

Zarah thought this must be what adults do when they flirt. They get right to the point—at least, Dr. Bluett was doing that. Zarah hadn't flirted since she was a teenager and doubted she had ever been good at it, even back then.

He sensed that he was making her nervous. They had worked together for over twenty years and shared a friendly, business-like relationship. The conversation he had begun could change all of that. He continued...

"Jack told me you are divorced."

"I'm legally separated." Zarah managed to answer this time without tripping over herself. Their conversation shook her—it felt like she had lost the ability to speak like a semi-intelligent human being.

"Why don't you just 'go for it' and get a divorce?" He was puzzled.

"My soon-to-be ex needs my health insurance until he gets his own. He's in between jobs."

"That's too bad. It puts you in limbo," he said.

"No, I'm not in limbo. I've gone on with my life," Zarah stated a bit defensively.

"Would you like to meet for a drink sometime? When are you off work next?" She thought his confidence level was second to none... or was it arrogance?

"I'm technically still married, Nate." Zarah could not believe that the esteemed doctor seemed interested in her. She felt her heart pounding and tried hard not to blush again.

"Is there a reconciliation in your future?" he sounded disappointed.

"No."

Zarah needed some time to process this. She would love to run her fingers through his thick blonde hair and kiss the lips, which had made her heart skip a beat for many years. Now, in his mid-fifties, Nate's British accent had yet to fade, and Zarah strongly suspected that he was aware of that fact and played it for all it was worth. He called her ZZ like everyone else in the hospital, but occasionally, he called her by her name. He softened the "a," which sounded like music to Zarah's ears.

"Are you dating anyone?" he asked.

"I've been too busy with my home renovation projects to contemplate dating. I bought an old house in Lansing... You should see it!"

"I'd love to," Nate said without hesitation. "Let me know when you are free."

"I've got to get some charting done," Zarah said as she nodded toward the computers.

"We'll talk later," he said as she turned and walked away.

What just happened? Did I invite him to my house? What did I start by meeting his stare? Why didn't I break eye contact?

She shook her head to snap herself out of it. She could never deny that Dr. Bluett had always made her weak in the knees or that she had spent more time than she should have to watch him as he walked out of the ICU.

In Zarah's estimation, Nate Bluett was the ultimate man —a brilliant surgeon with world-renowned skills, looks, and the personality to match. He knew it. He knew that he was *all* of that.

On the other hand, he was married. There were always rumors that he was separated from his wife, but those rumors changed occasionally. There were also stories that he was involved with several other nurses over the years. Zarah would not be a home-wrecker. She knew the pain of marrying a husband who was more interested in someone or something else.

She walked over and sat down next to Jack, who was wrapping up his charting for the day.

"So, what was *that* all about?" Jack said as he nodded toward the door to Andy's room.

"What was what about?" Zarah asked in the hope that he wasn't referring to the conversation with Nate.

"You and Blue Eyes seemed to be having a cozy conversation over there..."

"Oh, that was nothing. We were talking about my renovation projects." It was a lie of omission.

Her friendship with Jack was strong. He knew her better than almost anyone else and vice-versa. Besides her sister, Jack was probably Zarah's best friend. She could count on him for anything and knew she probably did not fool him with her evasive answer.

"Mmm," Jack nodded as he continued entering his final notes into the computer.

"Well, have a good evening, Zarah. I hope Andy remains stable for you." He pushed away from the workstation and walked out of the unit. He made no eye contact with her when he spoke or left, which was highly unusual. They typically parted with cheerful small talk.

"What's up with him?" Zarah whispered to herself. *Is he jealous?*

Jack had an on-again, off-again relationship with his girlfriend, Celeste. Celeste was ten years his junior. The age gap caused problems, and the fact that Celeste had two young children didn't make their relationship easy. Over the years, Zarah listened to and supported Jack whenever he needed to vent about the relationship.

Zarah had never admitted her attraction to Nate to anyone—especially not to Jack. Jack was Nate's good friend, and she didn't need that complication. It had been a school-girl crush, a pipe dream, a fantasy she had kept to herself. Her attraction toward Nate Bluett was not different from idolizing a movie star. Nate was a distraction that had kept her entertained over the years, and as far as she was concerned, Jack was on a need-to-know basis.

Twenty-one

Only a dream

HER SHEETS WERE damp from sweat. The strange dream had left her nearly breathless. She headed straight to the coffee pot. She measured an extra scoop—this morning's coffee must be strong.

It had felt so real. Was it a dream? Or was it something else? If she took the dream seriously, she would get off of the path she was currently on. If she ignored the dream and blamed it on random brain cells playing tricks on her, she could further explore where her life was heading.

She walked with her coffee out to the back porch. The orioles were already fighting for position at the grape jelly feeders, and several bluebirds were splashing in the birdbath. She sat close enough to admire them but far enough away not to scare them. As she drank her coffee, her mind drifted back to the dream…

She flew at an unfathomable speed. She had a body, but it was not physical—she was made only of energy and light. She could not slow down, nor did she want to—she had no idea where she was headed.

She collided… with another light being. It was Nate. He had been on his way to meet her from the opposite direction. Their cosmic bodies smashed together with great force, but there was no pain—it was the opposite of pain. It was an overwhelming emotion, a euphoria beyond anything Zarah had experienced.

Their bodies entwined on impact and were held up only by the hands of the cosmos. There was no gravity, no sun, no stars, no moon—only light. There was no one around to contend with. No patients, no wives, no husbands. They had traveled to the one place that existed only for them.

They joined with a kiss, and every lightning bolt that had ever struck the earth pulsated through her very core.

She suddenly began to choke… She instinctively pushed him away. She could not catch her breath. Something was lodged in her throat. She couldn't speak. She could only watch helplessly as Nate floated further and further away. She wanted to reach out and pull him back, but she knew that something was wrong—something that had seemed so right had gone very, very wrong.

She laughed off the dream—it was only a dream. That day, she had a lot to do. It was spring, and she had trees and flowers that waited to be planted. First, she'd call Joe. She hadn't talked to him since their disastrous meeting at the coffee shop and the ensuing ugly scene in the parking lot. She'd shower first and get her thoughts together. She had an important question on her mind. Sadly, she suspected she already knew what his answer would be…

"Joe, it's Zarah. Did I catch you at a good time?"

"It's as good a time as any. What can I do for you?" It was ten o'clock, and his speech was already unclear.

"I need to ask… Are you taking advantage of my health insurance, Joe?" she asked matter-of-factly.

"No."

"No?"

"No, I have *not* used your insurance, Zarah. Is that a problem?" His defenses were up.

"It *is* a problem, Joe. We are legally separated for that reason alone. Do you plan to get health insurance when I convert the separation to divorce?" Joe was eligible for veteran's benefits but would not apply for some reason.

"No, I have no plans for my health insurance. Don't worry about it, Zarah. Stop treating me like a child!"

"I'm not treating you like a child, Joe," she answered. "I'm asking for a simple answer to a simple question. I'm going to the courthouse this afternoon, Joe. We should be divorced within a week or two."

"Don't do it, Zarah! Damon is getting married soon."

"What does that have to do with us?" She was confused.

"Everyone at the wedding will know we are divorced!" he pleaded.

"Look, Joe… you've had nine months to use my health insurance. Hell, I even paid the damn insurance premium for you! That was the deal. I've done my part, and you have done nothing. I need to move on with my life."

"I won't sign the papers!" Joe slurred out.

"You don't have to sign a thing. The initial document for legal separation is the only thing necessary to convert to divorce. You don't have to sign anything; I do *not* need your permission to do this."

She felt the usual sting of pity for him. Would she ever live a life without worrying about Joe?

"Joe… Is everything okay?"

"I'm fine, Zarah, and I'm sure everything is going great for you," he said sarcastically.

"Goodbye, Joe."

She stared at her phone. Why did he hate her? Over the years, despite his emotional absence, she was kind to him and did her best to make a good home for him and their boys. She had tried everything to bring back the man she thought she once saw and the rare days he seemed to be engaged in their marriage had been an act. Maybe the desire to live a different lifestyle ate him up, little by little, every day.

That afternoon, she drove to the courthouse. Two weeks later, she received their final divorce decree in the mail.

Twenty-two

A song for eternity

THE BREATHING TUBE had been removed, and the intracranial pressure monitor and cooling mattress were no longer necessary. Only one IV pump and a feeding pump remained.

After five long weeks, Andy was finally stable, and he was ready to be transferred out of the ICU. His four siblings and his father were at his bedside, and Zarah saw beaming smiles on their faces through the sliding glass doors.

Zarah knew that Andy had a long row to hoe. He would need months of physical, occupational, and speech therapy.

"Good morning, Jack," Zarah said as she sat beside him for report. "Looks like our boy is moving on!" The report she would receive from Jack would be quick, as another head-injured patient was in the Emergency Department and was due to arrive in the ICU the moment Andy's room was vacated and cleaned.

"Good morning, ZZ! Yes, Andy will be transferred to the third floor any minute now. He's packed up and ready to go."

Andy was the kind of patient that made a nurse's job rewarding. His recovery could have quickly gone a different way. However, the staff had gotten him through a critical period, and there was hope that Andy could make close to a full recovery and lead a reasonably normal life.

"Jack... my divorce... it's final," Zarah blurted out the moment Jack finished giving report.

"Are you okay?" Jack asked as he gently placed his hand on her knee.

"Yes! I'm fine! I'm more than fine! I knew the document was coming, but it was still a shock to open the envelope and see it in black and white."

Zarah slid the glass door open to tell Andy's father and siblings that the transporter had arrived to take Andy to his new room. This moment was always bittersweet. Often, families bond with the staff, and the thought that their loved one would now be in the hands of strangers could be terrifying.

"Jack is giving report to Andy's new nurse as we speak," Zarah informed Matt. "Linda is an awesome nurse. I've known her for years."

"Will she know how to care for Andy?" he asked.

"Andy will be in the best hands! Linda has over twenty years of experience and is the nurse I would handpick if Andy were my son. They will do things for Andy in the step-down unit that we don't do in the ICU."

Andy had no comprehension of the gravity of his situation. His speech was unintelligible. He could say "yes," "no," and "Andy," but that was the extent of it. He smiled a lot at his father and siblings, but he most likely would not remember one day that he spent in the ICU under Jack and Zarah's care.

His father, Matt, will. He will remember every single agonizing second of this, the most horrifying event of his life. He will remember finding his eldest son Andy face down on the concrete patio. He will remember that he could not wake Andy up. He'll remember that his right pupil was fixed and dilated when he looked into Andy's eyes. He'll remember screaming for his children to call 911, performing CPR, and that it felt like forever for the ambulance to arrive. He will remember the emergency room at the local hospital and how the doctors and nurses surrounded Andy's bed, forcing him to step back and out of the room. He'll remember Andy being whisked away for a CT scan and that it took hours for a doctor to walk into the waiting room to speak with him…

"Andy sustained a severe head injury… There is significant bleeding in his brain… The bleeding is putting pressure on his brain, causing it to shift… He needs emergency surgery. The best thing for Andy would be to call the Flight For Life helicopter team and transfer him to Lansing General."

He would never forget the long drive to Lansing General Hospital, sitting in the waiting room for ten hours and finally being told that Andy was out of surgery. He will never forget the relief he felt when told that Andy had survived the surgery and the moment he walked into the ICU to lay eyes on his son for the first time…

Andy's head was wrapped in gauze with tubes sticking out. He wouldn't have recognized Andy as his son if he had not known better. There were tubes down his throat and tape across his face. There were tubes in his arms, IV pumps, and other machines he could not identify.

There was a tall, blonde nurse at Andy's bedside. She smiled briefly and pointed to a chair on the opposite side of the room.

"Come in. Please, sit down over there, Mr. Werner. I'm Zarah, Andy's second-shift nurse."

She was deep in thought and not ready to speak to him. She wrote in a chart, checked the rate and medication of every single IV pump, and then studied the monitor over Andy's head after infusing medication into one of the IV lines.

No, he will never forget one moment of the past five weeks—the experience forever changed him. The hospital ICU staff, especially Jack, Zarah, and Dr. Bluett, had brought him from the lowest point of his life to the most hopeful.

"Zarah," Matt choked out. "Thank you… for everything."

Zarah smiled. "I'll visit Andy tomorrow to see how he is adjusting to his new room… This is a *good* thing, Matt. This is a huge step in the right direction for Andy."

She hugged Matt, then hugged each one of his children. She would miss Matt, but there was always another patient and another family. After a while, they all faded from memory—only the special ones stood out. She would not forget Matt and his cowboy good looks for a long time to come.

That evening, the ICU doors swung open. Zarah looked up from her charting… it was Nate.

"What are you doing here so late, Dr. Bluett?" Zarah asked.

"The surgery went longer than I expected," he stated.

"Why aren't you on your way home?" she asked.

"I was hoping to see you. Are you off on Friday?"

"I am. Why?"

"Do you want to go for a motorcycle ride?" He raised his eyebrows as he waited for her response.

Zarah did not know Nate's intentions but didn't want to overthink it. It had been a long time since she had fun, for fun's sake. She thought that he must be, once again, separated from his wife, but she didn't ask. The magic of the moment would disappear if she did.

"Sure, that sounds like fun." She gave Nate her phone number and told him where she lived.

"I'll pick you up with my sixty-five Triumph. Do you have a helmet or riding clothes?" he asked.

"No, I don't."

"I'll bring them for you."

Zarah returned home after her shift ended. She threw her keys on the kitchen table. It was eleven p.m., and she only wanted to shower and crawl into bed.

Unexpectedly, her cell phone rang… It was Jack.

"Hi Jack, why are you calling me this late?"

"Hey, ZZ! A few of us are at Harry's bar… want to join us? I thought you could use some fun!" He was talking loudly over the music and laughter in the background.

"Jack, I'm so tired. I just got home!"

"Come for one drink, Zarah! We're only five minutes from you. I'll come and get you!"

"No, no. I can drive myself. Who is all there?" she inquired.

"Everyone! We are celebrating Celeste's birthday, and we can also celebrate your divorce! Come on, Zarah! Find your second wind. You are off tomorrow, right?" He sounded like an excited little boy.

"Okay, yes, I *am* off tomorrow. Give me a few minutes to change."

"Ugh," she said after she hung up the phone. She had no ambition to leave the house this late evening, but Jack had a point. She had off tomorrow and could sleep in. A little fun would do her good. She took a two-minute shower, put on a pair of her favorite blue jeans and a loose floral top, and slipped on a pair of sandals. She had no time to fix her hair, so she brushed her ponytail into place. She put on minimal makeup and, of course, her silver hoop earrings.

She stopped in front of her full-length mirror… "This will have to do!"

She arrived under thirty minutes from Jack's phone call and saw a group of her co-workers milling at the bar.

"ZZ!" she heard Jack yell out. She saw him waving from a booth and walked over to join him. He was sitting next to his girlfriend, Celeste. They looked happy together, but Zarah knew that could change.

"Happy birthday, Celeste!" Zarah said as she bent over to hug her.

"Happy divorce, Zarah!" Celeste added.

Nate was sitting across from Jack and Celeste in the booth. He was alone.

"Take a load off, Zarah!" Jack ordered. "What can I get you to drink?"

"A beer would be nice… Surprise me," she answered knowing that Jack was a beer cicerone want-to-be.

Until now, Jack knew nothing of Nate's interest in her. If their relationship went any further, she would tell Nate to keep it that way. She sat beside Nate in the booth, as there was no other place to sit.

"Hi, Nate. I thought you were heading home." She felt her face flush and was thankful that the lighting in the bar was dim. She rarely called him by his first name.

"I was home, then Jack called me," he answered.

"Does your wife approve of you leaving the house at this late hour?" Zarah asked.

"There was no wife at my house today, Zarah," Nate said with finality.

She would never grow tired of his pronunciation of her name—he made her name sound like English royalty. But what did he mean by *no wife at my house today*? Did his wife no longer live with him? She couldn't pry any further—she didn't know him well enough, and Celeste was sitting across from them. To ask further questions would be inappropriate and could raise suspicions.

"Your post-op patient in room seven is doing well," she changed the subject.

"That's nice, but let's not talk shop," Nate said.

She had no idea what to say next, and she was glad that a band was playing in the far corner of the room—any conversation over the music would be difficult. She was rarely at a loss for words, but recently, Zarah could barely form a coherent sentence whenever Nate was around. She was tired after working a ten-hour shift anyway, and mindlessly sipping beer was all she felt capable of doing.

Jack returned and set Zarah's beer down in front of her. He then quickly turned to Celeste, "Let's go, Celeste! You have to dance to '1999' on your birthday!" Jack grabbed her by the hand and led her to the dance floor. The dancers on the floor were hopping in unison with every beat of the song.

Nate and Zarah were alone in the booth to watch the drunken crowd. They laughed a few times at one of their coworker's lack of dancing skills. Once the lively song ended, the band announced that they would slow down the pace. Jack and Celeste stayed on the dance floor.

From the first note, Zarah recognized the song that the band was about to play. The magical harmonic F sharp could not be mistaken for any other introduction. It was a song that described great love between a man and a woman, and if ever there was a song that could be played directly from her heartstrings, it was this one.

♪♪ *You'll remember me... as the west wind blows...*

Was this a cruel trick by the universe, or was it a moment that would change her life forever? She felt the music reach deep into her soul. Did Nate feel it, too? They sat side-by-side, watching the couples on the dance floor move slowly in each other's arms.

♪♪ *Then she took her love... there to gaze awhile*

As she listened, she imagined herself walking hand in hand with Nate through a golden field. He must have felt something, too, as at that moment, he moved his left leg until it touched Zarah's right leg. She reciprocated and let her leg relax into his.

Besides the handshake when Nate introduced himself to her over twenty years ago and possibly their fingers touching when she handed him a patient's chart, this was their first physical contact. She felt his body heat radiating through his jeans.

♪♪ *Won't you stay with me... Won't you be my love*

Zarah didn't want to move—she wanted to stay in the booth forever and have the song play into eternity.

♪♪ *See the west wind blow... like a lover soul*

Nate relaxed into the booth, then nonchalantly lifted his arm to rest it across the top of the bench behind her. A casual observer would see two friends enjoying a beer together. Her ponytail brushed his arm every time she turned her head.

♪♪ *I never make promises that I keep, and there have been some that were broken... And I swear there are days still left... When we'll walk in fields of gold... When we'll walk in fields of gold...*

The room felt as if it was floating. Zarah had only taken a few sips of her beer, so she knew that the sensation had not been alcohol-induced... It was Nate-induced.

When the song ended, Zarah knew it would replay in her heart for as long as she lived, and if nothing more transpired between them, she could always let her mind wander back to that moment in time. The band shifted into a country rock set, and the room's mood changed completely. Jack and Celeste returned to the booth.

"Awww, you two make such a cute couple!" Celeste said out of the blue as she climbed back into the booth.

Neither Zarah nor Nate commented on her odd and inappropriate statement, but out of the corner of her eye, Zarah could have sworn that she saw Nate smile after Celeste said it.

Nate's thigh remained pressed into hers, but no one knew their secret beneath the heavy wooden table. If he wasn't going to move his leg, Zarah was not about to move hers either.

Twenty-three

Motorcycle ride

FRIDAY AT ONE o'clock sharp, the rumble of a motorcycle approaching the house caught her attention. She peeked out the front blind—it was him.

"Damn, you are punctual, Dr. Blue Eyes," she whispered nervously into the blinds. As promised, he had a second helmet strapped to the passenger seat. He was dressed in black leather, and Zarah thought she may never have seen a more attractive man. He removed his helmet and hung it on the handlebar. She quickly stepped back from the blinds as he began to strut toward her front door.

Nate was not disappointed when Zarah opened the door. He rarely saw her in anything other than light blue scrubs. She wore a floral sleeveless shirt and snug-fitting blue jeans. Her wavy blonde hair fell loosely past her shoulders—not the typical studious ponytail she wore daily to work. He thought she had lost too much weight for a while, but she must have regained her appetite—her curves had returned in all the right places.

"This is a nice house, Zarah. Who does your gardening?"

"I do. I love to get my hands dirty."

"I'll have to keep that in mind!" he teased.

"Come in, Nate." Zarah suppressed her laugh as she opened the screen door. Nate passed within inches of her as he entered, and she suspected he did it purposefully. She slowly inhaled his scent as he passed.

"You can throw your jacket over a chair."

Zarah felt as though she was an actress in a play. Was this happening? Was one of the most famous surgeons in the country—in the world—in her house? She pulled herself together and tried to appear as cool as a cucumber.

"Would you like a tour of the house?" she asked. "I'll bet you aren't aware I'm a handyman!"

"Well, you are definitely *not* a man, and I have overheard you talking to your cohorts about what you've been doing to this place. I'd *love* to see what you've accomplished thus far," His curiosity was piqued.

She turned around. "This is the living room. When I moved in, this hardwood floor hid under an ugly old carpet. I hired a professional to sand and refinish it."

Nate's eyes scanned the room. It was airy and bright. An off-white leather couch was against the far wall. Mid-century modern end tables and a matching coffee table in front were on both sides of the sofa. The table tops held only the essentials—a lamp, a book, and a bowl of polished stones. White wooden blinds were tipped to let in the perfect rays of afternoon light.

"And this is the dining room," she said as she turned around. The dining room table and chairs were also mid-century modern.

"Very nice, Zarah. Is this furniture vintage?"

"Yes, I found the pieces either online or at estate sales. I wanted to match the furniture to the original era of the house. I love the dovetail details," she said as she ran her hand over the tabletop.

"I'm impressed," Nate said.

"You should be!" she said playfully. "I refinished every piece, which had to be carefully hand-sanded because the veneer is so thin." She'd stopped herself from saying any more about her furniture—she could talk for hours about furniture refinishing.

"This way is the kitchen."

Nate took off his jacket, tossed it on the back of a dining room chair, then followed her.

"This might be my favorite room in the house." She put her hands on her hips and let the room speak for itself.

"The cabinets are beautiful. Are they hickory?" he asked.

"Yes. They were already installed when I moved in. I think that's why I fell in love with this house. The rest of the house was trashed. I should show you the 'before' pictures sometime."

"I'd like that."

He scanned a nook in a corner of the kitchen filled with healthy succulents of every conceivable size and shape. Several plants hung from the ceiling with their foliage draping down well past the sides of the pots.

"You love plants," he stated.

"I do!" she said enthusiastically. "I especially love succulents. I can ignore them for weeks, and they don't die. Everyone assumes I have a green thumb."

"Do you have the same white blinds throughout the house?" he inquired.

"Yes. I wanted one room to flow into the next."

"You've accomplished that, Zarah."

From the moment he walked into the house, he felt like he had entered a tranquil oasis. It was as if Zarah's home enveloped him with a warm hug. It was so Zarah. He could easily imagine kicking off his shoes, laying on her couch with a book, or simply closing his eyes and taking an afternoon nap.

Zarah contemplated showing him the rest of the house. All that was to see were the bedrooms.

"Well… continue!" Nate said with a boyish smile.

"It's a small house. There isn't much more to see and keep in mind; it's still a work in progress." Zarah said as she walked toward the back of the house with Nate following behind. "This is the second bedroom I use for an office."

A mid-century modern-style desk was centered in the middle of an off-white area rug outlined in green and white azaleas. Several large plants were in the far corners of the room. A laptop computer, a pencil holder, and a neat basket of papers were on the desktop.

"You're so organized, Zarah! If I open a desk drawer, will I find where you keep all your clutter?"

"Go ahead and look! It's only me living here, so it's fairly easy to keep the place clean and organized," she stated.

Nate walked over to the desk and opened the top drawer. "I'll be damned. You have got to be the most organized person I know."

"Of course I am!" she laughed. "And across the hall…" she said as she turned around, "is my bedroom."

Nate loved the slight creek of the hardwood floor when he stepped into the room. Her furniture was, once again, an understated fifties style, and the room was airy and fresh. A fluffy white comforter coordinated with the white wooden window blinds and various blue pillows were haphazardly placed at the head of the bed. "Did you refinish this bedroom set, too?" he asked.

"I got lucky. This set was in excellent shape when I bought it. I only had to give it a coat of Danish oil, and it looked brand new."

"Your house has a zen-like quality." He admired Zarah's simplistic lifestyle.

"Well, thank you. That is exactly what I've been aiming for. I'm happier when I keep things simple," she explained.

"That looks like a comfy bed!" he added with a mischievous grin.

"Stop it, Dr. Bluett," Zarah said playfully. His suggestive remark came as no surprise. He and Jack were cut from the same cloth.

"Do you want something to drink, Nate?" she asked.

"Yes, but nothing alcoholic when I'm riding a motorcycle."

With iced tea, they stepped out to the back covered porch and sat at the white wrought iron table. She adjusted her chair to face Nate. He was beginning to seem like a regular person instead of the god-like being she had built him up to be over the past twenty-some years.

They talked about a new addition that the hospital was planning to build and about the progress of the post-op patient she had cared for in the past week. She wanted to get off the topic of work, so she changed the subject and asked him about his vintage British motorcycle collection— something she knew was near and dear to his heart.

"I overheard you talking to Jack the other day... You recently bought another bike?"

"Yes, I did! I bought a 1951 Norton."

"Does it run well?" she asked.

"It needs work. Believe it or not, it had only one previous owner. He recently died, and his son sold it to me."

"How many bikes do you have in your collection?" she asked.

"I'm not sure, but I'd say somewhere near thirty."

"What do you do with all those motorcycles?" Zarah asked.

"I ride them! Haven't you walked through my pole shed to see my bike collection during one of my parties?"

"Jack and I walked through. But I didn't count them. I do recall that your collection filled up most of the building."

Every summer since Zarah began working in the ICU, she attended an annual party hosted by Nate at his palatial lake house. The parties were well-attended by doctors, residents, nurses, therapists, and even the cleaning staff—Nate invited everyone. Even though he was a world-renowned surgeon, he held himself above no one. It was no more unusual to witness Nate conversing in the hospital hallway with the janitor than to observe him talking with the hospital CEO. He took an interest in everyone, and no matter their position, they earned Nate's respect if they did their job well.

Zarah never ventured inside his house during the parties, but she was always curious about how the prominent Dr. Bluett lived. Once, while standing outside with a group of her co-workers, she stole a glimpse through his kitchen window—it was nearly buried with papers, books, and what looked like general stuff.

Zarah never found a graceful opening to initiate a conversation with his wife, Vicky, nor say much more than a polite hello. As welcoming as Nate was, Vicky was not. Zarah found her standoffish as she socialized only with a small group of people she had invited.

Zarah could never figure out why Nate had chosen Vicky as his wife. A defense attorney, Vicky had a reputation for being a bitch and an all-around hard-ass. Zarah often saw Vicky at one event or another and rarely saw her smile. It wasn't even that she was pretty—she was quite plain.

Zarah had hoped that Vicky would have added a woman's touch, and maybe some much-needed order, to Nate's life. But the following year, Zarah could not help but steal another glimpse as she walked past the same kitchen window. The scene remained the same, maybe even more chaotic than the previous year. Zarah surmised that the house was strictly utilitarian for Dr. Bluett and his new wife, and perhaps they were a good match for each other after all.

An hour of conversation passed quickly.

"Are you ready to ride on an awesome 1966 Triumph Bonneville?" Nate asked with a grin.

"I am!"

As Zarah locked her front door, Nate began digging in his saddlebag. He pulled out a woman's black leather jacket and handed it to Zarah.

"This should fit you."

Was he giving her a jacket that belonged to his wife? The reality of what she may be doing felt like a slap in the face.

"Whose jacket is this?" Zarah said with a blank expression.

He saw her concern. "Zarah, I have about ten leather jackets in different sizes. I *never* take a passenger on my bike without protective gear. You'll find gloves in the pockets… And put this helmet on."

Zarah loved his take-charge attitude—he knew no other way to be. He got on the bike and revved the engine, then nodded in her direction so she could hop on. She wrapped her arms around his waist, and they left the neighborhood.

"Where are we going?" Zarah yelled over his shoulder when they reached the end of her street.

"You'll see!"

Forty-five minutes later, they were well away from the city. The countryside was hilly and rolling, and trees lined both sides of the streets. He drove the bike into the parking lot of a quaint little diner. They went inside and sat down across from each other in a booth.

"I'm starving," he said as he opened the menu.

"Me, too. Have you ever been here before?" she asked.

"No."

A waitress came to take their order. She stared at Nate for a few seconds... "*You* look so familiar..."

"I've got that kind of face," he answered without looking up from the menu.

Did he take me to this restaurant because it's far from town? Because the chances of being recognized here are slim to none?

She wanted to ask him if he was still with his wife. The most recent "office gossip" was that Vicky had moved out. Was that true? Or was he sneaking around behind Vicky's back?

Being with Nate was intoxicating. For selfish reasons, she pushed any curiosity aside and would assume that he was, as the rumors had it, separated from his wife. She did not want to know the truth.

"I'll take a club sandwich," he said as he returned the menu to the waitress.

"That sounds good. I'll have the same."

She could not stop her attraction for Nate, no more than she could have stopped the disdain she felt toward Joe as their marriage crumbled. However, in all the years they worked together, Nate and Zarah's relationship had remained professional, and their conversations were primarily focused on patient care.

There was *no* comparison between Joe and Nate—they were as different as two men could be. She had never known anyone more intelligent or ambitious than Nate, and she could not deny that those attributes were a huge turn-on.

"Are you coming to my annual party this year?" he asked. "I'm buying a pontoon boat, and I'll give you a ride if you're a good girl," he said with a sassy smile.

"When is the party?"

"The last Saturday in August."

"Well, that's months away. I'm sure I'll go with 'my people' as I typically do."

Zarah's thoughts began to spin wildly... *What will be my place at Nate's party? Will he walk up to me and put his arm around me... in front of everyone? Will their jaws drop open? Will people whisper behind my back and accuse me of being a home-wrecker?*

Or will the opposite happen... Vicky will be there. Nate will smile at me only when the coast is clear, and we will treat each other exactly as we do in the ICU.

Neither situation was good. She was divorced. She had found the courage to free herself from a loveless marriage. Sneaking around was unnecessary. What was Nate doing? She had no idea and could not yet bring herself to ask. She wouldn't worry about the party now.

After finishing their meal, they got back on the Triumph and rode back to Zarah's house. When Zarah got off the motorcycle, she locked eyes with Nate.

She had not planned on asking him, and something in her mind screamed, "Don't do it!" But her words escaped involuntarily as if they had a life of their own...

"Do you want to come in?"

Twenty-four

Slow down and slow down

OCCASIONALLY, ZARAH WOULD meet up with Jack for a coffee on their day off, as they never seemed to have enough time during work hours to discuss everything they had on their minds.

Besides being her friend, Jack was the big brother she never had. He was there for her whenever she needed him during her divorce.

In the years they had worked together, Zarah and Jack's sense of humor seemed to grow more off-color with every passing week, and every week, they had to laugh as they re-drew their line in the sand as to what they accepted as appropriate work-related conversation. Jack could have Zarah in stitches at a moment's notice to break the tension in the ICU, and Zarah learned to give it right back to him.

Their humor may have sounded crass or even offensive to anyone who overheard, but their humor was what got them through the type of work they did. And at times, if you didn't laugh… you would cry.

When Zarah began working in the ICU, she occasionally hid in the galley to compose herself in privacy. Patients often arrived in rough shape. The nurses would gather around a new admission's bedside to remove stones embedded in their skin after a motorcycle or automobile accident—they called it "road rash." Sometimes, a new patient resembled roadkill more than a person. The tests and procedures that quickly followed seemed callous and inhumane. Tubes and IV lines were inserted to allow access for the drugs that would follow. Zarah was always thankful when the patient was heavily sedated—that way, they were not aware of what was happening to them.

It took over a year for Zarah to become a stoic nurse. She developed the self-survival skill to not sympathize deeply with her patients—tears were not what helped them. It was easier for her to care for older patients—they had lived long lives. The younger patients always tugged at her heartstrings, but she learned to keep her emotions in check.

She was ten minutes early, and Jack texted that he was running late. She didn't mind the time by herself. It was a beautiful day, and she found an outdoor table under a shade tree where she would patiently wait.

Her phone buzzed in her purse—it was Nate. He had called or texted every day since their date.

"What are you doing?" his text read.

"I'm waiting for Jack at a coffee shop. What are you doing?" she texted back.

"I'm about to scrub in for a long surgery. You won't hear from me for the rest of the day." Another text quickly followed, "Did you tell Jack about us?"

"No! Did *you* tell him?" she texted back.

"No."

Nate and Jack frequently huddled together, talking and laughing in the ICU. They were as close as two friends could be.

"Let's keep it that way. Good luck with the surgery," she typed back, then put her phone on silent mode and returned it to her purse.

She was relieved that Nate had not told Jack about their relationship. She wanted to keep whatever it was they had quiet—at least for now. She still had no idea what their relationship even was. If he was still married, then he was cheating on his wife. And if Nate was cheating on his wife, she was having an affair with a married man.

"Ugh," Zarah said to herself. The thought that she may be "the other woman" made her uncomfortable in her skin.

At a table not too far away, she watched an older couple who were obviously in love. The woman rubbed her hand on her partner's back as she gazed into his eyes and said something that made him smile. Would she ever have that with Nate? Could this scenario be in her future? Was Nate her cosmic reward for the suffering she had gone through with Joe? What price would she have to pay, though? Would she have to pay with her reputation? Would hospital employees always look at her sideways and whisper to each other as she passed them in the hallways?

The memory of the other evening was clouding any rational thought process. She had relived the events of that night over and over and over…

Nate parked his motorcycle in her garage and then asked her to close the garage door. They entered the kitchen, removed their jackets, and dropped them to the floor. For a few moments, they stood and stared at each other.

"I have a confession to make, Zarah. I've always had a crush on you."

"I had no clue." She could not believe her ears. He went on...

"You were married. Then I heard you got a divorce, and I saw you watching me that day when you were standing at the assignment board..."

"Well, Doctor Bluett, I also have a confession to make... I've always had a crush on you, too!"

"Seriously?" he asked.

"Seriously," she replied.

"I wasn't aware you were going through a divorce, Zarah. You did a commendable job at keeping your problems to yourself."

"It wasn't hard to keep my personal life separate from my work life—I'm happy," Zarah explained.

"That's part of the allure," he smiled.

"What's part of the allure?"

"That you are happy."

Nate took several steps toward Zarah, put his hands around her waist, and guided her slowly backward until she leaned against the countertop. He then lifted her so she could sit on the kitchen counter. She wrapped her legs around him and pulled him close. They were eye to eye.

"I've always thought that you have the sexiest philtrum," he said as he studied her mouth.

"The sexiest what?" she asked.

"The grove that starts here... and ends there," he said as he outlined the area above her lip. "And it leads right to your sexy lips."

"Are you giving me an anatomy lesson, Dr. Bluett?" she asked playfully.

"I am."

"Are you aware that the nurses call you Dr. Blue Eyes?" she asked.

"I've heard that... I've been called worse," he smiled.

"Zarah, I want to kiss you." He was not asking for permission, and he began to kiss her before she could say another word.

His kiss was urgent... more urgent than she had anticipated. She expected a few moments of tenderness, but that was not what she got. He braced the back of her head with his hand as his lips pressed on hers with more pressure than was comfortable. His tongue searched as if he was starving. This was not the "first kiss" from Nate she had anticipated. She had no part in it whatsoever—she was merely the receiver. What was happening?

Zarah's experience with men was close to nil. Nate was only the third man she'd ever kissed. Was Nate so arrogant that he thought he could do no wrong? Was she destined to only be with men who didn't know how to kiss? She pushed him away.

"Nate!" she gasped.

"I'm sorry; you've got me very excited. Can we move to the bedroom? He flashed her a boyish grin.

"Yes, of course. But slow down, Nate! What's the hurry?!"

The mood lightened as they began to get undressed. She stood naked and self-conscious in front of him. She had given birth to two babies, and gravity had taken some toll. She reached up to close the blind.

"Zarah, you are beautiful. Leave the blind open."

Those words were foreign to Zarah, coming from the man who made her heart race for many years—the man she thought she could never have.

They laughed like two teenagers as they climbed into bed. Zarah immediately got on top of him and stroked his hair off his forehead.

"I've wanted to do this for a long time," she said.

"Fuck me?"

"No! That is presumptuous of you, Dr. Bluett. I've always wanted to run my fingers through your hair!"

They both laughed at his crass remark. She knew that he prided himself in his edgy sense of humor.

"So… what does it feel like?" he inquired.

"What does what feel like?" she asked.

"My hair."

"Mmmmmm, it's nice." Zarah grabbed a hold of a handful of his hair on the nape of his neck and gave it a playful tug.

"Hey, I kind of like that!" Nate informed her.

"Then I will have to do it again sometime, doctor. A good nurse always takes care of her patients. "

"I'm your patient? Does that make you my naughty nurse?" He liked where this was going.

"You are my patient when you are in my bed."

Zarah allowed herself to tuck her face into his hair and breathe in his essence. She smelled the faintest shampoo scent and thought he must have showered before picking her up today. She breathed deeply several times, trying to memorize the moment.

He ran his hands slowly up and down her back.

"Mmmm, that's nice…" she whispered in his ear. She relaxed into the warmth of his body and allowed herself to be mesmerized by his touch. She thought his hands might be the sexiest part of him—the same hands that performed intricate surgeries and saved countless lives.

He kissed her now more tenderly as his hands followed the curve of her waist, her hips, her breasts.

Zarah caught her breath. A sensation grew deep within her as if every hormone in her body was in alignment, and every nerve fiber was about to explode.

Their bodies began to move in a rhythm all their own— a primal rhythm that neither of them could control. It was as natural as breathing. Zarah pushed up off his chest and continued to move with him. There was no turning back. She reached down and guided him in.

She felt her eyes involuntarily roll back in her head and felt as if she was leaving her body. She heard a cry—it was her own. Every cell in her body vibrated, and nothing in her life had ever felt like this...

"My turn," she heard him say.

Nate flipped her beneath him and steadied himself on his arms. She watched his face above her. His beautiful face, the face she had admired for so many years, the man that had walked directly up to her over twenty-five years ago, on her first day as a new nurse, held out his hand and said, "Hi, I'm Nate Bluett."

"Zarah!" Nate cried out... He had experienced it, too.

Seeing Nate above her was too much. The twenty-five-year-long foreplay was over, and Zarah set free all the emotions that she had been suppressing for a second time. She wrapped her arms around him and did not let go.

"Wow, twice?" Nate said as he fell off of her onto the bed.

"Twice!" Zarah exclaimed.

She had found the reason she was alive—to be Nate's life partner. She had no idea how this would be accomplished—it could be a rocky road ahead for both of them—but she was confident that she felt something deep in her heart for this man...

"ZZ!" Jack's voice snapped her out of her daydream. She was relieved. She needed to concentrate on other things besides going to bed with Nathanial Bluett.

"Hi, Jack!" She beamed at him and stood to hug him.

She knew that, if possible, Jack must be one of the soulmates one incarnates with. During his divorce, Zarah had been his confidant. They had both helped each other when they were at their lowest points. Now, they had come full circle.

He returned within minutes with a large cup of coffee.

"Do you want something else? They have cookies!" Jack asked, his facial expression no different from that of an excited young boy.

"I'm good! Sit down, Jack. We have world problems to solve!" she laughed.

Jack sat next to her and patted her on the knee.

"So… What's new and exciting in Zarah-world?" he asked.

"Nothing much," she lied. *Everything* was new and exciting.

"You've been so distant lately, Zarah. It sure seems like something is on your mind," he said in an attempt to figure out what was weighing so heavily on his friend.

"It's nothing. Maybe the stress of the house renovations and work is finally getting to me."

"Are you sure, Zarah, because it sure seems like something else… Does it have anything to do with me?"

"No! Everything is fine, Jack." She wanted to steer the subject in a different direction quickly. "Tell me… What's going on in Jack-world?!"

She could not yet tell Jack about her relationship with Nate. She had no idea how he would react to the news. Jack wasn't stupid—he was sensing that something wasn't quite right in her life. She would have to smile and pretend that everything was fine—she had a lot of practice doing that during her marriage. She'd have to give a lot of thought to telling Jack about her relationship with Nate and have to start acting normal again. Other people would also begin to notice if Nate questioned her about a change in her personality.

The next hour flew by as if nothing else in the world mattered. It never ceased to amaze her how at ease she was with Jack. She would have never guessed that a woman could become best friends with a man without things getting confusing or turning sexual. But they seemed to have accomplished just that. She could call him anytime with any problem, and vice-versa.

Deep into their conversation, she decided to ask Jack about Nate nonchalantly. Jack may be aware of Nate's personal life details, and she could get information about his current marital status in that roundabout way. The stories floating around the hospital about Nate's marital status were either gossip... or self-delusion.

"So, what's going on with Blue Eyes?" she casually asked.

Jack was puzzled. "Why do you ask?"

"I'm just curious. I've heard rumors. Is he separated from Vicky again?" She immediately felt guilty for asking. She was never the kind of person to thrill to someone else's bad fortune to benefit herself. Who was she becoming?

"I have no idea," Jack answered.

"You guys talk all the time! How do you not know?"

"We don't talk about our personal lives."

She felt uneasy—she had used Jack to gain information. She vowed she would never do that again.

"ZZ, there is something... I have to tell you..."

"What is it?"

The last time she saw him this contemplative was when he told her he was filing for divorce.

"I broke it off with Celeste. Things were getting very complicated."

"Well, I can't say that I'm all that surprised. You two had a rocky relationship."

"There is something else I must explain to you, Zarah..."

"What is it?" She locked eyes with his. His tone was far too serious.

"During the past few years, we've met like this almost every week. We get along so well. We have so much fun together."

"We do! I don't know what I would do without you!" she said reassuringly, placing her hand over his.

"ZZ... Zarah... what I am trying to say is... I've fallen in love with you."

"What?! No! You don't love me like that!" Zarah had not seen this coming, and she was stunned. "Jack, you know that I love you, too. You might be the best friend I've ever had!"

"I'm sensing a 'but' coming..." he said as he broke eye contact.

"You're my friend. I guess I've never romantically thought of you..." That wasn't a decisive enough answer, and she knew it left too much room for interpretation. "Wait... Am I the reason that you broke up with Celeste, Jack?!"

"No, Zarah. Our relationship had run its course."

They both paused to collect their thoughts.

"Zarah, could you love me... that way?"

She could not cross that line with him or put her finger on a single reason at that moment.

"Jack, you're my best friend..."

That was not the answer he wanted to hear.

"Then I was under the wrong assumption," he added. "Silly me... You've been so mysterious at work. Whenever I ask you what is wrong, you give me a vacant stare or tell me, 'Nothing is wrong.' I thought you were holding back your feelings *for me*..." His voice trailed off.

"Jack, I don't know how to begin to process this..."

She had never intentionally led Jack on. Yes, they had pushed the limits of their friendship. There was barely a day that went by that she did not cross a line in the sand with him. She had often told him, "I have *never* talked this sassy with anyone before." She had always assumed that joking around was their way of easing the tension of their stressful jobs.

"Then what is it that you've been so tortured over, Zarah? Sometimes, you look like you're carrying the world's weight on your shoulders."

"I have a lot on my mind." She skirted the issue again, and Jack knew it, but she could say no more.

"I should get going," he stated flatly. He was sorry he had told her he had fallen in love with her. He needed to put distance between them.

"Jack!"

Zarah didn't have any words to offer to turn the situation around. She never thought she would lose Jack's friendship. In her mind's eye, she saw them sitting at a coffee shop when they were old and gray. What would she do if she could not fix this? How would she be? He was the first person she sought out when she got to work. He was always happy to greet her, and he *always* found her to bid her good night before he left for the day. They had worked together, side by side, on some of the most mangled bodies anyone could imagine. They shared their thoughts on the best way to care for their patients. They had laughed a million laughs and cried a million tears together. Could one sentence, one misconception, end it all?

"See you on Monday." He looked down at the sidewalk and walked away.

Twenty-five

Enough

NATE HAD BEEN coming to her house once or twice a week for months, and up to this point, neither one had brought up the subject of his marriage.

As usual, he was bringing steaks and an expensive bottle of wine tonight. She would toss the salad while he grilled the steaks on her back porch. It had become their routine. After dinner, they would talk for a couple of hours until the bottle of wine was empty. Then, like every single time before, they would end up in bed.

He arrived promptly at seven. She opened her garage door, let him drive his pick-up truck in, then closed it behind him. She was sure now that she was hiding him. Tonight, she would finally ask.

She wanted to go places and be out in public with other people like normal couples do. She wanted to discuss her boyfriend with her friends and not have to filter every word that crossed her lips carefully. She had no reason to hide... unless she was involved in something illicit.

She let herself enjoy dinner with him. They briefly discussed a difficult patient from the past week. Then, the conversation shifted to his childhood and what it was like to grow up in England. He talked about attending medical school at the Imperial College of London and moving to Baltimore to complete his residency at Johns Hopkins. Zarah thought he was born with a silver spoon in his mouth. His father was also a surgeon, and his mother stayed home to raise him and his sister.

"I've never been to England," Zarah said sadly.

"I'll take you there!" he answered.

She wished that to happen, and she thought he meant what he said, but something told her that a trip to England with Nate was not in the cards. She took a deep breath—now was the perfect time to say what had been on her mind for so long.

"Nate, we've been seeing each other for months, and all of this time, I've avoided a subject..."

Nate's face turned pale—he knew what she was about to ask, and he was surprised it had taken her this long to bring up the subject.

"I've heard so many rumors over the years... What is the status of your marriage? Are you single? Are you separated from Vicky? Are we a couple, or are we having an affair?"

Zarah had become more emotional than she thought she would—the last thing she wanted was to come across as desperate.

"Zarah, I can't tell you what you want to hear right now," he said with finality.

"What do you think I want to hear?!" she retorted.

"That I'm divorcing Vicky." His voice trailed off.

"Nate, *I* don't have to sneak around. *I* am divorced. But it has become painfully obvious to me that you do." Zarah could not hide the sarcasm in her voice.

"I know you love me, Zarah…"

She did love him more than she had ever loved any man, but she would not admit it to him—not this way.

She had gone through the hell that had been her divorce. She imploded the only life she'd ever known. She reinvented herself, almost as if she started her life from scratch. She had done all the hard work—and now she was looking directly at a man who did not dare to do the same for himself.

"Go home, Nate. Go home to your wife," she said with finality.

He reached over and took her by the shoulders. He pulled her in and held her.

"Zarah, can't we continue this? This has been the best sex of my life," he whispered into her hair.

"Mine, too."

"One more time?" he sheepishly asked.

"Go home, Nate."

Zarah walked toward the door. With her arms folded across her chest, she stared at the floor as she waited for him to put on his jacket. He leaned down, kissed her cheek, and walked out without another word.

Later that week, Nate studied the patient assignment board to determine which nurses had been assigned to his post-op patient. It was "ZZ."

"Zarah…" he said as he approached her. "How is my post-op in room three?"

"He's doing well. His vitals are stable. He is alert and oriented times three. His dressing is clean, dry, and intact," she matter-of-factly rattled off.

He should have thanked her then and moved on to check the status of his next post-op patient. Instead, he paused as he gathered his thoughts.

"Zarah… what are you doing Saturday?" he whispered with the same boyish grin that Zarah had always found impossible to resist. His eyes had never appeared bluer nor more bereft.

"Nate, not here. Room eleven is empty."

Zarah took a few steps into the room and closed the door behind them. Fortunately, all the other nurses were busy. If any of her co-workers had seen them walk into the empty patient room, it would have been a dead giveaway that something was happening between them. She quickly pulled the privacy curtain and turned to face him.

"*We* aren't doing anything this weekend. *We* are over," she said, emphasizing the words "we."

"Are you serious, Zarah?" he asked.

"And by 'over,' I mean no more of '*that*,'" she said as she drew an imaginary circle in the air between them. "I want to date someone who can be seen publicly with me. When you are divorced, give me a call. Maybe I'll still be available. But I can't promise anything."

"Zarah…" Nate began. He looked thoughtful as if he had a natural solution for the problem. "What if I took care of you…"

"What do you mean, 'take care of me?'" She had no idea what he was trying to say.

"Financially…" he said.

"What?!" Zarah double-checked to ensure the heavy glass sliding door was closed. She was about to raise her voice. "I'm *not* your prostitute, Nate! And I have my own money!"

His statement should have insulted her, but she stifled a laugh instead. The offer was his last-ditch effort to keep their affair going. She knew that Nate would happily stay in their affair—maybe for years—maybe forever.

"I'm sorry, I didn't mean to insinuate that you're my hooker. But think how easy your life could be. You wouldn't have to work."

"I love my job, Nate. I don't need your money, and I can't imagine anything worse than sitting home like a princess on a pillow awaiting the prince's return! I won't live for the scraps you throw my way when it's convenient for you."

"She was unfaithful to me, too," he said as he stared down at the floor.

"Vicky? She was unfaithful to you?"

"Yes... more than once."

"Are you two playing some game? Who can hurt who more?" She felt panic set in... "Does Vicky know about me?! Was I just a pawn in your game?!"

"No, Zarah. She knows nothing about you."

"Nate, I ended my marriage, but you either don't want to end yours, or you don't have the balls," she whispered loudly, her face inches from his. "I can't determine which is the correct scenario... Probably both."

Not only was he cheating on his wife, but he was cheating himself of the life he preferred to be living.

"Zarah, you know how I feel about you. I don't love Vicky, but we've been married for a long time... It's complicated. The relationship that you and I have is very different."

"The relationship we *have,* Nate? Don't you mean, 'the relationship we *had*?'"

She did love Nate and probably always would, but that wasn't enough. She had lived in a loveless marriage for so long and never knew what she had missed. She was not about to settle again for a relationship missing a vital piece of the big picture. If she couldn't "have it all," she was perfectly content remaining single.

She had enjoyed every single second of her time with Nate. Being with Nate woke her to the fact that someone could be attracted to her. In all the years she had been married, no other man had ever given her a second glance. But then, she never gave out the vibes she had given to Nate.

Their relationship was wrong, but she had no regrets. She wouldn't have missed it for the world.

"Goodbye, Nate."

She peered through a crack in the curtain. The coast was clear. All of the nurses were still busy. She slid the door open and walked out of the room as if nothing had happened.

Twenty-six

Cowboy in town

THE TRANSPORTERS WERE running an hour behind schedule. Zarah's patient, Mr. Johnson, had been discharged to home. He needed to be taken by wheelchair to the hospital's main entrance, where his family was waiting to pick him up. His room was required for the following admission, which was already en route via helicopter. Zarah decided to take him down to the main entrance to expedite the process.

She helped Mr. Johnson out of the wheelchair and into the car, then stepped back to wave goodbye as his wife drove him away. She wished him well—he was a lovely man.

Her mind focused on returning to the ICU as quickly as possible. There was equipment to gather and medications to prepare. The new patient had sustained a severe head injury, and he would take all her concentration. The doctors and her co-workers would descend upon him the moment the Flight For Life crew wheeled him into the room. She turned around abruptly to head back to the ICU.

"Whoa!" she heard someone say. "You need backup lights, Nurse Zarah!"

It was Matt, the father of her former patient, Andy, and she had run smack into him in her haste.

"Wow, sorry about that! What are you doing here, Matt?" she asked.

"I just dropped Andy off for rehab."

Zarah and Jack had been Matt's lifelines during the weeks when Andy remained unresponsive in the ICU. Without them, he would have felt helpless. He was forever grateful for the care she and Jack provided to his son and for the support they offered to him. How would he have lived through that terrible time without them?

"It's so nice to have literally bumped into you, Zarah!" Matt laughed. He glanced down at her left hand and noticed she no longer wore her wedding band.

"How is Andy? I rarely get updates on my patients once they leave the ICU."

"He is doing well!" Matt smiled. "He is walking with minimal assistance, and his speech is much improved."

"I'd love to get an update on Andy now and then. May I give you my phone number so you can call me occasionally to let me know how he's doing?"

She scribbled her phone number on a scrap of paper in her scrub jacket and handed it to him.

"Zarah, I have to ask... I could never figure out... Are you married?" While Andy was in her care, she had always tap-danced around the subject of her personal life, but now she seemed somehow different.

"I was married, but I'm not anymore," she answered.

"Well, then... What if I use this phone number to call and ask you for a date?" Matt asked with a grin.

"That would be nice!" Zarah smiled as that was precisely what she was hoping for.

"What are you doing Saturday? There is a new restaurant downtown I've been wanting to check out," he said hopefully.

"You've got my number... Call me with the details! I've got to get back to the ICU. Duty calls!" They exchanged a brief, polite hug goodbye.

As she walked away, she felt light and happy. Maybe getting on with her life after Nate wouldn't be so hard. By coincidence or fate, the handsome cowboy had walked back into her life.

Twenty-seven

Disappoint a friend

MATT LIVED AN hour's drive from Zarah's house. They scheduled a standing date every Saturday night between his dental practice and overseeing the care of his five children. Zarah didn't mind. Her job and her never-ending home rehab projects kept her occupied, and a date every Saturday night fit nicely into her life.

She still saw Nate nearly every day that she worked. He always sought her out when he entered the unit and nodded in approval when he made eye contact with her. Her heart skipped a beat whenever he did so, but she was now a different person... stronger and wiser. She suspected that Nate would remain with his wife—life was simpler for him that way. It took courage to leave a marriage... Something he did not possess.

Instead of the usual smile and head nod, Nate approached Zarah as she sat in front of a computer studying lab values on her patient…

"How are you, Zarah?"

"I'm fine, Nate. You?"

"I'm good… I miss our time together…"

She would *not* engage with him in a conversation about their past sex life. He would like that too much.

"Is there something I can do for you, Dr. Bluett?" she said in a business-like tone.

"My party is next weekend. Are you going to come?"

Zarah had never missed one of Nate's parties. Her co-workers were planning on going, and it would seem out of character if she didn't attend.

"May I bring a date?" she asked smugly and watched for his reaction. He paused an uncomfortable length of time before answering.

"Of course, bring a date, Zarah." With that, he gave her a forced smile, asked her about his patient in Room 5, and then told her to "Have a wonderful day" before exiting the unit. He didn't like her request.

"Too bad, Blue Eyes… too damn bad. You can't have it your way anymore," she whispered to the computer screen as she pretended to be engaged in reading about her patient.

It had been weeks since the fateful meeting with Jack at the coffee shop. Their relationship was different now. She felt insignificant to him—he avoided being assigned to the same patient as Zarah. He spoke to her, but their conversations were strictly business.

She saw him washing his hands in the room of an unconscious patient. Nobody else was around.

"Jack!" she loudly whispered as she approached.

"Well, hello ZZ. What can I do for you?" She was irritated—he was not dropping the act. He was hurt, and she knew it was her fault. She would have to force him to talk—she wanted him back in her life.

She entered his patient's room, closed the door tightly behind her, and pulled the privacy curtain.

"Jack, you've got to stop this…"

"Stop what?"

"Jack! Please, drop the act!"

He paused momentarily while he dried his hands and chose his words carefully.

"Zarah, I'm okay," he finally said.

"You are?"

"You did me a favor. I read your signals wrong. I saw what *I* wanted to see and not what was happening. But I can't figure out what was, or still is, going on with you. You're different… Something isn't right. I can't pinpoint what it is… And you won't tell me." He stared into her eyes, hoping she would finally relent and tell him what she was hiding.

"It doesn't matter, Jack. Something was going on in my life, but it's over. I can't discuss it yet. I will explain it to you someday, I promise."

Jack wasn't satisfied. He didn't like the puzzle that he had watched her become. She wasn't being truthful, and her evasiveness was ruining their friendship.

"Jack, I'm sorry I can't get romantically involved with you. We've been best friends for years. I can't cross that line. You're like a brother to me…"

"Oh, great!" he laughed. "That is exactly what I wanted to hear." He was smiling, but it was not a happy smile. It was a sarcastic smile.

"I know I've hurt you, Jack. But I want you back in my life! I miss you so much…" Zarah's voice trailed off.

Jack reached up and grabbed Zarah by the shoulders.

"Okay, Zarah. I can be friends again but may not be the same man. You understand, right? It will take me some time to work things out in this thick head of mine... I still have feelings for you, but I am working on it."

"Thank you, Jack."

"Hey..." Jack lightened the mood. "Are you planning to go to Nate's party next weekend?"

"I am going, and I'm bringing a date. Remember our patient Andy in room five a few months ago? The boy who fell out of the window?"

"Oh, yes, yes. Isn't he a little young for you?"

Zarah laughed. Having even a sliver of Jack's humor back was so good.

"No, his father, silly. We've been dating for a few weeks, but it isn't anything serious."

"The cowboy!" he laughed, "Well, that's good, Zarah. You *should* be having fun." Zarah couldn't read if he was truly happy for her or if he was telling her what she wanted to hear. At least he was trying.

"We'd better get back to work. Everyone will wonder what we are doing in here," he said as he mischievously wiggled his eyebrows.

Zarah was relieved. Without talking, their friendship had no chance. At least now, *nearly* everything was out in the open.

She watched Jack walk toward the nursing station. She could not comprehend why she couldn't "cross that line" with him. He was handsome, kind, gentle, and, most importantly, honest. He was everything she would want in a partner—he checked every box. Over the years, she had seen other co-workers fall in love and even get married. They seemed to make it work. If she had had romantic feelings for Jack, wouldn't she have felt those feelings long ago?

Twenty-eight

Three's a crowd

MATT PARKED HIS pickup truck on the grass. Fifty cars or more had already arrived, and more cars were lined up behind him.

"Wow, this party is a big deal!" he exclaimed.

Zarah searched the crowd for her co-workers and spotted them gathered in the tent where the beer was being served.

"There they are," she said to Matt as she pointed in their direction. "You never did get to meet Andy's third shift nurse, and I see her in the beer tent. I'll introduce you."

Matt was honored that Zarah had asked him to the event. Dr. Bluett had been his son's surgeon, and Matt had the utmost respect for the man who had saved his son's life.

She saw Nate standing in their midst as they walked toward Zarah's co-workers. They appeared to be clinging to his every word and, as typical, broke into laughter at anything even remotely funny he said. They all adored everything about him.

In the opposite direction, Zarah also saw Nate's wife, Vicky. She was with a small group of people that Zarah didn't recognize. Her heart began to pound, and she thought she might turn around and leave. Her conscience told her that she owed Nate's wife an apology, but at the same time, she knew that was probably the stupidest idea she'd ever had. She had convinced herself that she wasn't aware of his marital status when they began their affair, but then... she never asked. She felt the raw sting of guilt the moment she spotted Vicky. Did Vicky have any clue that Nate had been unfaithful to her?

Zarah consciously decided to avoid eye contact with Nate's wife... and, God forbid, she would *not* strike up a conversation with her. But would avoiding Vicky make her appear guilty? She would blend into the crowd that was Nate's adoring fan club.

Nate spotted her as she walked toward the group. She was walking with a man who looked vaguely familiar, and he was holding her hand.

Zarah was glad she brought Matt along. She would show Matt a lot of attention and give Nate an eyeful. She knew her attitude was childish, but she didn't care. She wanted to show Nate that she had moved on, and the opportunity to make Dr. Nathanial Bluett jealous was irresistible.

"I've got to fire up the pontoon! It's time for a booze cruise!" Nate abruptly said to his captive audience as Zarah and her date drew nearer, and then he turned and left.

Zarah introduced Matt to her co-workers. She knew that some of them were checking him out, and they would ask her many questions about him when they returned to work later in the week.

Jack had yet to arrive. *Has he changed his mind about coming?* It would be abnormal if he didn't show up. Like her, Jack had never missed one of Nate's summer parties. She hoped she didn't upset him by telling him she was bringing a date. But she didn't want to blindside him either —she wanted to give him fair warning.

In the distance, she saw Jack's truck pulling into the parking lot. He was alone, and Zarah assumed his relationship with Celeste was over. She watched as he exited his car and began walking toward Nate. It wasn't unusual that Jack would seek out Nate before looking for anyone else—the two men were thick as thieves.

"I've got to go talk to Dr. Bluett!" Matt suddenly exclaimed.

"Now?" The timing was *terrible*. "Maybe talk to him a little later," Zarah encouraged.

"He was Andy's surgeon! He saved my son's life! I've got to thank him!" Without another word, Matt released Zarah's hand and began to walk in long, quick strides toward Nate. Jack was also walking toward Nate at the same pace.

She watched as Matt, the man she was currently dating, strutted toward Nate, the man she had recently ended an affair with, and Jack, the man who had only weeks ago declared his love for her. All three men had something in common... Zarah.

Nate faked a smile as Matt approached—he still could not place him. All he knew at that point was the man had arrived with Zarah, and he was probably sleeping with her. A flash of jealousy overwhelmed him, but he maintained total composure.

Matt reached out his hand and introduced himself to Nate.

"Dr. Bluett, I don't know if you remember me... I'm Matt Werner... Andy Werner's father. He's the kid who fell off the roof in the middle of the night. You were his surgeon..."

"Yes, I remember you, Matt. How is Andy?" Nate asked as Matt vigorously shook his hand with both of his.

"He's doing well. We're seeing progress every week!"

Seconds later, Jack arrived at Nate and Matt's side.

"Jack! It's so good to see you again! How is my favorite first-shift nurse?! I don't know if you remember me..." Matt said as he wildly shook Jack's hand.

"Yes, I remember you!" Jack forced out. "What brings *you* here?" Jack asked, even though he already knew the answer. He nonchalantly studied Matt up and down. *What is it about this man that Zarah likes?*

"I'm Zarah's date! Lucky me!" Matt said while smiling from ear to ear. "Dr. Bluett," Matt said in a more serious tone. "There are no words to thank you for what you've done for my son."

"Well, you can thank the excellent nursing staff, too," Nate added as he nodded toward the crowd where Zarah stood.

"Believe me, I thank Zarah every chance I get!" Matt half-laughed. Nate suddenly felt uncomfortable in his skin, and Jack thought he might lose his lunch.

Zarah watched on in disbelief as the three men talked. Her feelings for Nate were still strong, but their relationship was over. Only recently, Jack told her he was in love with her—she was still trying to mend their relationship. Then there was Matt—the man she was currently dating. Matt was the only one who could be open about their relationship—he had no reason to hide.

How would this conversation go? *Will Nate slip up and mention his connection to me? Will Jack?*

She imagined all three of them turning their heads to stare at her—all three faces filled with anger. Her heart skipped a beat. *It's silly to think that way. Nate would never mention our relationship... Would he?*

Somehow, she and Nate had managed to keep their affair a well-guarded secret. No gossip about their circumstance was heard at the hospital, and nobody else got hurt. He had a wife, and she was standing some twenty feet behind him. She didn't think Nate would say anything to the other two men. Mentioning their relationship with Matt and Jack would add way too much complication to Nate's life.

What were the odds that the three men in her life would be standing within feet of each other and conversing? She was looking at a mind-blowing triangle of the three men in her life. She took a mental picture. Not one of them knew what had transpired between Zarah and the other two. She held her breath while waiting for them to finish their conversation and move on.

Matt enthusiastically shook hands for a second time with Nate and Jack. Then he turned and began to strut back toward her.

"Sorry I left so abruptly, Zarah. I had to thank Dr. Bluett and Jack for caring for Andy."

"That was nice of you, Matt. I'm sure they both appreciated it."

Zarah sighed with relief—all had gone well, and she laughed to herself that she had been so paranoid.

Matt grabbed Zarah's hand and then kissed her on the cheek. He was a fun person to pass the time with—someone to do things with—and someone to show Nate Bluett that he wasn't the only man in her life. She was feeling a bit guilty… Was she using him?

"Matt," Zarah began as he drove her home that evening. "I think we should get on with our lives…"

"What do you mean, Zarah? Are you breaking up with me?" he asked with sadness.

"I've enjoyed our time together, Matt. I know it's a huge effort for you to arrange to spend time with me. You have your practice, family, and Andy's rehab five days a week. I think you need to focus on your family right now. You are a super nice man…"

"I hear a 'but' coming," Matt nervously laughed.

"But I don't see us together in the long run," Zarah explained.

"I see. I've enjoyed our time together. But you are right," he admitted. "Sometimes it is hard to get away to see you."

They drove the rest of the way home in silence.

It was nearly midnight after Matt dropped her off at her home. She felt relieved that she had ended their relationship, and Matt had taken it well. Sex with Matt *had* been an education—she would have to give him that. Zarah never knew how many sexual positions existed, and she believed that Matt showed her just about every one. But there was one thing missing... Zarah never once felt the heat with Matt she felt with Nate, and Matt sensed it, which only made him try harder to satisfy her.

Her phone rang... it was Jack.

"Hi, Jack!" she answered. "Are you driving home?"

"Yes, I'm driving home," he said sarcastically. There was an uncomfortable pause, and Zarah felt her heart skip a beat. "Zarah... It was Nate! Is that what you've been hiding?! You're having an affair with Nate Bluett?!"

"Jack!" Zarah half-cried. She had no idea what led him to the conclusion... He was spot-on.

"Nate couldn't keep his eyes off of you tonight. He was irritable, and he wasn't himself. He asked me if you were serious about the cowboy. He watched you and your boyfriend's every move like a hawk..." Jack was hysterical.

"He's not my boyfriend. We broke up on the way home tonight," Zarah explained.

"I can't believe this!" Jack screamed into the phone. "You're in love with Nate?! And I thought you had feelings for me?! I'm an idiot! Tell me I'm wrong, Zarah. Tell me that this is all my imagination!"

"Jack... Nate and I *had* a thing... But it's over."

"How long has this been going on, Zarah?!"

"A long time."

"So… all those times at work when you looked like you were in agony, and all those times that I asked you if something was wrong… It was Nate you were thinking about?"

"Jack… please… You and I were doing so well! We were mending our friendship. I don't want to lose you again!"

"We were doing well, Zarah. But I'm not stupid—I always knew you were hiding something. But I never suspected for an instant that you were in love with Nate Bluett!"

"It's over!" she screamed into the phone. "I've always had a silly schoolgirl crush on him from the first moment I met him. After my divorce, we started to see each other."

"You mean you started to fuck each other!"

"Jack! Please! Nate and I had much more than a seedy affair. I'm sorry you confused the torment I was going through with feelings I was hiding for you. You know I love you, Jack… Just not that way!"

"I know." He was beginning to calm down. "I love you, too, Zarah."

"Are we okay?" She did *not* want to begin mending their friendship again at ground zero.

"I will be. At least this situation is making some sense to me now."

Twenty-nine

Ian

IT WAS THEIR birthday tradition—lunch at a restaurant they had never been to. Zarah spotted Liz the moment she walked in. Zarah was glad she had called ahead for a reservation. The view of the lake out the large rear window was breathtaking.

"Happy birthday, sister!" Liz said as she hugged Zarah.

"Happy birthday, sister!" Zarah echoed back.

Liz handed Zarah a small gift box the moment she sat down.

"Here, I can't wait. Open your birthday present!" The box was as light as air. Zarah shook it.

"An empty box?" she curiously asked.

"Open it! I couldn't resist..." Liz sat at the edge of her seat.

Inside the box was a piece of paper. Liz enthusiastically began to speak before Zarah had the chance to unfold it.

"It's a three-month subscription to dreamdate.com!" Liz excitedly stated.

"A dating website?" She knew her sister's intentions were good, but Zarah was unsure that a dating website was a good idea.

"I've already set up the profile for you. Check this out…" Liz began to fumble with her phone. "All we have to do is activate it."

"Is this safe?" Zarah said with uncertainty, then saw disappointment in her sister's eyes.

"Zarah, this could be fun! I'll help you every step of the way. You need to get your mind on other things besides home renovations and that silly love triangle you've found yourself in!"

Zarah knew that Liz was right. She and Jack were friends again, although he could still be a little aloof sometimes.

Her heart still skipped a beat whenever Nate walked into the ICU, and she still caught herself watching him whenever he walked out. But her thought process had changed, and she no longer felt like a silly schoolgirl with a big crush on teacher.

She had never heard a word from Matt after telling him their relationship was over, which was for the best.

"Maybe you're right, Liz. This might be fun. My gift for you isn't quite as exciting."

Liz loved the blue sweatshirt that Zarah had bought her. It had the word "sisters" embossed across the back.

"I bought one for myself, too. Now we can be twins!" They both laughed. The two women shared similar features, but Zarah stood three inches taller and was blonde compared to Liz's thick, brunette bob.

Back at Zarah's house, the sisters logged into dreamdate.com. Zarah was impressed—Liz had put in considerable effort when creating the profile page. She had used current photos of Zarah—one of her in a black dress and a glamour shot they both had taken on their last birthday. Zarah hit the "accept" button.

"Let the fun begin!" Both sisters nervously laughed and began scanning the profiles of the single men who lived in their area. Liz had a keen eye and would catch details that Zarah missed. Zarah gave her sister the nickname "Sherlock Holmes."

"Look at the date on this picture. It was taken ten years ago," Liz pointed out.

"What age group do you want to search, Zarah?"

"Let's search for five years younger to five years older than I am."

"Are you sure? You could pass for ten years younger than your actual age!" Liz stated.

"I'm sure. I want to have something in common with the men I date," Zarah added. "Ugh! Another half-naked one!" She did not like the men who posted pictures without a shirt on. "And this guy has a mustache…"

"No mustache? Seriously, Zarah? You know that makes you sound very shallow," Liz complained.

"I need to be attracted to someone. I'm sorry, but I don't care for mustaches. A goatee is a different story."

They continued to flip through the profiles. They ruled out anyone with young children who lived too far away. Zarah found four profiles she liked out of two hundred single men within a twenty-mile radius.

"Now, what do I do?" Zarah asked.

"Now you 'wink' at them, and if they like you, they 'wink' back at you."

"Oh my gosh, this *is* fun!" Zarah laughed. She winked at all four.

Within twenty-four hours, three of the four men had winked back, and each had sent a message. All three men wanted to meet her, and before Zarah knew it, she had lined up three dates for the upcoming weekend.

Zarah insisted that the first "dates" should be casual and in a public place—somewhere they wouldn't be rushed and would have time to talk. A coffee shop or a pub during daylight hours felt like safe options. Also, she didn't want the men to spend money on her—she would pay for her drink.

As emails flew back and forth to her prospective dates, Zarah asked each man for his surname and then researched them to ensure she wouldn't meet up with someone who had anything questionable in his past. Liz suggested she run a hard copy of their profiles and jot down notes after their first meeting. She thought it could become confusing when trying to keep track of all the details such as their job, children, where they live and what they do for fun.

"Oh my gosh," Zarah laughed. "This is like running a business!"

She did as her sister suggested and printed a copy of each of the three men's profiles, then put them into a file folder.

She hoped she would meet someone she liked—someone she could do things with. She was happy alone, and she loved living by herself. But she wanted some adventure and someone to share experiences with.

She was curious. What would it be like to be in a normal relationship? Did one even exist? She had missed out on something important that she believed people are meant to experience... A relationship with someone you love *and* trust... Someone who was painfully honest.

The first man she would meet that weekend was Ian. He was handsome in his profile picture. He was divorced, had no kids, was six-foot-two, and had a sexy goatee.

Zarah arrived at the pub they had agreed upon and parked her car on the far side of the parking lot. She didn't want him to see her vehicle or license plate number if she didn't like him.

She recognized Ian the moment she walked into the bar. He stood up and waved to get her attention. As she approached, she was not disappointed. He was as handsome in person as on his profile—maybe even more so.

"Hi, I'm Zarah," she said as she extended her hand.

"Ian Elliot," he said with an approving nod. "Have a seat, Zarah. What can I get for you to drink?"

"What are you drinking?" she asked.

"Gray Goose on the rocks."

He's drinking vodka... Joe liked vodka.

"Hmm... that would be a bit too strong for me... But I would love a Cosmopolitan!" she said with a sassy smile. He was a nice-looking man—eye candy. If nothing else came out of this date, she would enjoy a few hours of conversation with a charming man.

She told him she was a nurse at Lansing General Hospital, and he told her about his job as the director of a local and popular talk-show radio station. He said he was married for a couple of years in his early twenties but gave no reason for his divorce. Zarah told him she was divorced for many reasons but didn't go into detail either.

"You have an interesting job, Ian! Do you get to meet all the celebrities who have shows on the station?"

"Of course... I'm their boss," he answered casually.

"That's exciting!"

"I could take you on a station tour sometime," he added.

"I'd love that!" Zarah had never met anyone who worked in radio. She was intrigued. He had an exciting career, and he seemed to be ambitious—qualities she admired.

"So... what is the elusive Zarah's last name?" he inquired.

She hesitated for a few seconds. She had not planned to give her surname at the first meeting, but Ian had an honest face.

"Zoelle… Zarah Zoelle."

"Zoelle? Your initials are ZZ?"

"Yes, everyone at work calls me ZZ."

"Your profile stated that you have kids?" Ian asked.

"Yes, I have two grown sons. They have their own lives. Do you have kids?"

"No… Kids were never in the cards for me. But I do have two fur babies. Black labs… Fibber McGee and Molly."

"Wasn't Fibber McGee and Molly an old radio show in the forties and fifties?" she asked.

"It was. I'm impressed you know that. Do you have pets, Zarah?"

"I had a dog but had to put her down a few years ago. I still miss her terribly."

"Actually… Dogs are my favorite people!" Ian half-laughed.

"Mine, too! They never let you down!"

"I'm on a committee at the radio station to raise funds to build a dog park. There aren't enough dog parks in the city."

"That's awesome, Ian," Zarah was impressed. *He is ambitious, and he loves dogs*.

"The project is still in its early stages, and the city is difficult to work with. Land within the city limits is expensive, so we are considering property outside Lansing… Would you like another Cosmo?" he offered.

"No! But thank you. I'll switch to water. I've got to drive home," she said.

"One is my limit, too. If I have more than one, I feel like complete shit the next day. It's not worth it."

She hoped he was telling the truth.

Two hours passed quickly, and she could not recall having ever enjoyed a conversation more. She definitely could picture herself spending more time with him.

Ian walked her out to the parking lot. Out of habit, she held her key ring in her hand, which included a tube of pepper spray—just in case. But she felt safe with Ian... He had a kind face.

"Where's your car?" he asked.

"Over there." They began to walk toward her car.

"What do you drive, Ian?"

"That's my BMW under the light post," he pointed out.

"This was fun!" she said as she turned around and leaned against her car. He was tall—six inches taller than she. She felt her pulse rate rise. He was strikingly handsome under the parking lot lights.

"What are you doing tomorrow night?" he asked.

"Nothing," she lied. She had another "date" lined up but would happily cancel it. What were the odds that the first man she'd meet on a dating website would be someone she'd be attracted to?

"I'd like to take you out for dinner. May I have your phone number so we don't have to communicate through the dating service email?" he asked. He entered her number into his cell phone. "I'll call you tomorrow with the details."

"I'll meet you at the restaurant." Zarah had enjoyed the evening more than she ever expected. Still, she had heard too many online dating horror stories, so she would remain cautious and drive separately until she got to know him better.

For the first time that evening, they stopped talking and gazed at each other curiously. He leaned over and kissed her gently on her lips. He had not planned on kissing Zarah goodnight—it was *not* his style to move fast.

"Good night, Zarah," he said as he opened the car door for her.

"Good night, Ian," she said, smiling at him.

The following morning, Zarah had plans to help her handyman take down the old yellowed fiberglass roof that covered her back patio. She had picked up two extra shifts last week to cover the cost of the supplies and Gary's hourly wage.

All the while they worked, she kept her phone in her pocket, awaiting Ian's call. She was slightly irritated by late afternoon and figured she was being stood up. Finally, at five o'clock, her phone rang.

"Sorry, I had to work today," Ian explained.

"On Saturday? That's just wrong," she laughed.

"Live talk radio only pauses on Sundays when we play re-runs."

"I listened to your station this morning while working with my handyman. There were a few interesting shows today."

"Thank you, although I have no control over what comes out of the host's mouth," he laughed. "Have you ever been to Bowdie's? I heard that they serve killer Cosmopolitans." She imagined he was smiling in his cute, sexy way.

"That sounds good to me."

"Seven o'clock?" he asked.

"Sounds good. I'll meet you there."

Zarah fussed over what she would wear and finally settled on black dress pants and a lightweight blue-green sweater. She took a little extra time applying her makeup and fixing her hair.

Ian waited for her at the bar when she walked into the dimly lit restaurant and waved her over.

"You look *very* nice, Zarah," he said.

"Thank you, you look nice, too," she smiled shyly. Complements were still something she was adjusting to.

A waitress walked them to their table a minute later, and Ian gave her their drink order.

"I'm famished..." Zarah said as she began to study the menu.

"I can't imagine that you eat much, Zarah. You're very slender," he said a little flirtatiously.

"I have a healthy appetite, and I never stop moving," Zarah laughed. It was a true statement. She was working on her house if she wasn't at the hospital. She explained the day's project to Ian...

"Something amusing happened today during the installation of the new porch roof... The sheets of polycarbonate are large... about four by eight feet. When we got to the last sheet, neither of us could figure out how to install it—we had boxed ourselves out because the last piece was to be installed next to the existing roof. We should have started there instead of ending there. Gary and I stood dumbfounded with our hands on our hips for the longest time. Finally, I climbed onto the roof, and Gary slid the piece onto the rafters. I had to stretch for all I was worth to screw the stainless steel screws into place. I really couldn't see what I was doing. But the structure seems to be sound. I'll find out for sure with the next big wind. I guess you had to be there to appreciate the humor."

"I've never dated a 'handywoman' before." Ian sounded impressed.

As they ate, Zarah went into further detail about her job at the hospital. She knew from experience that trying to explain her career as a Level One intensive care unit nurse to someone who didn't work in the medical field was nearly impossible.

"Why did you divorce your husband?" he asked curiously.

"There were too many things he loved more than he loved me." That was the cleaned-up version she prepared to recite to people who asked too many questions.

"Wow, a twenty-eight-year marriage down the drain—he must have majorly fucked up." Ian tried to comprehend the finality of it all.

"I will tell you this… He drank too much," she admitted. "What about you, Ian? Why did you divorce? "

"I was only married for a couple of years in my twenties. It ended, and I don't recall why we divorced. It was so long ago. So there is not much to tell," he said dismissively.

The subject made him appear uncomfortable, but Zarah's curiosity piqued.

"Have you had any serious relationships since then?"

"I had a live-in girlfriend for twelve years."

"Why did *that* relationship end?" Zarah did not want to appear nosy, but she did not want to waste time on someone with issues—she had enough of that in her marriage to last a lifetime.

"I think she wanted more than I could give." *Again, dismissive.* "What about you, Zarah? Any serious relationships since your divorce?"

"I was involved with someone I work with for a while, but that ended."

"What happened?" he asked.

"We were in two different places." She could be dismissive, too.

After dinner, they walked hand in hand down the street to a popular pub. They were lucky to find two unoccupied seats at the bar—the place was standing room only. A lone guitarist in the room's far corner played folk music, and laughter and music filled the air.

Ian had to yell to the bartender when he ordered a "Gray Goose on the Rocks and a Cosmo for the lady." When the drinks arrived, they swiveled their stools to face each other and wove their legs to be as close as possible—their faces inches apart.

Zarah had to adjust to the fact that they did not have to duck for cover or hide the fact that they were out in public together. It felt surreptitious—as if they were doing something illegal or naughty.

"So, this is how adults are supposed to date!" she shouted.

"What?!"

"Nothing! It was nothing." She was glad that he hadn't heard. The statement would have made her sound like a dating rookie.

She hadn't thought of Nate once since she met Ian. Sitting at the bar with him, with their legs entangled, was the most exciting thing she had done in a long time.

They talked and laughed until the bar was about to close, then left hand in hand and headed for the parking lot. Zarah wanted to wrap her arms around him and sensed he was feeling the same. The term "magnetic attraction" came to mind—that was precisely what she was feeling.

The parking lot was dimly lit, and nobody else was around. He pulled Zarah close and kissed her... It was the kiss that Zarah always dreamed was possible. His lips were perfectly matched to hers. They stopped only to take a few steps toward his car, then leaned against the hood and began to kiss again. Zarah never wanted the kiss to end. She had always thought she would recognize the man she was supposed to be with by his kiss alone—the kiss she had always hoped existed.

For the next few weeks, Ian was attentive, and Zarah had no desire to date anyone else. He called her several times weekly and arranged to take her to dinner the following weekend.

Zarah logged into her dreamdate.com account. She had put her dating profile on hold a week after she met Ian. It dawned on her... Did Ian also put his account on hold? She quickly found his profile. He was still on, and she saw that he had recently added a few more pictures of himself and edited his site… "Looking for someone who likes to travel…"

"Ugh!" Zarah said disgustedly to the computer screen. She quickly logged out. She had canceled dates with two seemingly charming men to be with Ian. Maybe that had been a mistake.

It was early in their relationship, and the last thing she wanted was for someone to believe she was "needy." She was anything but. This type of dating was new to her. Were there "online dating rules" she was not made aware of?

Ian was scheduled to arrive at her house that evening at six. Zarah had purchased a new grill and spent the afternoon assembling it. He had treated her to dinner several times, and she wanted to cook for him for a change.

The calendar read that tonight was a "blue moon." Zarah thought she was lucky when she found a bottle of Blue Moon wine at the grocery store that day. The irony made her laugh. She would serve it to Ian tonight with their dinner.

His car pulled up her driveway at precisely six o'clock. He knocked, then let himself in. Zarah was in the kitchen tossing a salad together.

"That looks delicious!" he said when he saw her in the kitchen.

"I'm making a chopped salad," she informed him.

"No, not the salad… I meant the girl tossing the salad looks delicious," he said as he raised his eyebrows to appear flirtatious.

Zarah laughed. She loved his sense of humor.

Ian went outside to check Zarah's handiwork on the grill, then shook his head when he saw she had assembled several pieces incorrectly.

"This grill is all wrong!" he shouted back into the kitchen.

"Then please fix it, Mr. Elliot! I'll get my toolbox for you... " he fixed the grill and lit the coals in under ten minutes. Zarah handed the pork chops to him out the back door.

After dinner, Ian kicked his feet up on an empty chair. He looked content.

"Did you read the label on the wine? It's 'Blue Moon wine!'"

"And?"

"There's a blue moon tonight," Zarah said with some frustration. She had wanted him to catch the synchronicity, but she had not impressed him with her clever choice of wine.

"Ian..." She turned her chair to face him. "We've been dating for about a month, and I've noticed you still have your profile on dreamdate.com."

"I'm not dating anyone else, Zarah," he said defensively.

"Then why is your profile still up?" she asked.

"I don't know. I guess I hadn't thought of taking it down."

"Well, you must have checked it recently," she said sarcastically. "You added several pictures and mentioned that you like to travel..." He did not reply. "Ian, how long have you been on the dating website?"

Startled, he locked his eyes on hers. "Is this an inquisition?"

"No! We're both adults and can do whatever we want. I don't know how online dating works. Are there some unwritten rules that I'm not aware of? If there are, I wish someone would explain them to me. You're the first man I've dated from dreamdate.com, and I put my profile on hold a week after we began dating."

"You didn't have to do that," he flatly stated.

She had yet to learn if he was planning to take his profile down or if they were dating exclusively. She was glad that they had not been intimate.

"Ian," her mood turned serious. "You are the first man to make me forget about the surgeon."

"Can't we just continue what we've been doing, Zarah? And see where it leads? Do we have to put a label on this?"

"No! Of course, we don't have to put a label on this," she said as if she couldn't care less. She did *not* want to come off as someone desperate for a boyfriend. She wasn't sure she wanted a boyfriend and did not wish to be legally bound to another man again. She couldn't say what she wanted from Ian—all she knew was that she wanted him in her life.

After dinner, they took their dishes to the kitchen and set them in the sink.

"I'll wash them later," she curtly informed him.

He leaned back against her counter, then gently pulled Zarah toward him. He began to kiss her again, more passionately than ever before.

"Let's go to your bedroom," he said.

"A 'make-out session' is all you're getting, sir. You're still active on the dating website." She set her boundaries, but she wished she didn't have to. She hoped that at that moment, he would tell her that he would get off the dating site and date only her.

She grabbed his hand and led him into her bedroom.

They laid down side-by-side. Zarah tucked herself in the crook of his arm, and for a few minutes, they stared up at the ceiling fan. He seemed to be deep in thought.

He got up on one elbow and outlined her face gently with the back of his fingers, then leaned over and again began to kiss her.

Their hands began to explore each other. Zarah was ready to experience more of what this man had to offer. She reached under his shirt and ran her hands over his chest; then she reached for the top button of his shirt. His hand immediately came up and stopped her.

Abruptly, he got off the bed and began to straighten his clothing.

"It's time for me to go."

This made no sense to Zarah. Why would he stop at that moment?

"What do you mean, 'It's time to go?!'"

He did not answer her and began to walk toward the kitchen.

"Ian!" Zarah yelled behind him. "I don't understand. Why are you leaving?"

He took his keys off the kitchen counter and began to walk toward the front door.

"Ian!" Zarah again said firmly. "I don't want you leaving this way."

He set his keys down and turned around. She waited for what seemed like forever for him to speak.

"If we have sex," he began, "that means we are in a relationship."

"Does it?" she answered coolly. She maintained her composure as if nothing he said surprised her.

She wanted to beg him to stay—to finish what they started. She had never felt this physically attracted to anyone before, but she'd rather be damned than tell him.

She picked his car keys off the table and handed them to him.

"Go," she said firmly. She could not watch him walk out the door, and she wondered if she would ever lay eyes on him again.

That evening, Zarah called her sister. She needed Liz's viewpoint on what had happened.

"It isn't normal for a man to act like that, Zarah." Liz held back nothing. "You need to forget about him, Zarah. There are other fish in the sea!"

"I don't want to date anyone else. I have a mad crush on Ian," her voice trailed off.

"Then tell him that!"

"I can't do that. I'd scare him away forever."

"What are you going to do?" Liz felt sad for her sister. Her husband Cameron was the love of her life. They had their share of troubles, but he was a good man, and his day revolved around making her happy. Liz wanted her sister to experience that kind of love, and until now, nothing Zarah had experienced had even come close.

"Keep yourself busy, Zarah. Get back to your house projects. You've been neglecting them since you began dating 'Nike-Man.'"

"Nike-Man?" Zarah was confused.

"You've heard the Nike commercials... 'Just Do It!'"

"Oh!" Zarah laughed for the first time. "You're killing me, Liz. It is time to return to my home projects... but I'd light a match to this house to have Ian in my life."

"Zarah, you've got a few weeks left on dreamdate.com. Turn your profile on again, and have a little fun!"

Thirty

A swim in a pool

BEFORE HER SHIFT began, Zarah chatted with a group of her co-workers. They always enjoyed hearing what house project she was currently working on. She was unaware that Nate was approaching the group from behind her, and he caught the tail end of the conversation.

"Zarah has a beautiful house!" Nate enthusiastically announced to the group.

Zarah quickly turned around and consciously controlled her jaw from dropping open in disbelief. What was he doing? Did he admit to everyone that he had been at her house? She had no idea how to backpedal out of this. Her co-workers would quickly figure out that Nate had been at her home, and the hospital gossip could spread like wildfire. Nate's wife could find out... and Zarah would be forever known as the tramp who broke up their marriage.

Nate stood there, matter of factly, as if he had said nothing unusual. Zarah had to think fast…

"Oh, that's right, Nate," Zarah spoke up clearly and a bit loudly so that nobody would miss what she was about to say. "I had forgotten that I gave you a tour of my house the day you picked up the firewood." She threw darts at him with her eyes, hoping he would get the hint and shut the hell up. She was amazed with herself that she had fabricated the lie with split-second timing.

Zarah's co-workers knew she had multiple trees taken down in her yard, and she had been asking everyone if they needed firewood. Her lie made perfect sense, and nobody appeared suspicious after she told it.

Her co-workers began to walk toward the assignment board as they had only minutes left before their shift started. Zarah hung back until she was the only person left in the hallway with Nate.

"What are you doing?!" she said in an angry whisper.

"What do you mean?" he sounded clueless.

"The comment you made about my house!"

"Well, you *do* have a nice house, Zarah."

Zarah thought she made it clear that their relationship was over. Nate could have just started a world of trouble for them both.

"Are you still dating the cowboy?" Nate asked with an expression of hopefulness in his eyes.

"No… But I am seeing someone… Sort of." Not even Zarah knew the honest answer to that question. "Nate, you have to stop this. I'm not your mistress, and I don't want to get a reputation for being a home-wrecker."

Zarah surprised herself—she felt no anger toward Nate. She just wanted him to behave.

"I miss you, Zarah… I miss what we had," he said sadly.

"What *did* we have, Nate? We had to hide our relationship! We couldn't go out in public. We couldn't even go for a walk in my neighborhood! Everything happened behind closed doors!"

"Was that so bad, Zarah? I thought our relationship was pretty fucking amazing."

"It was, Nate. But the 'we' part? That never existed. Maybe all either of us wanted was sex, and it's time to admit that."

"Point taken." With that, he turned and walked away, and she still could not help but watch him take a few steps before turning to join her co-workers at the assignment board.

Over the next several weeks, Zarah accepted several dates. The first man was overly buff; all he could talk about was working out. The second man looked nothing like his profile picture, and she thought he was at least ten years older than he claimed to be. His skin was deeply tanned—he appeared to be upholstered in leather. Her third date fell asleep at the dinner table after eating. He had ordered a few too many drinks during dinner. Fortunately, she had brought her car and slipped out of the restaurant without saying goodbye. The last date she accepted was with a man who couldn't stop talking about his ex-wife—Zarah suspected he was still hung up on her.

Zarah followed up with each of the men with a polite email. She found a painless way to "break up" with someone she'd only met once or twice… "I'm sorry, but my old boyfriend is back in my life." Of course, it was a white lie, but she felt nobody got hurt, and they would blame her for the rejection instead of themselves.

Zarah's relationship with Jack had improved to the point that she could entertain him with stories of her online dating experiences, and he found her stories downright amusing.

"Two weekends ago, I had dates with 'Meathead' and 'Leather-Man,' and this past weekend, I dated 'Sleepy' and 'Whiplash-Man,'" she said, half-laughing for giving silly nicknames to the men she had dated.

"Whiplash-Man?" he couldn't figure that one out.

"Yes, he couldn't stop looking back at his past. I'm sure he must have strained his neck. He's still hung up on his ex-wife. I don't get it... They all looked so normal on their profiles."

"What about the guy you were dating for a while... the radio station guy..." Jack could not recall his name.

"Oh, you must mean Nike-Man. His name is Ian."

"Why do you call him Nike-Man?" Jack inquired.

"Because he wouldn't 'just do it,'" she whispered as she made air quotes. Jack was still puzzled. She leaned in and whispered again, "He wouldn't have sex with me."

"What a stupid man! I would have had sex with you!" Jack answered a little too loudly. He quickly added, "I'm sorry, Zarah. I shouldn't have said that. Old habits die hard."

Zarah was not offended by his comment and was delighted that she and Jack seemed to be back in the relationship they had once shared.

Jack had recently begun dating Diane, a respiratory therapist, and Zarah was relieved that he had finally found someone who seemed to be a good match for him. She was age-appropriate; her daughters were away at college, and she loved to do the same things he did.

After several weeks of no contact from Ian, Zarah's phone rang... It was him.

"Hi, Ian," she answered as casually as possible.

"How are you?" he asked as if no time and no issues had passed between them.

"I'm good, Ian. How are you?"

Her heart was pounding hard, and she put her hand on her chest in an attempt to slow it down.

"I'm good. Would you like to go out this Saturday?"

"Are you asking me on an actual date?" she said with feigned sarcasm.

"Hilarious, Zarah. Yes, I am."

"I have plans for Saturday," she lied, not wanting to seem too anxious. "I could meet you on Sunday."

"Do you want to come to my house first?" he inquired.

Zarah had never seen his house, and she was curious how he lived. She thought that, quite possibly, this was the next step in "Ian world" toward an actual relationship.

"Sure, what time?" she asked.

"Come around two." He gave her his address and driving directions. "And bring your swimsuit," he added.

"Why?"

"I have a heated pool in my backyard with a built-in whirlpool."

"Do you think that I am going to go in the pool? Alone? With you? That is pretty presumptuous!" she half-laughed.

"Well... You don't have to if you don't want to." He sounded disappointed.

"I'll bring my swimsuit, Ian," she assured him. "I'm just teasing you."

When she arrived, Fibber McGee and Molly, Ian's two black labs, greeted her. They were nearly out of their minds, excited to meet the new visitor.

"Do you keep these poor dogs locked in a cage all day?" Zarah laughed.

"No, they are just happy to meet you. They are spoiled. They have the run of the house all day when I'm at work. I told them all about you." Ian said with a mischievous grin.

"You did? Well, I hope you told them only the good things!" Zarah said as she crouched down to meet the dogs eye to eye. "Your dogs are adorable, Ian!" she laughed as the dogs tried to lick her face. Her mind flashed back to memories of her little Rosie. Would she ever stop missing her?

The dogs followed them from room to room as Ian gave Zarah a tour of his house. She was pleasantly surprised. Over the past ten years, he had transformed every room and done all the work himself. He was neat and organized. They had more in common than she had previously thought.

"You must have knocked a few walls out. It's open and airy for a circa fifties home," she observed.

"I did. The living room used to be tiny, and the kitchen was secluded and dark. So I knocked out the wall that separated the two rooms."

"Very nice, Ian. And I love your hardwood floors. Did you lay them yourself?"

"I did. And out there is the pool," he said as he pulled the curtains back.

"Nice!" Zarah exclaimed. "Your yard is beautiful, Ian. I especially like how the trees and bushes seem strategically arranged to block any view from inquiring neighbors," she half-laughed.

Zarah left to change into her swimsuit. She tied a sarong around her hips, as she still felt a little too timid to prance around half-naked in front of him.

"Cute," he playfully said as she walked into the backyard.

"Thank you, sir."

Ian had brought a bottle of wine, a plate of crackers and cheese, and two wine glasses.

"Would you like a glass of white wine, Zarah?"

"Yes, that would be nice." She studied his profile as he poured the wine.

"I haven't eaten much today. I could get silly," she warned.

"Silly is good!" he said with a mischievous smile.

Zarah felt as if she had known Ian forever. She could not imagine him not being in her life. He had disappeared for weeks, and she still couldn't comprehend that. She would not bring up his absence. It would ruin the mood. At that moment, it felt like no time had passed since their last time together.

She removed her sarong and tossed it over a chair. They walked down several steps into the pool and sat down. Steam was rising from the water.

"The water is so warm!" she delighted.

He reached across her and pressed the start button on the whirlpool. They tangled their feet together, leaned back, and looked at the sky.

Zarah couldn't decide if it was the half-glass of wine she drank or the warm water that swirled around her, but she was feeling something.

"Wow, this wine is potent. I've only had a few sips, and I feel it! Are you trying to get me drunk, sir?" she teased.

"You're on to me," Ian laughed. "Do you want some more?" he asked.

"Sure!" She held out her glass, and he topped off both glasses.

They small-talked at length about their jobs and the past week's events. He answered a few of her questions about the radio station celebrities, but he was cautious not to reveal too much—it would be unethical.

Several minutes passed without speaking. They both seemed to enjoy being in each other's company.

"So... I made you forget about the surgeon?" Ian said out of the blue. Zarah's heart began to race—she had almost forgotten she had said that to him.

"Yes, you did, Ian," she answered timidly.

He placed his wine glass on the pool deck, then took her glass and put it next to his.

"Zarah... What do you do to me?"

He wrapped his arms around her and began to kiss her. The kiss that she had thought about a thousand times since the first. The kiss that made her want to abandon all self-control.

He reached behind her and found the tie to her bikini top.

"May I?" he asked.

"Yes."

He pulled on the tie in slow motion until her top was freed. Zarah reached down to remove the rest of her suit.

"No, leave it on," he said firmly.

He reached down, removed his swimsuit, and set it aside.

Zarah's hands took advantage of the unspoken permission he had given her. For a man in his mid-fifties, his body was in beautiful shape. She felt every inch of him and discovered nothing wrong or dysfunctional about him.

The kissing became more passionate. If it were possible to climb inside of him, she would have. At that moment, he was the only man, and she was the only woman on the planet. Passion at that level was foreign, otherworldly, and something that Zarah knew she could never live without again. What had she been missing all of her life?

She shifted position and sat on top of him. As she kissed him, she felt the pulsation of their bodies wherever they touched. She wanted nothing more than to finish what they had started, and she suspected he felt the same.

Their bodies moved in unison as if to the beat of a distant drum that grew louder and more intense. And, despite the presence of a single layer of clothing between them, she was seconds away from total ecstasy.

Unexpectedly, he reached for her arms and firmly guided her off of him. He stood up and reached for a towel.

"What are you doing, Ian?" Zarah was puzzled. Did he want to move to the bedroom?

"It's time for you to go," he said flatly.

"What?!" Zarah exclaimed. Had he done it to her again?! He had brought her to the brink for the second time, then abruptly stopped. She couldn't believe she had let this happen. She was disappointed beyond belief, but she would not give him the satisfaction of telling him.

"Right… yes. It is time for me to go," Zarah said firmly as she got out of the pool and wrapped a towel around herself. She reached down to pick up her bikini top, then went straight to the bathroom to change into dry clothes.

She fought back tears. She felt so foolish. Why was she so drawn to this man, and what the hell was wrong with him? *Is there something wrong with me?*

She walked into his kitchen and grabbed her keys off the table.

"Goodbye, Zarah," she heard him say.

She walked out of his house without replying. She fully expected to never speak to him again.

Come here, go away

It wakes me from sleep.
I reach for the pen, only half awake,
to write it down.
Then, it will stay on the page where I place it.
Maybe I can be as I was before you.
I have a photo, and if I stare long enough
your mouth seems to smile.
And your eyes.
If I move, they follow.
They look past the blue-green.
Where do I put this?
I've tried to bury it, and it rises to the surface.
I have cried to free it, and it returns.
It slams into me without permission.
It wakes me from my sleep.
It follows me around during the day.
It haunts me as I try to rest.
It has an insatiable appetite, never satisfied,
never enough, never lets up.
The apparition won't leave me, won't let me get back
to where I was before I saw
your mouth
and your eyes.
And when you walk away,
the silence.
Come to me or let me live
in peace again.
Let me talk to my friends
without looking for your mouth.
Let me glance at someone
without looking for your eyes.
And let me scan a crowd
without looking for the view
of you,
walking away.

K.D.Kinz

Thirty-one

The list

SHE WAS CLAWING at the foot of the mountain... searching... for something.

Every few seconds, she found another object and examined it closely. Did it hold any value? All the objects were useless. They were cheaply made. They were garbage. She tossed them to the side.

More frantically, she continued to dig. She knew it was buried somewhere and would have to work hard to unearth it.

All she knew was that she had never seen it, but she would recognize it... if she could only find it.

Near exhaustion and with a pile of useless trinkets beside her, she continued to claw her way into the mountain. But despite all her efforts, she barely made a dent.

Suddenly, she heard a voice. It was soft and fatherly. The voice was familiar. She had heard it before, but she couldn't bring to mind where or when.

"Looking for gold?" the voice said. "These are only inclusions you'll find along your way..."

The dream remained crystal clear—it had felt so real. She looked down at her hands. Her fingernails were clean. She laughed to herself... it was only a dream.

"Inclusions?" she asked as she leaned into the bathroom mirror. Her eyes were still puffy from sleep. She grabbed a hairbrush and pulled her hair back into a ponytail, then splashed cool water on her face.

Ian had called several times in the past week, but she didn't answer. Something was wrong with him. Would she ever figure him out?

Her three-month subscription to the dating website had expired. It was a thoughtful gift from her sister, but she would not renew it.

For the past month, she had dated Robert, a man who could not make eye contact with her—it was almost as if he had something to hide. She gave up on him and told him the standard line, "My old boyfriend has come back into my life." She probably should have told him the truth... She didn't trust him. On second thought, it wasn't worth her time —he'd never change. He was who he was.

The dating website had been a rollercoaster ride, complete with highs and lows, but she had no regrets. After all, it was how she met Ian. And even though their relationship fell flat, it proved to her that it was possible to move past Nate.

She planned to spend the morning gardening, and later, Liz was coming over for lunch. She was glad she had set aside time for her sister. Bouncing things off of her always made things better.

As she gardened, her mind wandered back to Ian in the pool. She still felt the raw sting of what had happened and wasn't getting past it. She wished that she could wipe the memory from her brain.

"What is *wrong* with that man!" Zarah said out loud as she yanked one weed after another. She found gardening therapeutic—maybe even better than seeing Dr. Foxen.

Liz walked into the backyard to find her sister frantically pulling weeds. "Zarah!"

"Oh, hi! Sorry, I lost track of time!" Zarah hugged her sister, careful not to let the dirt on her hands touch her clothing. "Give me a few minutes to wash up. Come in and talk to me while I fix our lunch. How much time do you have?"

"I'm off for the rest of the day," Liz said with a grin. "I'm all yours!"

Minutes later, the sisters walked to the back porch with their sandwiches, a bottle of wine, and two glasses.

"I love this new roof, Zarah. Did your handyman install it?"

"We installed it together."

"You've got to be coming close to being done with your home renovations," Liz stated.

"I am. The projects have been a great diversion. Without them, I don't know what I would have done with myself after the divorce. Every day, I had something to accomplish."

"Have you seen Blue Eyes at work?" Liz was curious.

"Every day that I am there!" Zarah half-laughed.

"Does he still make your heart go pitter-patter?"

"If I'm truthful, I will always have feelings for Nate. He woke me to the fact that other men could be attracted to me."

"What about Nike-Man? You haven't mentioned him in a while…"

"Oh, you mean Ian. He called several times, but I didn't answer, and he didn't leave a message."

"I'm glad you didn't answer. There is something wrong with that man. Who does that? Quits at the height of passion! That isn't normal, Zarah!"

"I know."

"Well... What *do* you want in a man?" Liz inquired.

"I don't know! Maybe that's the problem. I've been giving confusing signals to 'The Universe,'" she made air quotes.

"Then tell The Universe *exactly* what you want in a relationship!" Liz encouraged. "There is no better time than the present..." Liz lifted her wine glass to the sky. "The Universe is listening!" she announced.

"Oh, you've had way too much wine, sister!" Zarah laughed. "Mr. Perfect might not exist, and I don't think that meeting my soulmate—if there is such a thing—was meant for me in this lifetime. Maybe it will happen in the next life. Or maybe I've got some crazy cosmic debts that I am paying..."

Liz wanted Zarah to be happy like she was and her sister to experience a meaningful relationship.

"Okay, Zarah... seriously... How *would* you define Mr. Perfect?"

Zarah had never considered listing the qualities she wanted in a life partner. *What do I want?* She leaned back in her chair and gazed at the perfectly blue sky through the transparent porch roof.

"Mr. Perfect would have a 'cuteness' about him. Something about him would attract me to him. Maybe his smile or his eyes..."

"You wouldn't consider an ugly man?" Liz laughed.

"Believe me, if he has all the qualities I'm about to add to the list, I don't care if he looks like Quasimodo." They laughed, and she continued...

"I consider myself fairly ambitious, so Mr. Perfect should also be ambitious. I don't waste money, so I wouldn't want a man who spends foolishly. He'd have to like sex because I still do!"

"My sister is a nymphomaniac!" Liz teased.

"I still like that part of life. Maybe that will fade away someday, but I hope it doesn't until I am old and frail."

"I'll drink to that!" The sisters clinked their glasses together.

"I've run into good qualities in every man I've had a relationship with. If only I could pick out the good qualities from each of them and roll them into one man…"

"Even Joe had good qualities?" Liz was surprised to hear her sister admit that.

"Yes. Even Joe. We had some good times. I won't pretend we didn't."

"What *were* Joe's good qualities?" Liz curiously asked.

"He supported my decision to stay home for a few years to raise the boys. And he was supportive while I was in nursing school…"

"But after you began working as a nurse, it seems that was about the time things began to go south in your marriage," Liz said.

"Things went downhill quickly when I started to work, but our marriage began to go south from day one. Once I started working long hours, Joe was free to pursue every quirk he had ever suppressed."

Zarah could no longer keep *any* secrets from her sister. Keeping things to herself in the past was a big mistake— Liz could have been her ally if Zarah had given her the chance.

"Okay… I will be serious now, Liz… this could be fun!"

"Wait! Let me get a pen and paper!" Liz ran into the house and returned in under a minute. "I'm writing this list for you so you don't forget. So far, you said, 'He should have a cuteness, but it's okay if he looks like Quasimodo.

He should be ambitious, not foolish with money, a nymphomaniac like my sister…'" They laughed again and had to compose themselves before continuing.

"Okay, Zarah! What else should we add to the list?"

"Whoever is listening, pay close attention!" Zarah said playfully toward the sky. "This is my order to The Universe for Mr. Perfect…. He does not have to be drop-dead gorgeous, but it would be nice if he is taller than me. He should have a career that he loves, and it would be a bonus if he was a handyman and liked to fix up old houses!"

"Continue!" Liz encouraged as she feverishly wrote down every word her sister said.

"Mr. Perfect should be curious about the world… not a couch potato. He should keep himself in decent physical shape. He should have no bad habits. Moderate drinking is fine… there is nothing wrong with an occasional drink. But most importantly, he *has* to be honest. **Painfully honest.** I prefer be alone for the rest of my life than be with another liar."

"They've all been liars," Liz added as she shook her head. "What else?"

"That pretty much sums it up," Zarah said thoughtfully.

"Well, you did it, Zarah!" She slid the list across the table toward her sister. "Put this somewhere safe, sit back and let The Universe do its work!" Liz said light-heartedly. "Wait! We need to do one more thing to make this official!" Liz jumped off her chair, ran to the lawn, and picked a dandelion puffball. Then, holding it carefully, she returned to her sister's side.

"**Make a wish**!" Liz said excitedly as she held the puffball up to Zarah's lips.

Zarah had to smile. It felt like they were playing a silly game—something they did when they were twelve.

"Okay... I wish that The Universe finds Mr. Perfect for me!" Zarah took a deep breath and blew... The seeds floated up into the breeze.

Zarah topped off their wine, and then they sat silently for a few minutes, watching the bluebirds and golden finch splash wildly in the birdbath. Zarah broke the silence.

"I don't want to disappoint you, sister, but I think I'm going to forget about dating for a while—I'm going to take a 'man break.' I am perfectly happy by myself. Being single is a wonderful lifestyle. Maybe I've never known real love, and maybe I never will, but that's okay. I've come to terms with that."

"Don't confuse The Universe, Zarah!" Liz was irritated. "You just put your order in for Mr. Perfect!"

"And I hope The Universe finds him for me! But right now, I need to focus on my boys. After I divorced Joe, all my problems with him disappeared. But the boys... They had no option... I dropped their sick father right into their laps, and I think they are scrambling, trying to figure out how to deal with him. I think they feel responsible for him now. I discarded Joe, and they caught him. Liz, I didn't see that coming..." Zarah swallowed hard before she could speak again...

"I've been spinning. After the divorce, I felt like I was supposed to date... I was supposed to find another man. I don't feel that way anymore. I've been digging for gold, and all I've come up with are cheap plastic inclusions."

"What do you mean?" Liz asked.

"Oh, it's nothing. I had a silly dream... that's all."

Inclusions

As I am digging
As I am searching
Unearthing different
Shapes and voices

I pull out each one
And look with wonder
I want to care
Then find another

Is this the one
I want to keep now?
And then I drop it
To the floor

Expecting gold?
I heard Him say
These are inclusions
You meet on your way

And so I dig
And so I pull
Looking for the one
To match my soul

Cast aside inclusions
Of no use to me
I drop each one
And set it free

K.D.Kinz

Thirty-two

On his terms

ZARAH PUT DOWN her pencil to review the sketch she had finished for her new gardens. She would begin the project by removing fifty-plus years of the prior owners' neglected plantings. She studied library books to learn more about plants that grew native in her region and plants that would benefit the local wildlife, then added only native plants into her plan.

Her handyman had informed her that she had a few nosy neighbors who had nothing better to do than to watch her every move out their windows. Most of her neighbors were elderly, and Zarah was the new "kid" on the block. With her curious neighbors in mind, she strategically placed cedar trees in her garden plans to provide privacy. She had to laugh that, at her age, she could still stir up a little neighborhood gossip.

Her elderly neighbors were entertained as they sat outside on their lawn chairs, watching Zarah dig holes, rip out overgrown bushes, and trim trees. They whispered to each other… "Nobody has given that yard any attention in fifty years!" "Did you know she kicked her husband out?" "I've seen her sitting on her back porch having drinks with different men." "That woman can run circles around anyone."

None of the neighbors knew what to make of Zarah. She infused an energy into the old neighborhood that the old folks had never experienced before.

Zarah planted several oak and maple trees and hoped to set a good example for the neighborhood. She ordered a batch of fifty additional burr oak trees from the county, then passed them out to her neighbors along with instructions on how to plant and care for them. She hoped to add beauty to the entire neighborhood and, simultaneously, get acquainted with her neighbors and prove that she was not the scarlet woman some thought her to be.

After weeks of planting, she ordered a truckload of mulch, then spent days shoveling, hauling, and tucking it carefully around her new plantings.

Transforming her yard had been a tremendous effort, but it was exactly what she needed. With each planting, she felt a sense of satisfaction and a renewed hope for the future.

She stood back to admire her yard. She hated that the neighbor's overgrown silver maple and elm trees hung over her yard and continually dropped their seeds on her fresh-laid mulch. She knew that if she didn't remove the seeds promptly, she would have hundreds of tiny sprouts to pull out weekly.

In her peripheral vision, she saw a car pulling up her driveway. It was a black BMW. The car door opened, and Ian stepped out.

"You don't answer your phone," he said as he closed the car door.

"I've been busy." Zarah waved her arms to draw attention to the work she had done in her yard. She didn't smile, and she didn't know how to react to this unexpected visit.

"You did all of this yourself?" Ian was impressed. He knew Zarah was ambitious, but he never guessed she could single-handedly transform a once-neglected yard into a parklike setting.

"Yes, I did it myself. When I'm frustrated, I have a lot of energy," she said with an overt hint of sarcasm.

"Zarah, you are talented. If you ever quit nursing, you could design outdoor spaces."

"It's not talent… It just takes a little planning and a lot of elbow grease," she answered cooly. "I was just about to take a break. Do you want to come in for an iced tea?"

"I'd love that," Ian answered.

She brushed the dirt and mulch from her clothes. Ian reached up to remove some leaves that were stuck in her hair.

"Leave it," Zarah snapped. "I'll brush it out later."

Ian followed Zarah into the house. He leaned back against the kitchen countertop and watched her wash her hands and pour their tea. He remained reticent, and she sensed a sadness in him.

The sight of Ian standing in her kitchen was more than she could take. She wanted to either grab him by the shoulders and shake him senselessly or wrap her arms around him and never let him go. It had been weeks since the pool incident.

Zarah had taken many walks around her neighborhood with her headphones on, listening to contemplative music. The eighties song fit the situation with Ian perfectly…

🎵 *"Time keeps flowing like a river... Time keeps beckoning me... Who knows if we will meet again... if ever. 'Cause time... is flowing like a river... to the sea..."*

She hit the repeat button over and over again, trying to erase the ache in her soul. Ian was not emotionally available—she had to accept that fact. But moving on from him felt impossible.

He stood quietly and appeared uncomfortable—as if he had done something wrong. At the very least, Zarah thought he owed her an apology or an explanation.

"Ian..." Zarah said firmly as she handed him a glass of tea. "What the hell, Ian?" She hadn't planned on confronting him, but that was precisely what she was about to do. "What happened that evening in your pool? We were wrapped in each other's arms one minute, and the next minute, you told me to go home." She remained calm and in control and stated the facts.

He stared at her blankly, set down his tea, and began to pace the kitchen floor. He did not seem to have an answer for Zarah, which furthered her irritation.

"Ian! Is there something you want to tell me?!"

She let him pace for a while longer, and then, when she could not stand it any longer, she reached out and grabbed his arm, stopping him in his tracks.

"I thought we had something special, Ian. Was I wrong?"

"You weren't wrong, Zarah." She let go of his arm, and he began to pace the kitchen floor again. This time, she would not stop him. He appeared deep in thought, and she hoped he'd soon have something meaningful to say.

After several minutes, he stopped, leaned back against the counter, and looked at Zarah. He opened his mouth to speak but changed his mind and said nothing. He began to pace again... Zarah lost her patience.

"What do you want to tell me, Ian?" Zarah said firmly. "Are you not ready to give up seeing other women? Are you addicted to the attention you're getting from the dating website? Is there another woman in your life? Tell me!"

He stopped pacing and grabbed his keys off the counter.

"I should go." He leaned down and gave Zarah a quick kiss on her cheek, then walked out the door. She heard his car start and watched through the blinds as he pulled down her driveway.

His visit had left her in the same place she was before he arrived—with no answers. She would not wait for him. She would do her best to put Ian Elliot in the past and heal her broken heart.

She had no regrets. In the few months they had been together, she experienced something she had never experienced. She had always wondered, but now she knew the holy grail of kissing existed.

The passion they shared could not have been faked. But for some reason, he was running from her. He was set in his ways, and she shook his world. It would always be on his terms if she ever saw him again.

"Goodbye, Ian," she whispered into the blinds as she watched him drive down the road.

Thirty-three

A cutie-pie

IT WAS A relief to step inside the air conditioning at the Lansing Community Center on a hot summer morning. Zarah and eight co-workers had signed up for the conference, "Recognizing and De-escalating the Violent Patient." She arrived with plenty of time to register, get a complimentary coffee and bagel, and find a seat.

This was the part of nursing that was fun — extracurricular activities. The seminar would count as eight hours toward the continuing education that her nursing license required. Plus, she earned her regular hourly pay simply by attending.

She thought that the day's topic could be interesting. Some of her patients, and even some of her patients' family members, had become violent over the past years. Any advice she could learn on handling this type of situation would be most welcomed, but she doubted she would learn anything she wasn't already keenly aware of.

Her co-workers had already found their seats. She saw Jack as he waved to her and pointed to an empty chair beside him.

She felt blessed. The people she worked with in the "trenches" of the ICU were also her heartfelt friends. They had all worked together for many years, and she loved every one of them... especially Jack.

She would need to get a large cup of coffee. She worked a double shift yesterday and didn't sleep well last night. She couldn't quiet her brain. The evening replayed in her head all night as she tried to sleep, but she could not come up with an alternative way she could have handled the overconfident, arrogant first-year resident.

The entire night, her patient teetered on the verge of death. The resident she worked with was a "know-it-all" and would not take Zarah's advice. The intelligent residents listened to and took advice from the well-seasoned nurses. But this resident was obstinate. Zarah knew that the dose of the medication he ordered her to give was far too high and would harm her patient, so she stood her ground and refused to administer it. In a huff, the resident administered the medication himself, and within minutes, the patient crashed, and a code blue was called. Thankfully, her patient pulled through, but Zarah could not shake off the stress of the situation.

She charted the medication dosage and the name of the resident who had administered it. A concise record of the incident would absolve Zarah of any wrongdoing in a court of law, but it would not help the patient, whose prognosis was even more grim than before the incident.

The coffee line was moving in slow motion. She turned around... *Are the people behind me also irritated? Or is it just me?*

"This line is so slow!" she told the man behind her. "There should be an express lane for those of us who worked a sixteen-hour shift yesterday and need caffeine!"

She finally reached her turn at the coffee pot and filled her cup. She turned again to the man behind her.

"Enjoy the seminar," she said politely, trying not to spill her coffee.

"Let's hope it isn't boring," he replied.

He had a nice smile, and there was definitely something cute about him.

Zarah sat beside Jack as the first speaker approached the podium.

"I was standing before a cutie pie in the coffee line," she whispered to Jack.

It had taken several months, but she and Jack had repaired their friendship. The discomfort they both felt after he admitted his love for her had finally dissipated, almost as though it had never happened. They were friends again and felt comfortable talking about anything—even the people they were dating.

"I thought that you're on a 'man break...'" Jack whispered back.

"I am... I mean, I was. The 'man break' officially ended two weeks ago when my financial advisor asked me out."

The past several months without dating were peaceful. Zarah accomplished a lot and learned she loved not having anyone to answer to.

"So... do you like your 'financial advisor guy,' or is he just someone to occupy your time?" Jack asked.

"His name is Richard, and it's far too early to tell. All I said was, 'The man behind me in the coffee line was a cutie pie!' I *am* allowed to look, aren't I?" she said with a sassy glint in her eye.

After a couple of hours, they were dismissed for a break. Zarah and her co-workers grabbed a water bottle and went outside for fresh air.

"That's him!" Zarah said as she elbowed Jack. "That's the man I was talking about... The cutie-pie from the coffee line. Aww, he's all by himself."

"Go talk to him, Zarah!" Jack encouraged.

"No! That would be too forward." She needed more encouragement and subconsciously hoped Jack would give it to her.

"Zarah... Don't be a chicken!" Jack ordered as he gave her a little shove. As she began to walk toward the cutie pie, she heard Jack behind her mimicking a chicken clucking. She playfully flipped him off behind her back.

"You couldn't find a date for this?" she laughed.

"I was lucky to get the day off. I'm John... John Gray," he reached out to shake her hand.

"Zarah Zoelle. It's nice to meet you. Where do you work, John-John Gray?" she laughed at her quip.

"I'm an ER physician at St. Teresa in Bay City. Where do *you* work, Zarah Zoelle?"

"I'm an RN at Lansing General. I work in the neurosurgical ICU." Zarah was always proud to state that fact.

"That must be an interesting job!" He was impressed.

"It is! I love my job... most of the time," she said with a cautious laugh.

"I'm assuming you are with your co-workers. You look like a tight-knit group."

"We are. We all work the same odd schedule, so we *have* to be friends. Who else is going to like us?"

John smiled at her comment. "I hope the coffee eventually woke you up."

"It did! I barely slept a wink last night." Zarah paused, then went on, "Your name... it sounds familiar to me. I have received several transfers from the Emergency Department at St. Teresa, and I recall seeing your name on some of the charts. In fact..." her eyes widened as she paused to recall a memory. "I think *you* gave *me* report... about a year or so ago... on a young man who sustained a head injury in a motorcycle accident. Apparently, there wasn't a nurse available, so you called Lansing to give report. You told me that the patient was about to be loaded into the helicopter, and at the last second, I asked you if the patient had a Foley catheter inserted. You said, 'No,' then I asked you to 'please insert one before he is transferred.' Anyway, I hope I said please! Do you remember that conversation? I believe you were a bit irritated with me!"

"I *do* remember that conversation! What a small world!"

"So *were* you?" she asked.

"Was I what?" he was puzzled.

"Were you irritated with me? I figured you must have thought me to be Nurse Ratched," Zarah nervously said. She knew their conversation could end as quickly as it began.

He studied the sidewalk and pushed a small stone to the side with his foot as he chose his words.

"Well, maybe a little. The chopper blades were already engaged, and the crew stood impatiently by while I inserted the damn Foley. But I appreciated your viewpoint... You didn't want your patient arriving in wet sheets."

"I definitely did not!" Zarah said with a half-laugh.

She was amazed that their paths had coincidentally crossed, and she hoped their first conversation had not left a long-lasting negative impression on the handsome doctor.

"I can see the helicopter landing pad from one of the windows in my ICU," Zarah enthusiastically described. "When time permits, I watch it take off or land. It's a thrill sometimes to know that the patient they are arriving with will be in my care as fast as the flight team can unload and transport him up to the ICU."

"I always imagined being part of a flight team would be thrilling, but I've been told I'm too tall to fit comfortably in the helicopter. Also, I need to be available to pick up my daughter from school, so that job isn't an option. St. Teresa is near my daughter's school and her mother's house, so

I'm committed to working there until she turns eighteen.... Where do you live, Zarah?"

"Just east of Lansing... A ten-minute drive from Lansing General Hospital. I bought an older home a few years ago after my divorce, and I've been busy fixing it up with the help of a handyman. This past spring, I turned my focus to my yard. It had been neglected for only the past half-century."

The ten-minute break was over, and she saw her co-workers heading back into the building.

"It was nice to meet you, Dr. Gray. Next time you give me report, I promise I'll be much nicer," she smiled.

"And I promise to have already inserted the Foley catheter."

He was an intelligent man, and unlike most of the doctors she worked with, he seemed to have no airs, and she could not detect a hint of conceit. She thought he was very down-to-earth, yet he exhibited total confidence—intriguing and admirable qualities.

She headed back into the building and found her seat.

"So... did you have a nice conversation with the cutie-pie?" Jack asked.

"I did! His name is John Gray. He's an ED physician at St. Teresa, and the funny thing is... I actually took report from him a year or so ago! He was not happy with me at the time because I asked him to put a Foley in the patient only minutes before the helicopter was due to take flight. I believe he thought I was a bit demanding." Zarah half-laughed.

"You? Demanding? No way!" Jack added with playful sarcasm. "Did you give him your phone number?"

"No. He didn't ask for it. He lives in Bay City. That's an hour-long drive on a good day. I think he's divorced, but I can't imagine he doesn't already have a girlfriend.

After the seminar was over, Zarah made a beeline for her car. She wanted to get home to water her flowers and bushes, most likely parched from the hot summer sun.

She heard a voice from behind…

"Zarah!" It was Dr. Gray. He seemed to be a little out of breath. "This weekend is Irish Fest at the Lansing Fairgrounds. Would you like to go?"

"With you?" Zarah answered playfully. His face went blank—he didn't understand she was toying with him, or he was far too sensitive.

"I assumed from our conversation that you are single. I'm sorry. You're probably dating someone…"

"I *am* single. I'm teasing you! Yes, I'd love to go to Irish Fest with you this weekend," she assured him. "I'm assuming that you are single, too? I tend to stay away from the married ones." She laughed. There was so much truth behind her statement.

"Yes, I'm divorced. Would you be more comfortable meeting me at the fairgrounds?" he inquired.

"No, you can pick me up, Dr. Gray."

"Call me John." His eyes seemed to study her.

"John," she echoed. For some reason, she had always liked the name John.

Zarah gave John her phone number and address, and they agreed he would arrive at her house on Saturday at six. Zarah could not help but smile as she walked back to her car. What were the odds of meeting someone at a seminar? She looked forward to their date and suspected they would have much in common and similar stories to swap. It didn't hurt that he was easy on the eyes, either.

She had plans with Richard on Friday night, and now she had another date with the handsome doctor. She laughed to herself—her attitude had definitely changed. She would date two men the same weekend and did not feel guilty. She no longer had any expectations and would approach dating as something to do just for fun. After the ultimate disappointment of her failed marriage and then the rollercoaster ride of men that followed, she was not about to invest herself emotionally any longer. If men could date without emotions or commitments, so could she.

Thirty-four

Like a man

ZARAH WALKED THROUGH her gardens and pulled a few weeds while waiting for John to arrive.

Right on time, he drove up her driveway in an older model blue Camry. She tossed a handful of weeds, brushed the dirt from her hands, and greeted him.

"How was the long drive?" she inquired.

"Not bad. I like to drive. It's the only time I sit still, and it gives me time to think."

"Well, welcome to my home," she said as she hugged him. "Would you like a tour of my yard? I can show you everything I've planted this season. Most of the plants have survived despite me!"

"My first impression is that you have a green thumb, Zarah... What is that adage about gardening? The first year they sleep, the second year they creep, and the third year they leap."

"Well, my plants are definitely still asleep," she said with a smile. "I look forward to next spring when they creep."

"Your yard is beautiful, Zarah. I live in an apartment now and miss working in my yard."

"Well, you can come over and pull weeds anytime!" Zarah laughed. "There is no better therapy than pulling weeds and digging in the dirt."

As they walked, John asked about her flower, shrub, and tree selections. Zarah was impressed—he identified her plants by their botanical names. She laughed to herself, as she only knew their common names.

"Would you like to see what I've done to the inside of the house? I can give you the fifty-cent tour... As long as you're not a serial killer or anything crazy like that," Zarah half-laughed.

Unbeknownst to John, Zarah *had* checked Dr. John Gray out online last evening to find out if anything was scary about him. She found nothing out of the ordinary, and, as far as Zarah could tell, he was a respected physician and model citizen. He also had an honest face, and she knew if something were "off" about him, she probably would have gotten wind of it somewhere along the way through the hospital grapevine.

"I'd love to see what you've done to the interior!" John said enthusiastically. After seeing what Zarah had accomplished with the exterior of her home, his interest was piqued.

"I guess you could say that I'm as comfortable with a hammer as I am with a glass of merlot," she said as they stepped inside the house. "I have a handyman, and sometimes we work on projects together. But I've found that it's easier for me to pick up an extra shift and hire my handyman to do the work."

As they walked from room to room, John listened intently as Zarah described what she and her handyman had accomplished. Every room in the house had been transformed somehow, and her home was bright, airy, and inviting.

"Would you like to see the 'before' pictures of the house? I took photos when we... when I... first moved in."

She caught herself including Joe when she spoke of her past—it was a hard habit to break. On the other hand, Joe *had* lived in the house for a short while, and if she hadn't used the word "we," she would be lying.

"I'd *love* to see them," John answered enthusiastically. Zarah went into her office and retrieved the photos from a drawer.

"My ex-husband is in some of the pictures. We moved into this house together, but he moved out three months later. I had the silly notion that working on this house would save our marriage," she scoffed. "John, would you like a glass of wine on the back patio? We probably have a few hours before Irish Fest starts to rock."

"That would be nice," he smiled.

They walked onto the back porch and sat at the white wrought-iron table.

"Wow, a clear extruded polycarbonate roof!" John said as he looked up. "What a good idea!"

"My handyman and I recently installed it. I love that it provides shelter and a clear view of the sky. But unfortunately, the doves like it, too, so I have to climb up on the roof about once a month and hose it off."

"Well, I am impressed." He turned his attention to the photos.

"These were taken on the day I moved in. Be ready to be amazed... or appalled," Zarah half-laughed. "You would not have believed the state this house was in. The prior owners took their clothing but left everything else behind. They headed south immediately after signing on the dotted line. My ex and I were left to clean up their mess, and believe me, there was not one thing they left behind that was worth keeping. We filled a dumpster."

"Wow, you *were* left with a mess," he said as he flipped through the photos. "It's amazing what you've done in a few short years."

"Thank you!" Zarah took a sip of her wine. "So... what's your story, Dr. Gray?"

"My story? Well, I'm recently divorced. We were married for sixteen years. I don't know what happened... I thought I was a good husband."

Zarah saw a red flag. It was evident that it was his ex-wife who had initiated the divorce. But why? What was wrong with him?

"Do you have children?" she asked.

"I have a daughter, Kirsten. She was a baby when I married my ex, and I adopted her soon after. She was born with a metabolic disorder, and my ex needed help with the monthly blood monitoring and managing Kirsten's special diet. My ex-wife's first husband, Kirsten's father, died in a car accident before she was born."

"Do you see your daughter often?"

"I see her once a week when I pick her up from school, but I have to take her straight home."

"You *have* to take her straight home? Can't you take her out for a burger? Or for a walk in a park?"

"No… I'm just a taxi."

Zarah was puzzled—she couldn't quite figure out why John *had* to take his daughter directly home. His answer was ambiguous—she would dig a little deeper.

"Well, I suppose your ex-wife works, and she isn't always able to pick your daughter up from school…"

"No, she doesn't work," he stifled a laugh. "I pick Kirsten up when my ex is out shopping, taking a painting class, or doing whatever she does."

He had been married to a princess. She would try to keep an open mind about John's baggage—she had a bit of her own.

It was evident by the edge in his voice that he was uncomfortable talking about his past, and he quickly turned the focus to Zarah.

"What's *your* story, Nurse Zarah?"

"My story? Hmmm," she gathered her thoughts. She would give him the cleaned-up version. "My ex-husband liked his vodka more than he liked me. I warned him to get help and straighten himself out, but he didn't. I probably should have ended the marriage sooner, but hindsight is always twenty-twenty. Pure inertia kept me in the marriage for so long. And I had kids to raise."

"How old are your children?" he asked.

"Damon is twenty-seven, married, and is a mechanical engineer; Drew is twenty-five and works in Ann Arbor as a software developer."

"Wow, you must have had them when you were twelve!" he laughed. "I guessed your age to be somewhere in the mid-forties."

"You can add a few years onto that estimation, doctor," Zarah playfully answered. She didn't want to state her age on their first date.

"I'm *glad* your kids are grown," he said. "It seems to me that most of the single women in Bay City have small kids."

"Don't you like kids?" Zarah asked.

"I like kids, but I don't want to go through the experience of raising another woman's child again."

"I'm sorry, John. Wasn't raising your daughter a good experience for you?"

"There were good times when she was a little girl, but my ex reminded me, on a near daily basis, that I was not her *real* father."

"I don't get it, John. Legally adopting a child means you *are* the real parent."

"Tell that to my ex."

Raising her boys had been the most joyful experience of her life, and she wouldn't have traded it for the world. She sensed his sadness and turned the conversation in a different direction.

"Did anything exciting happen in your Emergency Department this past week?"

They volleyed stories about their jobs and talked nonstop until dusk. She loved the ease of talking to someone who also worked in the medical profession. It seemed to her that medical people spoke a different language they only understood. Medical professionals had a different outlook on life, knowing firsthand that life can end at any moment.

Early in her career, she discovered that medical professionals develop a macabre sense of humor that could easily offend a "regular" person if overheard. Their "sick" sense of humor is a coping mechanism that helps them face the surreal situations they experience daily.

"Well, we'd better get going! Irish Fest awaits!" Zarah said enthusiastically. "Here is to a fun evening ahead!" she toasted.

There was no lull in the conversation on the drive to the fairgrounds either. John told her about the cottage he had built in upstate Michigan eight years ago.

"Unfortunately, my ex-wife is getting the cottage in the divorce settlement. She has it for sale, and we agree that I maintain it until it's sold."

"Why would you maintain something that your ex-wife will own?" Zarah was puzzled.

"If I don't maintain it, she'll hire someone to do everything, and I would be responsible for paying half of the bills. I've been neglecting the cottage this summer, and I probably should ride up there soon."

"*You* built the cottage, John? With your own hands?"

"Yes… Sometimes my dad or friends helped, and I hired local farm kids to help put up the trusses."

"Did your ex help with the project?"

"Never," he suppressed a laugh. "I also built the house my ex and daughter currently live in before I met her. I probably should have become a carpenter instead of a doctor," he laughed. "I adore construction more than anything else and aspire to embark on another building project one day."

Zarah was beyond impressed. Only a few doctors she knew had talents beyond their medical skills. He spoke about his accomplishments matter-of-factly—as if anyone could do what he had done.

"So… the house your ex and your daughter live in… was *that* split in the divorce?"

"No, she got it in the settlement."

"That does not sound like a fair settlement to me."

Zarah could not help but express her opinion. Her head was swimming with questions. John had built the cottage and house his ex-wife and daughter now occupied and owned. Why did he lose all of that real estate in the divorce?

John was intriguing, but she suspected he carried *a ton* of baggage—maybe too much. She was going to have fun that evening at Irish Fest and had no expectations whatsoever. Expectations had gotten her nowhere in the past...

After years of marriage to Joe, Zarah had expected that he would eventually discover that he loved her more than life itself, and he would do anything in his power to change his life around and become the husband that Zarah desired. She had expected they would grow old together and sit side-by-side laughing at their grandchildren's antics.

Then, Nate... the man she admired for so many years. She expected that everything he told her was the truth. She believed him when he talked of building a life with her. She hoped he was her cosmic reward for suffering for so long in a difficult marriage.

Ian... the man with whom she had made the most incredible physical connection. The man she expected was "The One." She could have crawled into his arms and remained there happily for the rest of her life. She would never forget the intensity of her feelings for him... She expected that passion never to end.

In each relationship, she had expectations and never expected to reach this age, having only experienced games, lies, and deceit.

John took Zarah's hand after they entered the gates of the festival. They navigated their way through the crowds of people to buy a beer. They walked from stage to stage to listen to different Celtic bands and laughed at the skill it took not to spill their drinks.

John put his arm around Zarah, and she reciprocated— she was surprised at how rail thin he was. They swayed in unison to the music. The evening was fun as they blended into the sea of faces and laughed over nothing. They worked their way up to the front of the crowds to get the best view of the bands, and they danced like no one was watching.

As they drove back to Zarah's house, their ears were still ringing from the loud volume of the Celtic music. It was two a.m. when they arrived home.

"If you'd prefer to drive home in the morning, I could give you a pillow and a blanket, and you can sleep on my couch," she offered.

"The couch, huh?!" he joked.

"Yes, Dr. Gray… there will be none of that!" she teased.

He agreed to her offer, then heard her lock her bedroom door after closing it for the night.

The sound of the shower running the following day woke John. He got off the couch, folded his blanket neatly, then knocked on the bathroom door…

"Zarah, I guess I'll get going. I had a great time last night. Thanks for letting me sleep on the couch!"

"Wait!" The bathroom door quickly opened. Zarah was dressed in light-blue scrubs, and her wet hair was wrapped in a towel.

"You're working today?" John asked.

"Yes. I picked up an extra shift. I'm earning money for new kitchen countertops. But I don't have to leave until noon. Give me a minute to blow dry, and I'll have coffee with you."

John went into the kitchen and opened a few cabinets for a coffee cup.

"The cups are above the toaster!" she yelled from the bathroom.

"Found them!"

Zarah appeared several minutes later—her hair neatly brushed into a ponytail.

"You look nice in scrubs," he stated.

"Doesn't everyone look the same in scrubs, Dr. Gray?" she said playfully.

"No, they don't. Scrubs do, however, camouflage various flaws," he laughed. "Would you like to do something next weekend, Zarah?"

"That would be nice." It dawned on her… She had already scheduled a date with Richard on Saturday—this could get tricky.

"I have plans on Saturday but am free on Sunday."

"That's okay… We'll work around our schedules," John answered as if their disparate personal and work schedules didn't phase him in the least.

"What about the distance between us? The hour drive between Bay City and Lansing is brutal."

"I don't care about the distance," John said definitively.

Zarah put two slices of bread into the toaster—the ceiling light dimmed the moment she pressed down on the handle.

"Your wiring needs updating," John stated matter-of-factly.

"What do you mean?"

"Your lights dimmed when you depressed the toaster handle. I could fix that for you."

"You know how to wire electricity?!"

"Of course," he answered. "I'm sure that you need a few additional circuits. This is an old house, and I'm willing to bet your electrical panel has never been updated."

"I'm sure you're right, John. I'm embarrassed that I never thought of replacing the old wiring."

She was discovering that John was a man of many talents. He talked about his skills and accomplishments as if they were nothing extraordinary.

"Would you like to meet somewhere midway between here and Bay City next Sunday?" John asked. "I'll find a restaurant in Montrose."

Dating two men at once was going to present some challenges. But she would stick to her plan… no emotions, commitments, or expectations. She was dating like a man.

Thirty-five

Learning to juggle

AFTER DINNER AT an elegant French restaurant, Zarah and Richard walked hand-in-hand on Main Street in downtown Lansing. She naturally walked at a faster pace, so she slowed down to match his leisurely stride.

Zarah liked spending time with Richard. He wasn't what she had "ordered" on her "list to The Universe." He was her height and a little on the stocky side, but none of that mattered. He had admirable qualities. His kindness, intelligence, and ambition to grow his investment company impressed her. She believed he was honest and never left her without setting up their next date. His children were grown, and he rarely spoke about his ex-wife. He didn't seem to have a lot of baggage and instead focused on the future.

"Zarah, I'm in the market to buy a new house. Would you like to come with me and my realtor this week to view several houses I'm interested in? I'd *love* a female perspective." He told her what neighborhoods he was focused on—the houses in those neighborhoods were very high-end.

"I'll be working a lot this week, so I couldn't possibly fit that into my schedule, Richard."

Zarah did not think going with him for such a monumental decision was a good idea. Minutes into their walk, they came upon a jewelry storefront.

"Would you like to go in and look around? I want to buy you something…" Richard raised his eyebrows as he waited for her to reply.

"Thank you, but I don't need any jewelry now. However, it's very nice of you to ask." With a smile, she led him by the hand past the storefront. He was much more serious about their relationship than Zarah.

"Zarah, I'm not dating anyone else…"

"That's nice, Richard, I like you, too."

At that moment, Zarah was glad their physical relationship had not gone beyond kissing. She had answered him evasively and wondered if he had caught it.

The following day, Zarah met John outside a quaint little restaurant he had recommended. He greeted her with a polite kiss on the cheek. They were seated at a private table with a view of trees and a river beyond.

He seemed to choose his words carefully before he spoke. What happened to him in the past that made him so cautious?

"I'm not very hungry… do you want to split something?" John asked.

"Actually, I'm starving," Zarah answered without taking her eyes off the menu. John's indifference toward food puzzled Zarah. "You're too thin, John. Don't you eat much?"

"I'm not accustomed to eating a lot. My ex never cooked, so I lived on whatever I had time to prepare after work." He paused momentarily, then added, "My ex kept herself in good shape. She was the size of a twelve-year-old."

"A twelve-year-old? Was that attractive to you?" Zarah saw another red flag. *Had he lived with a woman who has an eating disorder? Does he think a grown woman 'the size of a twelve-year-old' is normal?*

They each ordered a Cobb salad and a glass of white wine. The restaurant provided the perfect atmosphere to have a leisurely meal and conversation. They talked for two hours, pausing only to eat their salad or sip their wine.

They had a lot in common. Zarah was the first woman John had ever met who had her own workshop and knew how to use tools. John was the first man that Zarah had ever met who could do just about anything.

Hand in hand, they walked on a path alongside the river behind the restaurant.

"John, I'm gathering that you didn't know your divorce was coming—your ex blindsided you." It was a lot to ask on what was only their second date, but several things he had said on their first date piqued her curiosity.

"No, I didn't have a clue. I came home one Friday from work to find the locks on my house had been changed."

"Oh, my God!" Zarah gasped.

All the color left his face, and Zarah's questions had been the cause. She opened Pandora's box, but did she want to know what was inside?

"My wife... I mean, my ex-wife... had a terrible temper. Anything could set her in a rage. No matter what I did, I couldn't make her happy."

"Did she let you into the house that day?"

"Yes, then promptly handed me divorce papers. We had made plans the evening before to head to the cottage when I arrived home from work. You can only imagine my confusion. She then told me I had two days to find an apartment and vacate the house and informed me that she had already packed my belongings. Whatever didn't fit into my car and trailer that weekend was never returned to me... I still don't get it... I thought I was a good husband."

That was the second time Zarah had heard that statement on so many dates. John was too fresh out of his divorce—he did not have the time he needed to heal his soul.

Zarah's two years alone had been invaluable, and she wouldn't have traded the solitude she experienced for the world. During that time, she evaluated what she truly wanted in her life, and only then did she discover that she did not need anyone else to make her happy.

"Was anyone around to help you during that time?" she asked.

"My dad helped me. He drove up early the next morning."

"You found an apartment and moved out in only two days?"

"I found the apartment on Saturday, packed up my car and trailer on Sunday, and moved into the apartment that same evening."

"Divorce is not for the faint of heart." Zarah wished that she could have found something more comforting to say. What transpired between John and his ex-wife seemed cruel, and he remained distressed over the events. At the same time, there was something about him that Zarah had yet to put her finger on.

John drove to Zarah's house on his day off to update her electrical panel. She left a key under the front doormat for him. He had to pick his daughter up after school later that day, so he would have already left when Zarah got home that evening. When she made toast the following day, the lights did not dim.

She sent him a text message... "Thank you for updating my ancient electrical panel!"

Several hours later, during his lunch break, John answered, "You are most welcome! I'm off tomorrow. I could drive down."

"I don't get home until close to midnight..." she texted back. "And you're still sleeping on the couch, Dr. Gray!" She inserted a winking emoji.

John replied with a sad-face emoji, which made Zarah laugh.

Dating two men was beginning to weigh on Zarah, and it was not nearly the fun she thought it would be. Both John and Richard had admirable qualities, and at this point, she could flip a coin to decide between the two. She was building a relationship with them both, and if she thought about her predicament too long, her stomach twisted into a knot. What began innocently enough had taken on a life of its own.

She had wanted to date without emotion, without commitment. She tried to date purely for fun—how she believed men dated. What she never saw coming was both Richard and John were nothing like the men of her past, and both had expectations in their relationship with her.

Was The Universe playing a trick on her? Was this a test? She had asked for "Mr. Right." Why did she meet two Mr. Rights? She was at a loss as to how to end the situation.

She would let both relationships play out a little longer. Maybe one or the other would screw something up— perhaps they would *both* screw something up—then her decision would be made for her.

She knew so little about John. He was so newly divorced... Was she his rebound girlfriend? She would not sleep with either of the men—that would add a level of complexity she didn't need. She would keep things casual and noncommittal.

John continued to fit Zarah into his schedule as often as possible. He occasionally drove down in the evening to visit Zarah when she arrived home near midnight. They would cuddle up on the couch and talk for a couple of hours, then he got into his car and drove back to Bay City. She didn't know how he was managing with so little sleep.

John arrived bright and early one Saturday morning to help Zarah remove her old kitchen countertops and help her take measurements for new countertops. Later that day, they shopped at the building center to find and order the perfect granite. The following day, he helped her remove the old sink, then cut a piece of plywood to hold her coffee pot, microwave and toaster temporarily.

"It's going to be a very long two weeks of washing my dishes in the bathroom while I wait for the countertop to arrive," Zarah sighed. "I don't think I'm a patient person."

John stood with his hands on his hips, studying the cabinets. "You should install a backsplash after the countertops are installed. That would give this kitchen a nice, modern look."

"Hmmm. I hadn't thought of a backsplash."

"And, Zarah, I hate to be the bearer of bad news, but your furnace and air conditioner are old—you need to replace both units before winter."

"I can hardly believe you are finding all this stuff to fix, John! I thought I was nearly done with this house!"

"You fixed the aesthetics. I see what needs to be updated with the house's inner workings."

Zarah's mind could not help but add up the amount of money the projects he was conjuring up would take, but she knew he was right.

John then asked her if she would like to take a drive the following weekend to see the cottage. Mowing the lawn was long overdue.

Thirty-six

Flashes before your eyes

IT WAS MONDAY morning, her first day back to work after several days off. She was running late and would have to drive with determination to make up for lost time. She merged onto the expressway in bumper-to-bumper traffic as she had done hundreds of times before. It began to rain —she turned her windshield wipers on and gripped the steering wheel with both hands. Nurses who were late more than three times in a calendar year received a letter of warning, and she had already been late twice.

She let her mind drift to the past week. She had to smile when she thought of how helpful John had been with her kitchen project. Then she switched gears and thought of how sweet Richard had been when he wanted to take her inside the jewelry store.

Dating two men simultaneously was getting more complicated by the day. Sometimes Richard called her when she was on a date with John, and sometimes vice-versa.

The sky turned black, and the rain began falling harder —she adjusted the windshield wipers. An eighteen-wheeler flew past her in the right lane—he was driving far too fast for road conditions.

"Slow down, buddy... What's your hurry?!" she said into the windshield.

In one mile, she would reach her exit. She hoped that she'd find a covered spot in the parking structure. She forgot her umbrella, and she'd have to begin her shift in wet scrubs if she had to park on the roof and make a mad dash for the entrance.

She kept a close eye on the semi-truck who had barreled past her. *Is he drunk?* She saw the truck's brake lights suddenly go on, and then the trailer began to sway to the left... The driver of the eighteen-wheeler had lost control.

Zarah slammed on her brakes to avoid hitting the trailer as it floated into her lane in what seemed like slow motion. She depressed her brake pedal for all she was worth—her tires made a horrible screeching sound as she attempted to stop her vehicle. She recognized what it meant to have your life flash before you in those few seconds. In her mind's eye, she saw her sons' faces, and she prayed that they would be okay without her.

Despite locking her brakes, her car remained straight, and, by what she could only describe as a miracle, her car came to a stop with roughly ten feet to spare. In disbelief, she stared up at the wall of the semi-truck trailer that now blocked all three lanes of traffic.

"Thank you, God!" she gasped.

Suddenly, her head snapped back and hit the headrest *hard*. The SUV behind her was not able to stop in time. Her car jerked forward several feet with the impact. Then she felt a second jolt and could only assume that the vehicle that had crashed into her car was himself hit from behind in a chain reaction. She was now mere feet away from the semi's trailer. She looked to her left and then to her right and saw terror in the faces of the drivers as they attempted to stop their vehicles before crashing head-on.

The sickening sound of screeching tires and crunching metal resounded further and further away and seemed to go on forever. She lost count of how many crashes she heard—many happened simultaneously. She wanted to put her hands over her ears to block out the horror of the situation.

Zarah sat perfectly still, afraid to move. She would be shoved into the semi's trailer if her car were pushed further. Should she get out of her car? Or should she remain frozen in place and pray?

The crashing sounds finally stopped, and except for a stuck car horn in the distance, the pounding rain and the beating of her windshield wipers, everything went eerily silent.

She did a quick self-check—she was not hurt. She found her cell phone on the car floor and dialed 911. She gave the operator her location and told her to send ambulances. She told the dispatcher she had no idea how many vehicles were involved in the pile-up, and two cars, one to her left and one to her right, had crashed into the semi.

On her left, a car with four older women inside had rear-ended the vehicle that had crashed into the semi's trailer. Once she felt it was safe to move, Zarah exited her car and stepped into the pouring rain to check on the women. She knocked on the passenger window and asked them to roll it down. An older woman in the back seat was hysterical. Zarah assured the women that the worst was over and help was coming. The driver of the vehicle was dazed and had blood trickling down her face. Zarah instructed the woman in the passenger seat to find something to use as a dressing and hold pressure on the wound until help arrived.

Zarah looked at the SUV behind her, which had crashed into her. The driver waved to Zarah. She waved back. At that moment, she could not have cared less about the condition of her car—it was definitely totaled.

She tried to assess the situation around her, but the driving rain obscured her vision. She turned to look at the cars that had smashed into the semi. She couldn't see inside either of them—they were partially wedged under the semi-truck's trailer.

It all felt surreal... Maybe she was an actress in a movie, or she was having a bad dream. Perhaps she died in the accident, and she was a ghost lingering at the scene of her death.

She was not thinking clearly. She got back into her car and reached for her water bottle. If she was going into shock, she knew to drink fluids to keep her blood pressure from dropping. She was soaked to the bone. She took a few deep breaths to calm and recenter herself—her heart was racing.

She grabbed her phone again and began to dial. She was relieved when he picked up on the third ring...

"Hi, Zarah!" He sounded surprised. She had never called him during work hours before.

"John! I was just in an accident on I-96!"

"Are you okay?!" She heard panic in his voice.

"Yes, I'm okay, but I'm in a pile-up!" She said quickly. "A semi-truck jack-knifed right in front of me! It was windy, and the road must have been slippery. Visibility was terrible—it was pouring rain. I was driving in the middle lane, and the cars to my left and right couldn't stop in time, and they are both stuck under the semi-truck's trailer!"

"I'm coming down. Where exactly are you?"

"No... Don't come. There is no way you could get to me. I'm fine. I hear sirens in the distance, so help is coming." The rain was finally relenting. In her rearview mirror, she saw flashing lights approaching in the emergency lane.

"Zarah... Is your car drivable?"

"I don't know. My tailgate is squashed, and I no longer have a back seat."

"I'm coming down... You can't drive yourself home!"

"I'm not going home... I have to go to work!" Zarah knew that many of the injured would be taken to the hospital, and she didn't want to leave her unit short-staffed.

"Going to work today may not be the best idea, Zarah."

"I've got to go in! Don't drive down—there is nothing you can do! Emergency personnel are arriving, and an officer is walking this way. I'll call you later…" *click*

The police arrived first, followed by fire trucks and ambulances. Several firefighters went straight to the semi-truck. The truck driver stepped down from the cab and seemed to be explaining the situation to the rescue team. Zarah made a mental note to inform the police that he had been driving like a bat out of hell.

Several firefighters went straight to the two partially lodged cars under the semi-truck's trailer. They wasted no time removing the car doors with a loud hydraulic tool. In a short time, they pulled a bloodied man from the car on her left and loaded him into an ambulance. Zarah was relieved to see that the man was communicating with them. The firefighters quickly turned their attention to the car to Zarah's right and pulled the driver from the vehicle within minutes. He was an older man, and from Zarah's viewpoint, she saw no signs of life.

EMTs quickly went from car to car to triage the situation. Zarah exited her vehicle and told them she was a nurse, was not hurt, and could help. It wasn't customary to allow an accident victim to help, but they were desperate. There were more cars than EMTs, so they gave Zarah a first-aid kit and disregarded the rules.

Zarah took a moment to call her supervisor and told her what had happened. Her supervisor told her she was taking her off today's schedule—she would be too exhausted after the ordeal she had just been through.

Several EMTs nodded at Zarah as she went from car to car to help identify the seriously injured. Eventually, five ambulances left the scene with flashing lights and sirens.

After what felt like hours, the scene was under control. Zarah walked over to talk to the man who had struck her from behind, and they exchanged insurance information. He was a banker. He had been on his way to work. He had a wife and two young children to get home to.

Two tow truck drivers stood with their hands on their hips, assessing the situation. Before they could clear the eighteen-wheeler off the road, they would have to remove the two cars lodged underneath. It took another hour to retract the two vehicles from under the trailer and clear the eighteen-wheeler from the road.

She picked up her phone and texted John, "I'm heading home soon. My supervisor took me off the schedule."

Once the road was cleared, Zarah started her car and was relieved when she shifted into gear—it was drivable. She maneuvered her car slowly through a narrow path the firefighters had cleared. Zarah was the first car to leave the scene. In her rearview mirror, she saw a trail of cars behind her. No one was in a hurry; she could only compare the scene to a funeral procession. She got off at the next exit, made a U-turn, and then headed home.

It was at that moment it occurred to her... This was the first time all day she thought of Richard. After the accident, her knee-jerk reaction was to call John. She knew what she had to do. She put her earpiece in and ordered her phone to "Call Richard."

"Hi, Zarah!" Richard answered in his typical jovial voice. She took a deep breath—she knew this would be difficult.

"Hi Richard, I have something to tell you..." She would not tell Richard that an old boyfriend had returned to her life. She had to tell him the truth... She had met someone else. He had been nothing but kind, and she wished him the best of everything. She did not mention the accident— she didn't want the conversation to be about her.

She had been so wrong... She was *not* cut out to date two men simultaneously, and she definitely was not cut out to date without emotion.

She drove to her house and saw John's car in her driveway. He was sitting on her front stoop awaiting her return, and he stood bolt upright when he saw her SUV approach. His jaw dropped at the sight of her crunched car and disarranged ponytail.

"Zarah!" John wrapped his arms around her when she stepped out of the car. "Thank God that you are okay!"

"I'm lucky to be alive," she whispered.

For the first time that day, tears welled up in her eyes. She felt a huge lump in her throat, and she could no longer talk. She let herself melt into the safety of John's arms.

They walked together into the house. Zarah clicked the TV on to watch the news. It had been a twenty-four-car pile-up, and there was one fatality. She knew who it was. She had been the last person to see him alive. She will never forget the fear on his face in what was the last second of his life.

"John, I don't want you to go home tonight."

"I don't want to go home tonight."

"And you don't have to sleep on the couch."

Flying

The height of observation
I have worked so hard to climb
Shows me almost way too much
Shows me where I am in time

I see the destination clearly
And I know what I have found
But can I land the path below
If I am so far off the ground

One breath in and one breath out
I'm gripping at the wheel
Is this truly what I want?
Is it illusion? Is it real?

Tossed to the left then to the right
My opponent aims for landing
I want to reach and help him steer
But in that way it would mean nothing

We're aiming for the landing strip
We're flying side by side
Will we reach the path this time?
Or will we both collide?

Maybe I should just pull up
To a height of observation
Or maybe roll the window down
And throw out my hesitation

K.D.Kinz

Thirty-seven

Beyond repair

THE PLAN WAS for Zarah to drive to John's apartment and park her car, and then John would drive them both north to the cottage. He waved to her from his apartment balcony as he saw her car approach. She was glad to spot him; all the buildings looked alike.

John's apartment wasn't at all what she had been expecting. A futon and a television on a TV tray were in the living room, and a circa-fifties yellow vinyl and chrome table and chairs were in the dining room.

"Wow, John. Your apartment is clean… I'll give you that! Did you inherit the table and chairs from your parents?"

"No, the dining room set was in our basement."

"It was in 'our' basement? I don't remember that!" Zarah didn't appreciate his choice of possessive adjective.

"I'm sorry," he quickly recognized his faux pas. "The table and chairs were in the basement of *my* former home. This furniture is temporary—this apartment is temporary. I have a year lease, and I'm contemplating buying a condo near the hospital when the lease expires." He paused. "Do you want the nickel tour or the fifty-cent tour?"

"The fifty-cent tour, of course! I'd love to see what you've done with the place!" Zarah half-laughed, but from what she already saw, she knew the answer was "Not much." His apartment appeared practical at best. She had expected he'd own decent furniture, but it was apparent that John was living with his ex-wife's cast-offs.

"Down the hall is the bedroom." He stood to the side to let her pass. "I built this bedroom set when I was in college. I had to take it with me, or the ex would trash it."

"This bedroom set is nice, John! Wow! You build furniture?! You are a man of many talents!" The set was a simple, elegant Swedish design, and she could not fathom how, as a college student, John had already acquired the skills to create it.

"Who taught you how to build furniture?" She was curious.

"I taught myself."

"Is this a picture of your dog?" Hanging in the hallway was a poster-size picture of a sheltie sitting on top of a snowbank.

"Yes, that's Corky. I haven't seen her since the weekend I moved out. I never got to say goodbye to her, and I'm sure the poor creature is wondering what happened to me."

Zarah's heart sank. She knew, too well, the heartbreak of losing a dog.

"Why haven't you seen the dog?"

"My ex keeps her inside the house whenever I drop my daughter off. She must lock her up in a room because she doesn't come to the door, which is totally out of character for Corky."

"Is this a second bedroom?" Zarah asked as she pointed to a closed door.

"Yes," he swung the door open. "I got a two-bedroom, two-bathroom apartment because I expected my daughter to stay with me on the weekends, but that has yet to happen."

She saw boxes and garbage bags piled nearly to the ceiling on the far wall of the second bedroom.

"What's with all the stuff?" Zarah inquired.

"I have *no* idea what's in them—this is the stuff my ex-wife packed for me. Except for my clothing, I wasn't allowed to pack anything. She followed me from room to room to ensure I didn't take anything I wasn't supposed to."

"Well, I wasn't even home when my ex packed up and moved out, and I'm still surprised when I search for something that isn't there," Zarah said with an uncomfortable laugh. "I didn't care what he took at that point."

"She kept most of my tools, artwork, pottery collection, and antiques my parents had given me. I owned all of that stuff before I met her. I still can't imagine why she wanted to keep it all."

"Well, don't cry for something that can't cry back for you," Zarah said, trying to make light of the situation. "Are you curious about what's in the bags and boxes?"

"No," he flatly stated. It was apparent to Zarah that he wanted to close the bedroom door and move on from the subject of his ex-wife.

During the two-hour drive to Tamarack Lake, they shared stories about their past work week. One of John's patients was an older man who had been the victim of a carjacking. He had sustained multiple lacerations and bruises from fighting off his perpetrator, but John expected him to make a full recovery. The perpetrator had gotten away, and the older man was afraid to be released from the hospital. Zarah told John about Cory, a sixteen-year-old boy in her care who had been shot in the head as he stepped off of the school bus. The seventeen-year-old kid who shot him told the police that he did it because Cory was too intelligent, he only cared about getting good grades, and he refused to join their gang. If Cory survives, he would never be the same again.

The conversation turned to the sale of John's cottage.

"Your face lights up whenever you talk about the cottage," Zarah stated. "How did you feel about losing it in the divorce?"

John had a lifelong attachment to Tamarack Lake. His family had a small cottage on the lake the entire time he was growing up, and they still owned it. Eight years ago, when a vacant lot on the lake became available, John bought the property and built his cottage.

"I'm fine with it. It's time to move on. What did you say, Zarah? Don't cry for something that can't cry back for you. That is exactly how I'm trying to deal with it."

"You are a better man than I!" Zarah sarcastically said. "It's big of you to do the maintenance on the cottage. I could *not* do the same favor for my ex."

"I'm aware of what needs to be done, especially at this time of the year when things need to be winterized. And if I don't do the work, I am court-ordered to pay fifty percent of the maintenance fees. It's just easier if I maintain it."

The situation could have made more sense to Zarah. John had built the cottage and didn't seem upset at losing it in the divorce. Was he hiding his feelings? The more Zarah thought about it, the more uneasy she felt about spending the weekend in a cottage owned by his ex-wife.

Zarah was taken aback as they drove up the cottage driveway—all the doors were painted bright purple.

"Yikes, someone likes the color purple! I mean... I *love* purple, but I *never* would have chosen the color to paint my doors." The words slipped out, and she knew she may have insulted John with her knee-jerk comment.

Upon entering the cottage, Zarah noted that purple was also the predominant interior color.

"Wow, more purple," Zarah said flatly. "This is crazy!"

"Purple is my ex-wife's favorite color," he said without emotion.

"That's obvious... but isn't it a bit much?!" Zarah wanted to keep her comments to herself, but as hard as she tried, she could not. Something felt off.

"I don't like all the purple either, but my ex fancied herself an interior decorator. I'll show you around..."

They walked from room to room, and purple dominated each room. Every room was painted in a shade of lilac to purple, every room contained a vase of artificial purple flowers, and nearly every item in every room was purple.

"Did you design the cottage, John?"

"I did." He answered matter-of-factly as if it was nothing extraordinary to design a home. "It's small, but it lives large," he added.

Zarah thought John had to be about the most unpretentious man she had ever met. He had so many talents, yet he never bragged of his accomplishments.

In the master bedroom, a collage of pictures hung above the headboard. Zarah stepped closer to study it, expecting to see pictures of John's family. Instead, every photo in the frame was of his ex-wife, and in every photo, she was striking a pose in a different bikini. She definitely was the size of a twelve-year-old child.

"I'm sorry, I haven't stepped a foot in here since the divorce. The collage... I forgot all about it." He reached over Zarah's shoulder and quickly snatched the frame off the wall. He looked embarrassed, and Zarah thought he should be.

Zarah was disgusted. It was apparent that John's ex-wife loved having her picture taken, and John must have been the photographer.

"John... I feel like an intruder here... I need to use the restroom." Zarah needed to step away from John for a minute. Maybe she'd splash a little cold water on her face. *We all have our baggage,* she told herself as she walked down the hallway.

After closing the bathroom door, she turned and was greeted by a row of no less than twenty bottles of fingernail polish lined up neatly on the countertop. "What the hell," she whispered in disbelief. It didn't matter that his ex-wife was not physically in the cottage. Zarah felt her vibes, and the vibes were saying, "Get the fuck out!" Oddly, she had felt the same negative vibes when she stood in John's apartment earlier that day. Maybe it was the unopened bags and boxes... Or something else.

John had a lot he needed to accomplish that weekend. Zarah felt childish for becoming upset over a collage of pictures—not to mention the egregious collection of fingernail polish. What else would she discover? She was almost afraid to look.

It all felt creepy… It was almost like the cottage was a shrine built for a spoiled princess. Zarah told herself to stop feeling that way—after all, John's ex-wife was a hundred miles to their south, living somewhere near John's apartment in Bay City.

"Sorry for my little meltdown, John," she said as she walked out of the restroom. "We don't have to leave. However, I couldn't help but notice that your ex-wife must love to paint her fingernails," Zarah said with slight sarcasm.

John looked over her shoulder, and his face tensed. He quickly squeezed by her in the doorway, scooped all the bottles into the top vanity drawer, then closed it.

"I'll have to put everything back exactly how it was before we leave," he said under his breath as he thought out loud… but Zarah had clearly heard him. *His ex-wife owns this cottage, and he isn't allowed to touch her stuff. How often does she come up here? Is she aware that he's here for the weekend? And does she know that he brought me along?!*

"If you'd rather, we can go across the lake and stay at my parent's cottage. But their cottage has been winterized, so that means no running water," he stated.

Zarah searched the front picture window to size up his parents' cottage.

"Where is the lake?" she asked. There was not a glimpse of blue water. A row of overgrown gnarly white pines was growing close to the cottage. Zarah thought the trees looked haunted, and if she studied them, she would discover that they had arms, claws, and fangs.

"I'm fine, John. We can stay here. I'm kind of addicted to running water." She conceded even though every bone in her body was screaming, "Run!"

John didn't waste any time and left Zarah alone in the cottage to make their dinner. She pulled open one drawer and cabinet after another and found no cooking utensils except paper plates and plastic cutlery.

"There is nothing to cook with in this stupid purple cottage!" she said to herself. "What did that woman do all day? She certainly didn't prepare any meals for her family!"

Zarah had packed a cooler with all the ingredients for a chicken salad for their dinner. She chopped the vegetables on a paper plate using a plastic knife and considered herself lucky when she found an old saucepan far back in a cabinet to toss the salad in.

That evening, John and Zarah walked the property that surrounded the cottage. He pointed out hundreds of native trees that he planted over the years.

"John, I *hate* those gnarly white pines. They are half-dead and blocking the sunlight. Not to mention you have *no* view of the lake.

"I hate them, too," he replied.

"Why haven't you taken them down?"

"My wife, I mean my ex-wife, wants them there."

"Why?"

"To block 'prying eyes' from seeing us."

Zarah couldn't help but wonder...*What had happened in the purple cottage that his ex-wife didn't want anyone to see?*

That night, Zarah thought she heard a noise from the cottage kitchen. John was fast asleep beside her. It must have been her imagination. She got out of bed and began to walk down the pitch-black hallway to find the bathroom. She felt her way along the wall for a light switch.

Then she heard another sound... She heard breathing...

"John!" she yelled out, but John did not answer. She frantically moved her hands along the wall to find a light switch when suddenly someone grabbed her wrist. Panicked, she tried to pull away, but the intruder was powerful and did not let go.

In a sliver of moonlight, her eyes focused on the face of the intruder. It was the woman in the collage. It was Karma.

"Oh my God! John! She's in the cottage!" Zarah screamed.

"Zarah!" she heard John's voice. He was shaking her. "Wake up! You're having a bad dream!"

Of course, it had all been a dream. She did not tell John what the dream had been about. Her heart continued to race as she came back to reality. She snuggled into John's arms. As she attempted to fall back to sleep, she thought how ridiculous the dream had been. How could she have such negative thoughts about someone she had never met?

In the morning, she would tell John that if he had to return to do additional maintenance on the cottage, he'd have to go without her. The cottage felt cursed—the very air was permeated with something she couldn't put her finger on. If she *had* to describe it, she felt evil surrounding her.

Several weeks later, John had an announcement…

"I'm going to buy the cottage from my ex-wife."

"That's awesome, John! I could never believe that you wanted to give it up. You have a life-long history on that lake."

"I do. I'm happy with my decision. We close the deal next Thursday," he said with a smile.

"John, I have a chainsaw… Let's take down those ugly pine trees next time we go!"

John had never known a woman who owned a chainsaw—let alone knew how to wield one.

Even if they didn't stay together as a couple, Zarah felt strongly that John should own the cottage. John's father had moved his young family from town to town to further his career—Tamarack Lake was the only constant John had ever known.

Two weeks passed, and their weekends off finally aligned. They packed up their chainsaws and headed up to the cottage right after John's shift was over. Along the way, they stopped at a hardware store and bought new locks for the cottage doors. On arrival, and without hesitation, John began to change the locks.

All day Saturday and most of Sunday was spent taking down the white pines. John sounded like an excited little boy as he looked out the front window toward the lake…

"Zarah, I can see the lake! With the pine trees gone, the other trees I've planted over the years finally have a chance to grow—they have light for the first time!"

After dinner, they walked to the dock for a glass of wine. It had been a productive weekend—the locks were changed, and seven old, gnarly, half-dead pine trees had been taken down.

John poured two glasses of wine and handed one to Zarah.

"Well, here is to the end of a great weekend!" John said. They clinked their glasses together. Zarah was exhausted from two days of physical activity, but she loved the work and was thrilled with the results.

"Cutting down the trees was the easy part," Zarah stated. "Hauling the trees away *after* they were cut down was where the real work began."

John didn't answer. His eyes were transfixed on his parents' cottage across the lake. He had spoken very little about his parents in the present tense, although he mentioned them often when he talked about his childhood.

"John, did you spend much time at your parents' cottage while you were here with your ex?"

"No."

"Why not?"

"Because my ex *hated* my parents, and she especially despised my father, although I have no idea why. My dad's a great guy, but she did *not* like his sense of humor."

"Why didn't you just take the boat and go across yourself?"

"Because she would get angry, and it wasn't worth the price I'd have to pay. The repercussions could last days." His face tensed.

Zarah suspected that John had a lot of fence-mending to do with his parents, and now that he owned the cottage and his ex-wife was out of the picture, he might have the chance to do just that.

Zarah would let the subject rest for a while—John was visibly upset. She, herself, was no stranger to family difficulties. She stared into the horizon, took a few sips of her wine, and let her mind wander...

She hadn't spoken to her parents in months. The last time that Zarah did call her mother, her mother seemed to want to talk far too much about Joe. "Joe came over to visit us." "Joe sent me the nicest birthday card." "We met Joe yesterday for dinner." Why did her mother behave this way? She had to be aware that her words were hurtful. Was she punishing Zarah for divorcing Joe?

Zarah feared that one of her last thoughts on earth would be that her parents, especially her mother, did not support her during what had been the most challenging time of her life.

How different would her life have been with the support of her mother? Of both of her parents? At times, she had begged Rita to believe her—the way a mother should.

The sad fact was... If Rita and Charlie believed Zarah, they would never admit to it. Rita repeatedly said, "We've never seen Joe drunk! Maybe he drinks a lot, but a lot of men do!"

Zarah kept the ugly details of everything that went wrong in her marriage a closely guarded secret from her parents. It was not worth her breath. She let them believe it was only his alcoholism that had broken their marriage— that should have been enough. If she had told them more, her mother would have laughed and made up even more excuses for Joe—much like she had made up excuses for Charlie all the while Zarah and Liz were growing up.

Zarah could not understand why her parents seemed to love Joe beyond anything rational. It seemed as if they had traded her, their daughter, to remain faithful to a man who had hurt her deeply.

None of it made any sense to Zarah... None of it.

"Zarah?" John broke her trance. "You look like you are a thousand miles away."

"I was… John, did your parents fully support you in your divorce?"

"Yes, they did. I called my dad the evening my ex told me I had two days to vacate the house. At that point, I was estranged from my parents, but they were both there for me the moment I needed them—no questions asked. I'm sure they were relieved my marriage was over."

"You're so lucky, John."

"Why do you think that I'm lucky?"

"You have parents who were there for you."

"Weren't your parents there for you?"

"My ex played on my parents' sympathy, and my mother and father fell for his act. That made my divorce twice as hard because, in their eyes, Joe was the victim, and I was the villain," Zarah said sadly. "Do your parents understand what went on in your marriage?"

"No, I didn't want to burden them."

"I'm still confused, John. What if you had told your ex, in no uncertain terms, 'I am going across the lake to visit my family?'"

"You don't understand… She would fly into a rage. She would scream, she would kick me… and spit on me." His face tensed as if he was reliving the experience. "The screaming could go on for hours. The whole goddamn lake would hear her."

"Wait…" Zarah thought for sure she misunderstood what he said. "She would spit? At you?"

"Yes, she'd spit like a fucking rabid animal."

This was the missing piece of the puzzle. This was why John was hesitant before speaking, and this was why he was estranged from his family. He was abused… by his ex-wife… a woman the size of a twelve-year-old.

"What did you do when she attacked you?" Zarah said softly.

"I caught her by the wrists and held her as far away from me as I could until she calmed down."

"How often did this happen?"

"Often."

"Define often."

"Once or twice a week."

Zarah had one more question that she hated to ask, but she had to…

"Did you ever defend yourself? Did you ever hit her back?"

"Never. Sometimes, her wrists got bruised because I had to hold them so tightly. The next morning, she would show me the bruises and threaten to call the police to report me."

"Oh my God, John." This was new territory. Zarah had never known a man who had been physically abused.

"She could have ruined me, my career… my reputation. I could have been tossed in jail."

"And your daughter… How did all this affect her? Did she witness any of it?"

"She witnessed a lot of it, and she took good notes. She basically treats me the same as her mother does."

"Meaning…"

"She hasn't called me 'dad' for years."

"What does she call you?"

"Loser or asshole." His voice trailed off.

John was a broken man. He had been abused verbally, mentally and physically. *How did he allow this to happen? Why didn't he leave the marriage when the abuse began? What kind of man puts up with an abusive woman?*

Zarah's mind was spinning. This was what she feared the most in a relationship… Something she could not fix. Was every man in her life going to have something abnormal about himself? Richard was probably the most normal man she had ever dated—and she dumped him.

Do I gravitate only toward flawed men? Do normal men not appeal to me?

At that moment, a large turtle swam past the dock. John quickly looked at Zarah, and his eyes gave away his excitement.

"Should I get it for you?!" he asked.

"Should you get what for me…?"

"The turtle!"

"Well… okay!"

Without hesitation, John jumped into the lake and disappeared under the water, only to emerge seconds later holding a very surprised Blandings turtle high above his head. He brought the turtle closer to Zarah so that she could touch it, then gently released it back into the lake.

No man had done anything like that for her before. John's personality was endearing, but was she up for dating a broken man? Maybe her relationship with John would be better if they were just friends... However, too much had happened between them to take that step backward.

The turtle capture had lifted their mood. John turned to face Zarah. He had an idea he thought she might like...

"Do you want to de-purple?"

"De-purple?" Zarah had an inkling of what he meant and hoped she was right.

"I have some boxes in the garage. Let's get rid of all the goddamn purple!"

They spent hours going from room to room and filling the boxes with his ex-wife's purple items.

"I'd like to repaint this place as soon as possible. Maybe you can help me pick out some nice, neutral colors?"

"Are you sure you won't miss the lilac walls?" Zarah teased.

She enjoyed helping John de-purple the cottage—no matter what happened to them as a couple, he deserved a fresh start, even if it began with a coat of fresh paint.

Later that evening, they drove to John's old house and placed six boxes of the purple items they had removed from the cottage on his ex-wife's driveway. Zarah thought that by returning the purple stuff to his ex-wife, his ex may reciprocate and return some of John's belongings to him... Or maybe even let him see his dog.

Minutes later, they returned to John's apartment—Zarah was surprised that John lived so close to his ex-wife.

Zarah gave John a quick kiss goodbye. She told him it was best she didn't stay the night—she was scheduled to work the next day, and she needed to get a good night's sleep in her own bed. She entered her car and dug in her purse to find her keys and earpiece. She needed to talk to her sister.

Zarah knew that she was not the person to help John deal with the trauma of his past. Coping with her baggage had been enough. As far as she knew, John had not gone for any counseling. She did not understand how he was coping—he could surely crumble at any moment. "There is no way," she whispered into her empty car as she searched for her keys, "to simply sweep that kind of abuse under the rug and expect to lead a normal life..."

She found her earpiece, put it on, and then dialed Liz. She started her car and headed for home.

"Answer, Liz, answer..." she said nervously into the windshield.

"Hi, Zarah!"

"Hey, sis, I'm sorry to call you this late in the day..."

"What's wrong, Zarah?"

"I think I'm only attracted to damaged men. I don't think I can do this anymore... I'm beginning to face that I am meant to be alone." Zarah said with one long breath.

"What happened, Zarah?! I thought you were up at John's cottage this past weekend?"

"I was... Liz, he admitted to me that his ex-wife abused him.... For years! I can't spend the rest of my life trying to fix another man. He is so nice but must be so f'ed in the head. How does a grown man—a brilliant man— let this happen? How does a woman the size of a twelve-year-old beat up a six-foot man?"

"Zarah!" Liz said firmly. "Would you hold it against a woman if she was abused?"

"I would tell an abused woman to leave her abuser!" Zarah said emphatically.

"Zarah, I hate to tell you this, but *Joe abused you*!"

"He never physically hurt me, Liz! This is different! Why did he stay with her... for sixteen years?! Is he under a spell or some sick and twisted mind control?"

"I don't know how to say this without hurting you, Zarah. John is a nice man! He has baggage, but *so do you*! Did you tell John what went on in *your* marriage? And you hung in there for much longer than he did. Why didn't *you* leave your marriage sooner?"

Zarah was at a loss for words. Was Liz right? Was it unfair of her to judge John so harshly?

"Zarah, give John a chance. He must have reasons for staying in the marriage—he most likely stayed to raise his daughter."

"You've made a good point, sis. I'll give this relationship more time and see where it goes." Another call was beeping in. "I've got to go. Someone is calling me—it's probably John. I'll call you tomorrow."

She pressed the receive button on her headset.

"Hello?"

"Hi, Zarah." It was *not* John... It was Ian.

"Ian... How are you? You might be the last person I expected to hear from."

"I've been busy at work, and it hasn't been *that* long since I called..."

"I've lost track," she stated half-heartedly.

Her heart was beating too fast. Why couldn't she shake the feelings she had for this man? Had he left an indelible imprint on her heart she would never be able to erase?

"Do you want to do something this weekend?" he asked.

"No, I can't, Ian. I'm dating someone."

"Oh... well... that's not good," he sounded genuinely disappointed, but Zarah felt a little satisfaction that she had, for once, beaten him to the punch. *Did he think I would sit idly back and wait for him?*

"Well, okay, Zarah. Take care."

"Bye, Ian."

She second-guessed her conversation with Ian the instant she hung up... *Why didn't I ever tell him how I felt about him?* Her rational mind and her gut instincts were in total opposition. While she had been contemplating how to answer his offer to go out that weekend, two phrases came to her mind. She did not choose the answer that came from her heart. *What turn would life have taken if I said yes? Was he ready to commit to dating? Was he prepared to tell me why he had stopped in the middle of passion... twice?*

Then, as if a little voice in her head spoke and snapped her out of her daydream, reality set in. Where had Ian been all this time, and what had he been up to? All work and no play? She highly doubted it. She had looked at his dating profile a few weeks ago... His profile was still live but had been inactive for over a month. It was all so confusing, and with every thought she had, a conflicting thought followed.

What was it about Ian? What was left if she took his magical kiss out of the equation? Someone she had fun with on sporadic dates? Someone she could not rely on? Someone who disappeared from her life for days or weeks at a time only to reappear when it suited *his* agenda? Was a kiss enough to live for? Wait for? She knew it was not. But what could she do to get him out of her head? At the time, no other man had taken her to the heights of desire Ian had. But again, no other man had cut off his affection as abruptly and severely as Ian had. So... what was it about him?

As she drove toward home, she could not help but rehash the frustration that Ian had caused in her life. On the one hand, she wanted to figure him out—she wanted answers. On the other hand, she tried to put him totally behind her.

Then it dawned on her... *I wanted Ian because I could not have him.*

It was as simple as that, and nothing in her mind disputed that conclusion.

Thirty-eight

The puzzle

IT TOOK SEVERAL months for Zarah to wrap her head around John's situation. He was a man of few words when it came to his past, and she didn't push him for answers to the questions she still had. However, she found that if she paid close attention, she picked up bits and pieces of his life and began to assemble the puzzle pieces of his past…

She surmised that John had married his ex-wife because, at the onset, he saw her as the perfect mate. She was beautiful and attentive in his eyes and needed help with her baby daughter. She was in a pitiful situation—a tiny, fragile widow. He thought she was heaven-sent and his reward for the heartache he suffered after the painful break-up with Helen, his girlfriend of ten years. He thought he was just the man to help her navigate the difficult life she had found herself in.

He was building a house he had initially intended for a life with Helen. The hole left in his heart after the break-up with Helen was enormous. Then he met Karma, and she inserted herself into his life. He didn't see her for who she was—he saw only who he wanted to see, and without question, he saw only the side of her that she presented to him.

During their marriage, she morphed into someone else—the opposite of the woman he had first met. She had been sweet and loving, but soon after he adopted her baby daughter, sweet and loving became a rare part of her personality. John acquiesced to every new situation. He was knee-deep in raising his special needs daughter, and he didn't believe for a minute that his ex-wife could handle the challenges of the testing and monitoring that was necessary so that Kirsten would grow into a healthy, self-sufficient adult.

One part of John's past that remained a mystery to Zarah was... What happened at the end of his marriage? What caused him to cave into her every demand? Why didn't he fight for his fair share of anything? He was living in a dismal apartment surrounded by her cast-offs. He avoided opening the door of the room filled with bags and boxes of mysterious contents. He saw his daughter only on rare occasions, and he never again saw his beloved dog.

For some reason, he didn't fight his ex-wife on any level. She and her unethical lawyers managed to abscond with seventy-five percent of their savings and investments—John had rolled over and played dead.

Since Zarah and John began dating, there was never much of a lull in their activities. John drove down to visit her whenever possible, or they went to his cottage for a weekend together. At Zarah's home, they tackled one project after another, and at John's cottage, they redecorated the entire interior, making it warm and welcoming.

Zarah spent an entire day painting all the purple doors to a tranquil bluish-green while John rolled on a neutral taupe to cover the purple garage door.

When they were done, the cottage was transformed, but Zarah could not help but still feel the ghost of his ex-wife around every corner. She knew all too well that if you picked off a layer of paint, *the purple was still there*.

When John and Zarah met, it was as if they got on the same path and began running in the same direction. She felt confident that, if she chose to, she could build a life with John. They were both ambitious and energetic, and in that way, they were a perfect match. But Zarah could not stop herself from remaining cautious about their relationship.

She had her baggage and was aware that she had made mistakes in her own life. Her ex-husband had conditioned her not to trust anyone, and Zarah was always on the lookout for the next person who would deceive her. Would she ever learn to trust again, and could she undo the mindset that was so deeply rooted in her personality?

John presented himself as a man who had it "all together." He was trying hard to move forward with his life. He did not speak a lot about his failed marriage, but on the rare occasion when he did, his entire persona changed… His face tensed, and it was painful for Zarah to see.

Recently, a question occurred to Zarah, and she contemplated for days if she should press John for an answer. The answer to her question would help her complete the complicated puzzle of John's past… But the answer he may give could also change everything.

Thirty-nine

Sleeping with the devil

JOHN PLANNED TO drive down to Zarah's house after he got off work that Friday. He had thrown a change of clothes into a paper bag. He didn't need anything else. Zarah had given him a shelf in the medicine cabinet at her house, where he kept his toothbrush and a razor. Zarah also kept her supply of necessities at John's cottage. They had fallen into a comfortable routine and began referring to each other as "boyfriend" and "girlfriend."

During the past months, Zarah explained her past marriage to John. She did spare him some details, as she didn't want to dredge them up again. She also told him about the affair with Nate and about the frustration she felt toward Ian during the time they dated. John listened to her explanations with total acceptance—more than Zarah thought she deserved. Why couldn't she accept *his* past as easily?

She set the table for dinner as she awaited his arrival. She made his favorite chopped salad and had pork chops ready in the refrigerator for him to throw on the grill.

They had both eagerly anticipated spending an entire weekend together. Their plans included visiting a tile store to select a new backsplash for her kitchen. Zarah loved walking through the hardware stores with John as much as most women loved walking through a jewelry store.

"Hi, Zarah," John said as he entered the house.

"How was the drive?" she asked.

"Long, but the commuter traffic moved along nicely." He walked up to her and gave her a quick kiss on the cheek.

The question was still on Zarah's mind—it had haunted her for days. It was as if she had a devil on one shoulder and an angel on the other. The devil told her to ask the question, and the angel told her to leave well enough alone. She was leaning toward the devil's advice.

"Let's have our salad first," she said, "hold off on lighting the grill for now."

"Wow, that looks good," he said as he sat at the table.

She knew that he had a grueling week in the Emergency Department. She would let them eat in peace before she brought up the subject... Or *if* she brought up the subject.

"John," she put down her fork. "I have a question to ask you..."

"What is it?" he asked.

One thing that Zarah had learned about John was that he did not sugar-coat his answers. He stated the facts as he saw them and let the consequences fall where they may. Sometimes, people were taken aback by his straightforward manner, but Zarah appreciated this about him. She never had to wonder if he had a hidden agenda.

She took a deep breath. "After you were separated from your ex, did you return to her... Did you sleep with her?"

John paused, but there was no other way to phrase his answer. He knew he was about to hurt Zarah, and for a few seconds, he considered concealing the truth.

"Yes, I did." His face held no expression, and the blood drained from his face.

Zarah felt her stomach turn. Her instincts had been correct. She could have *never* slept with her ex-husband once he moved out. Never.

She stood up from the table and began to clear the dishes.

"I knew it," she said softly as she walked to the sink. "Have you slept with her since we've been together?"

"No. Zarah, I have not."

Zarah turned to face him. She needed every possible detail of information to process this conversation, including studying his facial expressions.

"How could you have slept with her after she kicked you out? After she stripped you of everything and did her best to leave you for broke... After she abused you!"

"She was... familiar," he choked out.

"Familiar?! You slept with her because she was familiar? Where was your self-respect?!" Zarah wanted to remain calm, but she could not. She thought she was beginning to understand the convoluted mess that had been his marriage, but she hadn't figured out a thing.

"Did she sleep with you in your apartment? In the bed that *we* sleep in?" She had to ask but wasn't sure she wanted an answer.

"Yes."

"Go home, John," she returned to the dishes in the sink.

"Zarah... She'd show up at my apartment... uninvited."

"So you *had* to let her in, and you had to have sex with her."

"Zarah, please... That's absurd!" He paused as he chose his words. "I was hoping that by letting her into my bed, she would stop the divorce proceedings."

"You wanted to stay in that marriage?!"

"It's complicated," he said quietly, looking down at the floor.

Zarah didn't want to listen to his explanation anymore. He was shaken, but she felt little pity for him. Nothing he could say could make the situation better. How could the most confident man she had ever met think so little of himself? It was a quandary without a conceivable answer.

"John…if we end our relationship over this, would you sleep with her again? Because 'she's familiar?'"

He paused. "No, Zarah, absolutely not."

Zarah did not believe him for the first time since they started dating.

The following day, Zarah drove to the tile store. She would continue with her plans as she had before John entered her life. She walked the aisles and occasionally stopped to feign interest in one tile or another. She even found herself, at one point, stopping to ask John's opinion… But he wasn't there. She left the store without making a purchase. Maybe the following weekend, she would return when her head was in a better place.

Forty

Closure of sorts

"ZARAH, I NEED to talk to you."

Ian's voice on the phone didn't elicit the same response she had experienced in the past. Maybe it was because of the disappointment she still felt from John's admission last week, or perhaps she was giving up on men.

"What do you want to talk about, Ian? I haven't heard a word from you in eons."

"Can you meet me tonight? What I have to say should be said face-to-face."

Again, the devil was on one shoulder and an angel on her other. She knew she shouldn't meet with him—Ian was a road to nowhere. To become involved with him again would only lead to the same dead end. But curiosity was getting the best of her, and she could not imagine what he wanted to discuss.

"Where do you want to meet?"

"At The Rusty Goblet. Does eight o'clock work?"

"Sure, Ian. I'll see you tonight."

Zarah laughed to herself as she got ready to meet Ian. She picked out her sexiest black leggings and a light blue sweater that complimented her figure. She put on a pair of black suede boots with three-inch heels. She wanted to look her best. She wanted him to feel something when he saw her, and she wanted him to see what he had been missing.

She pulled open the heavy wooden door to enter the tavern. It took her eyes a few seconds to adjust to the dim lighting. She saw Ian sitting toward the far end of the bar. He already had a drink before him and seemed to be staring at his glass. He smiled and waved her over when he saw her.

"Hi, Zarah!" He leaned toward Zarah and kissed her cheek.

"Ian, how are you?" she said in a monotone as if she didn't care how he would answer. But then, why was her heart beating in her throat?

"I'm not good, Zarah. I've been thinking a lot."

"Have you? About what?"

"About you. About us."

"Us?!" Zarah had to stop herself from laughing. "I wasn't aware that there was an 'us.'"

"Zarah, please. This is hard for me."

"I'm sorry, Ian. You disappeared, and I got on with my life. You didn't think I was going to sit by the phone and wait for you, did you?" she said with a sarcastic half-laugh.

"Of course not, but *you* could have called me, too!"

It had never occurred to her to pick up the phone and call him. She was old-fashioned that way. She had maintained her distance from him, too, and pretended he didn't mean that much to her. She *could* have made an effort and called him.

"Would you like a Cosmo?" he asked.

"Of course."

He flagged over the bartender and ordered her drink. After that, he remained quiet for several minutes. Something was on his mind, and she had no idea where he was going with this.

"Zarah, I know there are things about me you don't understand…"

"That's an understatement!" Zarah said with purpose. "I was dazed and confused the entire time we were dating."

The bartender set Zarah's drink in front of her. She took a sip and felt the effects of the drink almost immediately. She hadn't eaten since Ian called earlier that day.

"So… what conclusions have you come to about 'us,' Ian? I'm curious."

"Zarah… I was attracted to you from the moment we met. I haven't felt this attracted to anyone in a long time… maybe never."

"I felt the same way, Ian. But it seemed as though you were pushing me away. The better things got between us; the worse things got between us. Does that even make sense? Or was it just my imagination?"

"You weren't imagining it. I *was* pushing you away."

"Then, you stopped… in the middle of passion… Twice. What the hell, Ian? Why did you do that?"

"Fear, I suppose."

"Fear? Of me?"

"Fear of a relationship. I've been a single man for a long time. I thought we were taking things slow," he said.

"Slow? We were so slow that we were almost in reverse, Ian."

"Then you began dating someone else… So I backed off."

It was cliche at best, but Zarah felt she never had closure with Ian. His disappearing acts were all the closure she got. His explanation would have been nice somewhere along the way—it would have made her life so much easier.

It would have quieted her mind when she tried to sleep at night. Maybe closure was what he was working up to.

She was bored with tap dancing around him. She never told him how she truly felt. It was time to. She took a sip of her drink for courage, then inhaled deeply.

"Ian..." she put her hand gently on his far cheek and turned his face to hers. She spoke clearly... "I *was* in love with you."

His face tensed up as if she had stabbed him with a knife. His eyes became glassy. He pushed his hair from his forehead and took a quick, deep breath to control his emotions.

"Zarah... it's you. I love you..." His voice trailed off.

There they were. The words Zarah would have done anything to hear. His words should have made her want to wrap her arms around his neck and bury herself in his arms. She waited for the familiar desire to overcome her. She waited for tears of joy to well up in her eyes. At the very least, she should have wanted to say, *Ian, I love you, too.*

He was sitting inches from her—the man she thought she would die for. She recalled telling Liz she would have lit a match to her house to be with Ian.

"It's too late for us, Ian. I'm seeing someone else."

"Is that how it's going to be?" he asked. His face flushed as he fought back the disappointment in her answer.

"I'm sorry, Ian. The man that I'm dating is honest. He's an open book, and he has no secrets from me. He tells me what he'll be doing if he is busy for a while. If he's gone for days at a time, he explains why. I always know where I stand with him."

Of course, she wasn't dating John any longer and wasn't sure she would ever see him again. But every word she said about him was accurate, and when she said the words out loud, she became fully aware of what she may have lost in her haste to judge.

"I see." Ian took the last sip of his drink, then slid his glass to the far side of the bar. "Bartender! Another, please!" He turned to Zarah. "Do you want another?"

"No, Ian." She waited a few moments, then said something she thought he needed to hear.

"Ian, I hope you will meet someone else, and next time, don't ignore her while you sort out your feelings. Life is short. Maybe even have sex with her!" she said with a nervous laugh, but Ian did not find the humor.

"Ian…" She waited for him to look at her. She wanted to convey her point so he wouldn't forget what she had to say.

"If you don't change your ways, you are going to be *alone*," she said as kindly as possible.

"I'll take that into consideration." He sounded a bit gruff.

"I've got to go." She stood up. "Do you want to walk out with me?" she asked.

"No. I'm staying."

"How long will you stay?" She was concerned. It wasn't like him to drown his sorrows in alcohol.

"I'll stay until they kick me out." He paused for a few moments as he stared at the drink in his hands. He turned his head to face her.

"Zarah… There *is* one other thing that I've been wanting to tell you…"

"What is it?"

He took a sip of his drink, thought for a moment, then clearly changed his mind.

"Never mind. It's nothing. It isn't important anymore in the grand scheme of things."

"Goodbye, Ian."

Zarah took her purse off the back of the bar stool, put her jacket on, and walked out.

Forty-one

One long lesson

ON HER FIRST day back to work after having three days off, she sat down next to Jack to get report. He seemed excited to talk to her. His relationship with Diane was going well, and he wanted to ask Zarah if she and John would meet him and Diane for a rock concert the following weekend.

"That will not be possible… we broke up," she matter-of-factly stated.

"What?! You two were the perfect couple. I *never* thought you'd kick John to the curb! What happened?"

"He had too much baggage." She gave Jack the short version.

"Well, Zarah, I hate to break it to you, but *you* have a bit of baggage yourself!" Jack said while pretending to speak through a megaphone. "Why would you hold *his* baggage against him? At our age, unless you've been living under a rock, we all have baggage!"

At that moment, the doors to the ICU swung open, and Nate walked in with the usual line of residents trailing behind. They all stopped dead when Nate paused to talk to Jack and Zarah. Zarah laughed to herself... The residents adored him, much like she once did. But now that felt like a hundred years ago.

"Why so serious?" Nate said to Jack and Zarah.

"Zarah kicked her boyfriend to the curb," Jack slipped out.

"Jack!" Zarah kicked him under the table. She did *not* want Nate privy to her business. To this day, Nate continued to seek her out whenever he walked into the ICU and would nod his head as if in approval if he could catch her eye. She would smile back in a friendly way, but at this point, it had become nothing more than a game... Leftovers from something that almost once was. Her feelings were in check, and she would never make the same mistake again.

"Another boyfriend kicked to the curb? That's too bad," Nate said with a sympathetic tone.

Zarah smiled at him, but it was not her friendly smile. It was a forced smile... A smile that said, "Do *not* go there."

Later that day, while driving home near midnight, a thought occurred to her... Dr. Foxen. He had helped her through the most difficult time of her life. She decided to call his office in the morning to make an appointment to see him. If she had an hour of his undivided attention, maybe he could help her understand the situation with John.

They had been doing so well, and their relationship was moving forward—or so she thought. He seemed to have wanted the same things she did. She never had more in common with any man than with John. The time they spent together had given her hope that healthy relationships existed. John was close to the man she had "ordered from

The Universe." He ticked every box. Should she have added, "He should have no baggage" to the list? No, that would have been a ridiculous request.

He could have lied. He could have covered up the fact that he had slept with the devil—they would have happily continued in their relationship, and Zarah would never have known the difference.

It had been a long time since Zarah walked into Dr. Foxen's office. It was the same—not a thing had changed. He stood up from his desk, greeted her with a smile, and extended his hand. She seated herself in her favorite chair.

"So…" she said with a heavy sigh.

"I must admit that I was a little surprised when I heard you were coming, Zarah. The last time I saw you, you had just filed for legal separation from your husband."

"I did, and I gave Joe ten months to use my health insurance. He never did, so I converted the separation to divorce. That seems like so long ago. So much has happened since… Do you recall the surgeon I told you about? I'm sure I thought I was in love with him, but that relationship ended badly."

"How did it end?" he asked.

"He had… he *has* a wife. I thought he was going to leave her. I thought their marriage was over when I began seeing him—there were rumors then that they were separated. I think he loved me, but maybe I'm fooling myself. I was probably a sex thing." Zarah gave Dr. Foxen a sheepish smile. He was, after all, an ex-priest, and she felt a little guilty after her confession.

"How do you feel about ending the relationship with the surgeon, Zarah?"

"Would it be terrible to admit I wouldn't have missed it for the world? The time I spent with Nate woke me to the fact that I was still alive…"

"Alive? In what way?" the doctor asked.

"That I was still attractive to men... That I could still enjoy a physical relationship. I didn't know that about myself. I thought that part of me was dead."

"Maybe he did love you, but he wasn't brave enough to end his marriage... like you did. It takes a lot of courage to end a marriage." Dr. Foxen explained.

"I met someone on a dating website soon after my relationship with the surgeon ended. His name is Ian. Oh my gosh, I was so crazy about him."

"What did you like about Ian?"

"Honestly? Hmm. He's attractive. I felt magnetized to him. Nobody had ever kissed me like he did, and..." she paused to switch gears. "Dr. Foxen... you're an ex-priest, and sometimes it is hard to be honest with you."

"Zarah, I'm an ex-priest. I left the church. I'm just a regular guy now."

"Okay, but don't blame me if you start to blush," she joked, then went on... "Ian was the sexiest man I had ever been with up to that point. He made me crazy with my desire for him. He took me to heights of passion that I had never experienced before... But then he would stop." The doctor saw the puzzled expression on Zarah's face.

"What do you mean by, 'he would stop?'"

"Just what I said. In the heat of passion, he stopped. He would tell me it was time for me to go home or say it was time for him to leave. We never 'consummated' our relationship, but we came damn close." Zarah paused. "I think I will go to my grave wondering what a relationship with Ian would have been like."

"Did he ever explain to you why he did that?"

"He once told me that having sex meant that you were in a relationship."

"Do you regret how things ended with Ian?"

"Yes, very much. But there is another reason I'm here..." Zarah readjusted herself in her chair while she gathered her words. "A few months ago, I met John. He is an ER doctor with a similar background in health care, so we got along famously. We quickly became involved in each other's lives. We were together all the time. I felt as if I had finally met someone on the same path... Someone who wasn't afraid of me."

"Afraid of you? What do you mean by that?"

"I'm independent... I've had to be. In midlife, I found myself divorced but quite capable of standing on my own two feet."

"That doesn't explain why you believe men are afraid of you, Zarah."

"I'm not helpless... I can figure out how to solve most of the problems that come my way. I have a good job and my own money. I'm not bragging... But this is how I believe men perceive me, and they seem to be intimidated. I truly think that men tend to gravitate toward helpless women."

"A man who gravitates toward a helpless woman would never be the kind of man to whom you would be attracted, Zarah. I'm afraid you'd have that kind of man for lunch!" Dr. Foxen joked, then went on... "So, go on... You're dating John now. How is that working out for you?"

"Are all men untrustworthy? I'm sorry, you're a man, but every man I have had feelings for has disappointed me somehow."

"What happened?" Dr. Foxen asked.

"He slept with his ex-wife."

"While he was dating you?!"

"No, before we met." At that moment, Zarah felt foolish. When she said the words out loud, it sounded far less dramatic than inside her head. She continued...

"A little background... John's ex-wife was mentally and physically abusive to him. What kind of man stays with a woman who does that? And he didn't fight her for *anything* in the divorce. Who stays with a woman like that?!"

"A man who has post-traumatic stress disorder," Dr. Foxen stated emphatically. "I'm sure that John had, or possibly *still* has, a strong trauma bond with his ex-wife... Does he hold it against you that you stayed with your ex-husband for twenty-eight years? Your ex broke every single wedding vow and then some. You stayed, Zarah... In a bad situation. Maybe you never went back to your ex after he physically moved out of your home, but you went back to him countless times while you were living under the same roof. Is there that much of a difference in the situations?"

"I did slap John with the label of 'untrustworthy...' Almost as if I was waiting for my first opportunity."

"Zarah, think about it... This has been your thought process your entire life... Trust no man!"

She was acutely aware that he was spot-on. If she didn't change her mindset, she would eventually label every man who would come into her life the same way.

Dr. Foxen's wisdom once again blew her away. He saw her problems from a different perspective. She understood his viewpoint, but only after he clearly explained it.

She *could* trust John. She could trust that John would always be painfully honest. If that wasn't the definition of trustworthy, she didn't know what was.

It had been a few days since she spoke with Dr. Foxen, and she knew what to do. She picked up her phone and dialed.

"Zarah!" John answered on the first ring.

"Hi, John. Hey... I'm sorry for how angry I got the last time we were together."

"Zarah, will you ever learn to trust me? I'm afraid that you will never trust anyone."

"I'm working on it. I have *a lot* of baggage, John. More than I've admitted. I'm just as wounded as you."

"I've missed you," he said quietly into the phone.

"I've missed you, too," she admitted. "I'm off tomorrow..."

"I can drive down later today when I get off work."

"I'd like that, John."

"I'll pack a change of clothes," he laughed mischievously.

"See you tonight, John."

After hanging up the phone, it occurred to her… The list she and Liz wrote to The Universe… And the wish she made when she blew on the dandelion. She had almost forgotten. That day, she had folded the list and placed it at the bottom of a dresser drawer. She never thought about it again. She entered her bedroom, dug the list out of the drawer, and began reading.

In Liz's handwriting, there it was… HE MUST BE PAINFULLY HONEST, written in uppercase letters. She almost had to laugh… John *was* the man she had "ordered" from The Universe. She asked for him, and she got him. "Be careful what you wish for!" she laughed, then looked up to the ceiling and added, "Thank you."

Forty-two

Packing up

JOHN TOLD ZARAH that the lease on his apartment was coming due. He was required to sign a new lease for another full year.

"I can't see you living in that dreadful apartment any longer, John. You're here all the time… Move in with me!" She surprised herself with her spontaneity as much as she surprised John—she had not planned on saying those words. But Zarah was happy with the life she and John were creating, and she had no regrets that she had asked him.

In the coming weeks, they discussed how they would combine their belongings. Zarah's house did not have a lot of extra room, but John had ideas for adding more shelving to her closets. He also wanted to build a large garden shed in Zarah's backyard to free up room in her garage for his car and tools.

They were as excited as two people could be. They talked about the chances that two people, in their mid-life, would meet at the same time they found themselves single. And what were the odds they would have so much in common—including their distressing past marriages?

Several weeks later, John's apartment was packed. They donated most of his furniture—he seemed relieved to be rid of the cast-offs. They loaded his tools and clothing into a rented trailer and decided to move his bedroom set to the cottage the following weekend.

All that was left were the unopened bags and boxes that remained behind the closed door of the second bedroom.

"John… Do you seriously want to bring those bags and boxes into my house without looking inside them first?"

"You're right. Let's get this over with."

John opened the door to the second bedroom and walked in cautiously as if he didn't want to rouse the bags from their sleep. He pulled the first one down from the top of the pile, opened it, and looked inside.

"What the hell!" He cautiously put his hand inside and pushed a few items around. "This is garbage!"

"You mean junk? Should we donate it?" Zarah asked.

"No, this is *actual* kitchen garbage." He pulled down a second bag, then a third. All the bags were filled with household garbage, and he was angry that he had housed the bags for the past two years.

Next, he opened the first of eight large boxes. He dug around and was surprised to find his old photo album and his photo box.

"Wow, these are photos of when I was a kid up to my college days. I'm amazed that she gave them back!" he said with a half-laugh.

"How big of her!" Zarah said sarcastically. It was way out of character for Karma to be so kind, and she couldn't help but suspect that his ex had an ulterior motive.

In the remaining boxes, he found nothing useful, most of the stuff he didn't recognize, and one by one, he tossed every box into the dumpster.

Forty-three

Hold back tears

HER CELL PHONE vibrated in her pocket. Five minutes later, it vibrated again. She ducked into the break room to identify who was repeatedly calling her. It was Ian—he had called four times. As she stared down at her phone, it rang again. This time, she answered.

"Hi, Ian, I'm at work. I can't talk…"

"Zarah!" he interrupted. "You abandoned me!" His voice was cracking, and he sounded distraught.

"Ian, what are you talking about?!"

"You abandoned me, Zarah! You left me alone!"

"Ian, where are you?" What he was saying made absolutely no sense.

"I've been admitted to the hospital."

"Lansing Hospital?"

"Yes, I'm on the fourth floor, room seventeen."

"Are you okay?!"

"No, Zarah. I am not okay."

"I'll be down in a few minutes." *click*

Zarah found the shift supervisor and explained that she had to leave the floor and that she would be back shortly.

She ran down the stairway and pushed open the heavy fire door to the fourth floor. She walked briskly toward Ian's room and entered without knocking.

"Ian!"

He was sitting at the side of the bed, wearing a hospital gown over his blue jeans. He had an IV infusing into his right forearm. He was unusually pale.

"What is going on?!" Zarah felt mildly panicked.

"I'm sick."

Zarah sat down next to him and grabbed his hand. She never saw anyone who looked more alone.

"I have cancer, Zarah... A rare type of blood cancer."

"How long have you known?"

"A long time... I was in my late thirties when I was first diagnosed. It's returned several times since then... And it's returned."

"What have the doctors said? What is their plan for you?"

"They said I need another round of chemotherapy, and that *might* knock it back again, but there is no cure."

"Where are Fibber and Molly?" Zarah inquired.

"At my neighbor's house."

"Do you want me to pick them up and take them to my house?"

"No. They'll be fine. I hope to be discharged in a day or two."

They sat for a while in silence. She had held countless patients' hands before, but this was different. She had a history with this man—a man she once deeply loved and still felt more for him than she should.

"Why didn't you tell me, Ian?" Zarah asked in a soft voice.

"Would you have wanted to date me knowing that I was going to die?"

Zarah paused. She knew the answer.

"I would have understood. Life is short. I see proof of that every single day that I work." She stopped herself from saying more.

"You abandoned me." He repeated as he stared down at the floor.

"Ian, what are you talking about?"

"You left me. Now I'm going to die alone."

"Ian, I will be at your side through all this if you want me to be!"

He had been so strong and on top of his game. Now, he was a shadow of the man she had known.

"Ian," she quickly stood up. "I *have* to get to work, but I'll come back around midnight tonight, after my shift, to check in on you. Then I'll stop in again tomorrow morning before my shift begins."

"Zarah, I gave the social worker your name as my power of attorney for health care. I hope you don't mind... I can't think of anyone else I'd prefer to make decisions if I can't speak for myself."

"Of course. We'll talk more about that tomorrow morning... when I have time. You'll have to tell me what you'd want done in different situations. I have to go—I'm getting a new admission, and my co-workers will be angry with me if I'm not there when he arrives."

Ian leaned forward and put his head in his hands. Tears fell onto his jeans. Zarah immediately sat beside him, put her arm around him, and leaned her head against his shoulder. She did not cry easily; sometimes, she thought her tears were all dried up. But at the moment, she fought to control her emotions.

"Ian, you are *not* alone... You'll *always* have my friendship."

He nodded his head. Zarah stood up again to leave.

"I'll see you later tonight, Ian. You might be asleep when I come down after my shift, but I'll make sure you are okay."

He looked up at her—his eyes were bloodshot.

"Ian, I will be at your side as long as you need me," she said softly. "I promise... I will not abandon you."

"Thank you, Zarah," he said in a crackling voice. She began to slowly close the door behind her when she heard him call out...

"Zarah!"

"Yes, Ian?"

"I love you."

"I love you, too, Ian."

What she wouldn't have given to have heard those words when love would have meant more than love for a friend. If it was possible to feel joy and sorrow simultaneously, that was precisely what she felt.

The evening Ian told her, "It's you, Zarah," still echoed in her heart, and the conclusion to their romantic relationship still felt raw. She could relive the heartbreak at hearing those words at any moment, but she had suppressed the memory. She had moved on—she had to.

She walked briskly back up to the ICU. *Is this what The Universe had in store for us all along? Have I entered into Ian's life to help him die? Is this the cosmic plan? Is this our closure?*

Then another thought occurred to her... *Was his illness the reason he didn't want to be in a relationship?* It didn't matter anymore—she could no longer dissect what had happened between them. It was too confusing. She had committed to him to be his friend through his illness and would keep her promise. John was probably the only man in the world who would understand this turn of events.

After her shift ended, she headed toward the fourth floor again. After pushing the heavy fire door open, she saw his nurse, Leslie, running from Ian's room. The code lights flashed above Ian's door, and she heard an overhead announcement…

"Attention, code blue, fourth floor, room seventeen. Attention, code blue, fourth floor, room seventeen."

Zarah ran the rest of the way down the hall to Ian's room.

"Leslie!" she yelled. "Is Ian a full code?"

"Yes!"

"Ian!" Zarah screamed when she entered his room. He did not respond. She felt for a carotid pulse… "No pulse!" she cried out. Instinctively, she jumped onto the bed and began chest compressions.

Leslie returned seconds later, pushing a code cart. Zarah stopped compressions, got off of the bed, and turned Ian on his side so that Leslie could quickly slide a rigid board under him to aid with chest compressions. Leslie slapped defibrillator patches on Ian's back and chest, and they both watched as the monitor analyzed his rhythm.

"He's in asystole!" Zarah resumed chest compressions.

"Leslie… What happened?" Zarah asked breathlessly in between compressions.

"I found him unresponsive when I came to take his vitals." Leslie's face was white as a sheet—this was a nurse's worst nightmare.

Within minutes, the Code Team arrived and took over chest compressions for Zarah. She slowly backed into a corner of the room to watch. She should not help in the resuscitation efforts—Ian was her friend, and it would be considered unethical.

She had been in code-blue situations countless times. She had broken ribs under the weight of compressions before, and it had always made her cringe. It was not the practitioner's fault—it's just what happens. But this time, the cracking of Ian's ribs under the weight of compressions made her physically sick. She felt as if she was murdering her best friend.

She watched as the Code Team worked to save him—they bagged oxygen into his lungs through a tight-fitting face mask and drew tubes of blood for rapid analysis.

She wanted to scream, S*top! You're hurting him!* Instead, she maintained her composure and stood stoically, observing as the team went through the algorithms of Advanced Cardiac Life Support to return Ian's heart rhythm.

She was all too aware that it was rare for anyone to be better off after being "coded." Most of the time, after the return of their heartbeat, patients remained unresponsive. They would be transferred to the ICU, and the family would be called in to make the painful decision to "pull the plug." What was the sense of it all? If the chances of returning to a normal life after this were close to zero, why do it when it only delayed the inevitable?

"Stop compressions!" the code leader ordered. He quickly analyzed Ian's heart rhythm on the monitor. "He's in v-fib. Prepare to defibrillate." Zarah heard the monitor beep, confirming it was ready to deliver a shock. "Stand clear!" the code leader ordered—everyone stepped away from the bed. "I'm clear, you're clear, everyone is clear!"

Zap!

Zarah watched Ian's chest jump from the power of the jolt.

"He's still in v-fib. Resume compressions! Give one milligram of epinephrine!" After several minutes, the code leader ordered compressions to be stopped once again so that he could analyze Ian's heart rhythm. "A-systole!" he announced. "Resume compressions! Get ready to intubate! Give two more amps of epinephrine!"

To continue was futile. Electrical shocks were no longer delivered to a person who had no heartbeat. She walked through the Code Team to the head of the bed and took her exam flashlight from her pocket. She pulled Ian's eyes open—his pupils were fixed and dilated, and there was no reaction to the light.

"Stop compressions," Zarah said sadly.

"That is my call to make!" the code leader answered.

"No... it's my call. I am his POA for health care. Please... stop compressions and do *not* intubate him. Let him go." She could not speak another word.

The doctor looked at Leslie to confirm that what Zarah said was accurate. Leslie nodded. The team stopped all activity.

"Time of death... 12:45 a.m." the code leader said quietly.

"I suspect that he threw a clot... This type of cancer can cause that to happen sometimes," the Code Team leader said kindly to Zarah before he left the room.

After the team left, Zarah told Leslie she would like to stay at Ian's bedside for a while. Leslie told her to take her time.

Zarah dimmed the bright lights the Code Team had flipped on when they entered the room. She straightened his blanket to keep him warm, then slid a chair next to the bed. She looked at his lifeless face...

"Oh, Ian," she whispered, holding his still-warm hand. "Was this your secret? Is this why you didn't want to be in a relationship?"

She had been wrong—her tears were *not* all dried up. She laid her head on the side of Ian's bed and buried her face in the blanket. She began to cry for everything that had transpired between them—an uncontrollable cry that happened when you were six years old and fell off your bike. A cry where your body takes over, and you cannot stop.

When she finally regained some semblance of composure, she sat beside Ian in the darkness—an hour passed. If John were still awake, he would be worried that she wasn't home yet. She dialed his phone... no answer. She was grateful that he was most likely fast asleep.

The door opened slowly—it was Leslie and another nurse. Zarah knew that they had come to put Ian into a body bag.

"Zarah, how are you?" Leslie said softly as she handed Zarah a large cup of water. "I know that Ian was your friend."

"We were more than friends." Zarah took a few sips of the water.

"I'm so sorry, Zarah. Does he have any family to contact?"

"He's got a brother, but they weren't close... They've been estranged for years. I suppose we should notify him anyway." Zarah gave Leslie Ian's brother's name, fully aware that Ian would not have approved.

Zarah rose to her feet. "Whoa, I'm a little dizzy."

"Sit back down and finish that glass of water before you leave," Leslie ordered. Zarah had to laugh. She knew that was how she sounded to her patients—kind of bossy, but necessarily so. She did as she was told and watched as Leslie and the other nurse rolled Ian's body from one side to the other, inserting him into the white bag.

Leslie and her assistant left the room. It was time to go. The transporters were waiting in the hallway with the cart to take Ian's body to the morgue.

Leslie had not zipped the white bag closed—Ian's face was still exposed. Zarah leaned over and kissed his cheek. His face was cold.

"Goodbye, Ian."

She reached down and finished zipping up the body bag, then turned and left the room.

Forty-four

One year later...

HAND IN HAND on the park bench, Zarah caught a glimpse of her ring as it sparkled in the sunlight. She had never been happier in her entire life than she was at that moment. It wasn't only the ring on her finger and their approaching wedding date that made her smile, but also the dozen or so dogs running and playing around them.

She returned home at three a.m. the morning after Ian died. She told John how she had found Ian unresponsive and that she had to start chest compressions on him. She told him about the heroic attempts of the Code Team to resuscitate him and how kind the hospital staff had been to her after his passing.

John listened and understood—she had loved someone before him. He held her in his arms that night as she recalled every detail of the event.

Was there any other man who would support her as she grieved the loss of a past love? She did not think so.

That night, she could not sleep. She thought about the events that had brought her to this point...

Her marriage had disintegrated, and as hard as she tried, she could do nothing to stop it from happening. Her two sons were the result of their union, so if given the choice, she would not turn back the hands of time. The suffering had been worth it for her sons alone.

She hadn't talked to her parents in over a year and was beginning to feel a softening in her heart. Had they done their best? Did their childhoods influence their parenting skills? Her father had been beaten by his father when he was a child. Her mother had been raised a strict Catholic—she married for better or for worse.

Zarah had raised her sons differently than she had been raised, but maybe she wasn't as perfect a parent as she had thought she had been. Quite possibly, her sons held resentment toward her for divorcing their father. Perhaps they felt stressed growing up, and she never perceived it. She thought she had hidden the problems in her marriage, but she could be wrong. Perhaps Drew and Damon's childhoods were not as Norman Rockwell-like as she felt they had been.

She decided to call her parents and ask them to meet her for lunch. It was time to talk. It was time for a fresh start. Life could end for any of them at any given moment in time. If her mother or father passed without her having the chance to make things right, she would have to live with that. Losing Ian had clearly shown her... After death, there are no more opportunities.

She thought about Nate—she harbored no hard feelings toward him. She believed he had loved her on some level—and maybe still did. She hoped he was happy with the choices he made.

Jack... she still felt sad about what transpired between them and maybe always would. But Jack had moved on, and he was in a good place. Last week, he told her he and Diane were moving in together. Zarah felt confident that she and Jack had repaired their friendship and were maybe closer now than ever.

With Ian, she discovered she could feel deep love, but she could not change anyone but herself.

A week after Ian's funeral, a lawyer contacted Zarah to inform her that she was Ian's sole beneficiary. Zarah never had a clue he was leaving everything to her—she had never given his money a second thought.

After several months of contemplation, research, and number crunching, Zarah and John were prepared with their ideas and plans and were placed on the agenda of the next city council meeting.

A local park, just outside of the city limits, was run down and rarely used. The playground equipment was ancient—most likely unsafe—and the trees and bushes were neglected and needed attention. The park was all but forgotten.

Ian had left Zarah a sizable amount—enough to hire landscapers, purchase and install fencing, park benches, and picnic tables, and convert an old drinking fountain into a water station. John insisted that they add shade trees into the final plan.

Zarah felt confident that Ian would approve of her plans if he could. He must have trusted that Zarah would find a way to put his money toward a worthy cause. He left her no instructions of what to do with her inheritance, but he had inserted a brief, handwritten note on a torn half sheet of yellow-lined legal paper within the pages of his will...

Dear Zarah,

If you are reading this, then you have inherited a small fortune. I trust you'll put it to good use.

Yours,

Ian

P.S. It was always you.

Zarah tucked the note under the lining of her jewelry box. She may never read it again but could not toss it away. The knowledge that it was there was enough.

The city council readily accepted the renovation of the park and the contingencies of Zarah's plans. With the spring thaw, the work began. Fencing was installed, the landscapers trimmed the trees and planted six large shade trees, and a creative plumber designed and built a water station. A dozen park benches and six picnic tables were brought in and strategically put in place. Then, with the remaining money, she created a trust fund to cover the cost of future upkeep.

She and John had each followed a crooked path to find each other. What would her life have been like had she met him sooner? Would they have had children? Would he have been a different man had he not lived through the abuse of his first marriage? Would Zarah be different if she had not married Joe? Would she have the same strength in her soul? Would she appreciate all the blessings she eventually received?

She turned to admire the inscription on the back of the park bench...

"In dedication to Ian Elliot"

She took her jacket sleeve and polished the brass plate. She would make sure it would always shine.

"Fibber and Molly! Come!" she called out to the dogs. "It's time to go home!"

She took John's hand in hers. "You must know how much I love you," she said.

"I love you, too, sweetheart." He leaned over and kissed her lightly on the cheek. John's kiss differed significantly from any other kiss she had ever received... There was love behind it.

The dogs obediently ran to her side, and the four began walking toward their car. Zarah carefully closed the gate behind her as they left the fenced-in area. She took a few steps out, then turned around to admire all she and John had accomplished.

Zarah knew that Ian would be proud. He had worked for years to accomplish something similar, but the committee he worked on gave up after several years of effort as the funds were just not there.

A sign had been installed earlier that morning at the park's entry.

"John, can you get a picture of the dogs and me in front of the sign?"

She turned around and looked up to admire the lettering. She touched the bold black letters. The sign maker had done a skillful job.

"Fibber and Molly, *come!*" Zarah said firmly as she slapped her thigh.

The dogs immediately ran to her side as if they sensed that they were celebrating something important. They obediently sat down and looked up at John.

"Be sure to get the sign in the background!" Zarah said with excitement in her voice.

Click

Later that evening, Zarah turned on her cell phone to check out the picture John had taken of her and the dogs at the park earlier that day. She had to laugh that the dogs' tongues hung out on opposite sides of each other, and she could swear that they were smiling.

John did a good job when he took the picture. She would get it framed.

The new sign was clearly visible behind her...

"Fibber McGee & Molly's Dog Park"

If you enjoyed this book...

PLEASE RETURN TO AMAZON TO LEAVE A REVIEW!

A five-star review would be most welcome, and a written review would make my day!

Thank you!

K.D.Kinz

Made in the USA
Columbia, SC
12 August 2024

40321067R00167